GREGOR'S REASON

HELEN BRIGHT

VINCI
BOOKS

In loving memory of Auntie Joyce

Vinci Books

vinci-books.com

Published by Vinci Books Ltd in 2026

1

The publisher and the author have made every effort to obtain permissions for any third party material used in this book and to comply with copyright law. Any queries in this respect should be brought to the attention of the publisher and any omissions will be corrected in future editions.

A CIP catalogue record for this book is available from the British Library.

Paperback ISBN: 9781036707705

The EU GPSR authorised representative is Logos Europe, 9 rue Nicolas Poussion, 17000 La Rochelle, France

contact@logoseurope.eu

By Helen Bright

The Night Movers Vampire Series

Bitten and Bound

Blood & Secrets

Gregor's Reason

Sergei's Angel

Chapter One

Chloe

The orders had been coming in since the shop opened at 8.30 a.m. I'd had others coming through by text on my mobile before that, since getting the news that Julia Staithes had her little boy, Rory, at 10.36 p.m. last night.

My assistant, Pam, worked all day instead of her usual six hours, and Emma, my Saturday girl, covered the till and gift areas.

Pam and Michelle—my young apprentice—were helping with the orders for the new mum and baby in the back room of my shop.

I'd taken over the little flower shop in Barrowfield when my aunt Joyce left it to me just over a year ago. I wasn't sure what to do with the place at first. When I'd gone through the books, it didn't seem like my aunt had made much of a profit in the last few years. Still, I didn't have the heart to change the little shop into something else.

I'd spent lots of happy school holidays here making up

bouquets with my aunt, and she'd always told me the shop would be mine one day. Sadly, Aunt Joyce suffered a massive stroke last July and passed away a week later without regaining consciousness. When her will was read, it revealed that my aunt had left me the flower shop, the flat above it, and her little minivan. She'd also left me her extensive earring collection, a pair of which I was wearing today.

I retained Pam and kept the shop as a florist for a while. After I'd sorted out all the legal paperwork, Pam and I sat down and discussed the ideas we had that could bring in more customers.

We diversified a little, adding various gifts, candles and small decorative items to our stock list—as well as party products. We also redecorated and gave the shop a new name, Chloe's Flowers and Gifts, and have been doing well financially for the last ten months.

I've taken a few floristry courses, and I really enjoy my work. I just wish my aunt Joyce could see how well her little shop was doing now.

I relish the challenges my new business has given me. I love what I do, and although the shop came to me in sad circumstances, it also came at a time in my life when I needed a change: a new direction and purpose.

I married my now ex-husband, Craig, when I was a loved-up twenty-six-year-old. We'd been engaged for over two years beforehand, and I thought I was so lucky to meet such a sweet guy after a previous abusive relationship. The boyfriend before Craig had become violent towards the end of our time together.

The emotional scars from that relationship lasted longer

than the injuries he gave me, and I swore off men for a while. So when Craig came around with his thoughtfulness and gentle ways, I thought my dreams had all come true. Granted, there wasn't as much passion as I would have liked in our sexy time, but I thought we could work on that, and passion wasn't everything, right?

Craig's family was quite wealthy and gave us enough money to buy our first home as a wedding gift. His mother and father were wonderful people and had Craig—who was an only child—later in life.

They were very much in love, and after being married for fifty-two years, they passed away within four months of one another. His father had a massive heart attack after losing Craig's mum to bone cancer.

That was three-and-a-half years ago. A month after his father's funeral, Craig sat me down to discuss something. I thought it would be about his parents' home and belongings; what I didn't expect him to tell me was that he was gay.

To say I was shocked was an understatement. I was so stunned and unbelieving at what he'd said that I burst out laughing. Afterwards, when I realised he wasn't joking, I went through a whole range of emotions and actions.

I cried, screamed, and shouted; I also threw a cream cake at the wall before ordering Craig to leave our home, but he wouldn't. He kept saying he was sorry; he didn't want to hurt me, and he would always love me—just not how a husband should love his wife.

It took over a week for me to calm down and at least two months to accept the unwelcome development. As I've said, Craig and I had very little passion in our relationship. I used to think he wasn't as attracted to me as I was to him.

Craig is tall, fit, and good-looking, with blond hair and

baby-blue eyes, and he often turned other women's heads whenever we went out.

Being short, plump and pear-shaped, I never felt confident about my looks. Although I'm not unattractive, my light brown hair and pale freckly skin make me a little ordinary, yet my blue-green eyes are quite pretty. But as it turned out, I could have been a Playboy model, and I still wouldn't have made Craig get all fired up and passionate. I didn't have the right genitalia to get his motor running.

After six months of coming to terms with Craig's sexuality—and with divorce proceedings underway—I moved out of our home. We sold Craig's parents' house, and I used some of the money from the sale for the rent on a modern apartment close to where I worked, and Craig was happy for me to do so.

My parents own a B&B on the Costa Blanca in Spain. They offered me a room in their home, but I wanted to stay in the UK to keep my job as a medical secretary, which I'd had for years.

Craig eventually met Jake, a great guy who made him truly happy. When we finally divorced, Craig ensured I had a reasonable settlement, so I was okay financially. Some people think I'm crazy to remain such great friends with Craig, but I still love him dearly—although only as a friend —and I adore Jake.

They helped me decorate the shop, and we still see one another regularly. Their friendship helped a lot when I gave up my job and made the sixty-mile move from the outskirts of Nottingham—where I lived previously—to the little flower shop in Barrowfield, South Yorkshire.

I've made quite a few friends in this village, the new mum Julia Staithes being one of them.

Chapter Two

Chloe

After Julia's husband, Alex, sent me the text last night to let me know about baby Rory's safe arrival, he was the first to place an order for Julia's flowers. Of course, this order also had to include a helium balloon, as was customary for the couple. Julia had bought Alex one on the day she proposed to him.

Alex wanted to say thank you to his wife for making him the happiest man on earth, for loving him and making him a father. I suggested red carnations instead of roses for the flowers because they were Julia's favourite. I also included baby's breath and various bits of greenery to bring out the red in the bouquet. Inside the arrangement was a small, heart-shaped red and white balloon on a stick that said, "*Thank You.*" The customary helium balloon was white with red lettering that said, "*I love you.*" Alex wanted this to be all about Julia, as he knew baby Rory would end up spoiled by everyone else. He was right about that.

The next order came from Joshua York and his fiancée, Keeley, not ten minutes after Alex sent his text. They requested a blue floral arrangement with an *"It's a boy"* helium balloon. Keeley also wanted to send a blue teddy from her daughter, Daisy.

Keeley and I are also friends. I'd provided the floral arrangements and fairy lights that decorated the secret garden at Gregor Antonov's manor house, where her engagement party was held.

Gregor was next to request an arrangement. Unlike everyone else last night, Gregor's request came via a phone call. What made this even more special was that Gregor was in Russia at the time, so it was good to hear his voice.

He's flying back to Yorkshire today, and he'll stay at his home in Rothley for at least two months. I was glad. I missed the flirty friendship we had going on when he wasn't around, and I hoped we would get the chance to spend more time together while he was over here.

I first met Gregor when I called at Rothley Manor to deliver flowers for Keeley—Gregor's PA—who was staying at the manor. Gregor took me on a tour around his home and flirted shamelessly while we discussed what type of floral arrangements would suit each room.

I couldn't believe it when, after my tour, Gregor asked if I would go out to dinner with him. I wondered why he was asking someone like me. I mean, Gregor is a tall, good-looking, sexy Russian billionaire, and I'm just a plain nobody who happens to own a flower shop.

Since moving to Barrowfield, I've taken more care of my appearance. I keep my hair short and styled in a pixie cut, and it's a shiny chestnut colour right now instead of the dull brown it once was. I have a healthy tan from all the time I spend outdoors at the flower markets and garden centres. Yet, for all that and the twice-weekly swimming sessions and Zumba class I attend, I'm still a little too chunky in the hips and thighs, and at nearly thirty-five years old, my boobs have started to gravitate in a southerly direction. So why would Gregor be interested in flirting and spending time with me?

Whatever the reason, I've been extremely happy about it. Gregor's not only nice to look at, with his short brown hair that has just a few flecks of grey at the sides, piercing blue eyes and GQ model looks, but he's also intelligent, charming, generous to a fault, and always treats me with the utmost respect.

Of course, I'd love him to rip my knickers off and take me up against the nearest hard surface whenever we're alone, but that's never going to happen. Unless I suddenly grew a few more inches in height, lost thirty pounds in weight, and got a head transplant. But a girl can dream if nothing else.

Gregor's bouquet for Alex and Julia has white carnations and deep blue gerberas interspersed with blue irises. He said he'd bought Julia sapphire and diamond earrings to celebrate the birth and show her how special she was—another reason women seem to swoon when in Gregor's presence.

Yet, for some reason, even though Gregor has all these outstanding qualities and was more swoon-worthy than a handsome A-list movie star, I found myself wondering just what his dark secret was. I suppose from my track record with men, anyone would understand my wariness. But there was just something different about Gregor; something that I couldn't quite put my finger on…

Chapter Three

Gregor

We landed at Doncaster Airport at 6.30 p.m. after a flight with the worst turbulence I've ever experienced. Even the ordinarily laid-back Sergei had looked anxious and worried until the aircraft came to a stop. Only Yuri hadn't seemed affected by our troubled flight.

Yuri loved the Gulfstream jet we'd flown in on. It was the four-fifty model, so it wasn't our largest. But it was still very comfortable—luxurious even, and I was reminded again how fortunate it was to acquire this fleet of planes at much less expense than buying them outright.

Yuri was a trained pilot, but he'd flown nothing near the size of this aircraft and hadn't yet expressed any interest in doing so. Perhaps I should ask why and encourage him to try it?

We collected our luggage from where we'd stowed it. There wasn't much, as we'd left a lot of our belongings behind on our last visit.

The pilot and cabin crew were staying here for two weeks—transporting another Born Immortal from the UK to Barcelona during this time. The immortal in question had used our services several times, and the pilot and crew we employed told me that he was a favourite passenger of theirs. This was good to hear, as we had only one other immortal on this crew, and I liked to know that the humans I employed were safe.

Exiting the aircraft, I immediately spotted Keeley waiting in the VIP area. Her smile was infectious, and my spirits lifted as I walked into her embrace.

"It's great to see you, Gregor," Keeley said while kissing my cheek.

Before I could reply, Yuri picked her up and twirled her around.

"Keeley, you are more beautiful than ever. How is my little Daisy, and the new baby, too? I cannot wait to see them," he voiced loudly.

"It's good to see you too, Yuri. Daisy and Rory are both good. We can call over to see them before I take you to the manor, and I have photos of the new baby on here," Keeley said, sliding her thumb over her phone screen.

Sergei snatched the phone up first and flicked through the photos with one hand, grabbing Keeley by the waist with the other.

"He is very cute. How much did he weigh?"

"Nine pounds, six ounces," said Keeley with a beaming smile.

"So, has he done it?" questioned Sergei with humour in his voice.

"The earring? Yes, he's wearing it, Sergei. But I have to say, it's so not Alex. I can't believe that's what you bet him," Keeley replied.

"What did you do now, Sergei?" I asked, but he couldn't answer me for laughing. Yuri spoke instead.

"Sergei bet Alex that his baby would be a boy over nine pounds. I bet a girl about eight pounds, and Nik and Josh bet girls, too. Alex said he thought a boy about eight pounds." Yuri laughed, then added, "Alex was so sure he was right from what they said at the last ultrasound that he told Sergei he could name his forfeit. Sergei said if he won the bet, Alex would have to wear an earring again, as he did in the 1980s. I didn't think he would do it."

"Alex wanted me to shave off my hair if I was wrong, and I accepted his bet, so he had to accept mine," Sergei insisted when he finally stopped laughing. Keeley shook her head at him and proceeded to show me photographs of Alex and Julia's son as we walked through the airport.

Keeley insisted the baby had Julia's mouth but had a look of Alex and Freya around the eyes. Yuri and Sergei nodded, agreeing with Keeley. But to me, he just looked like a baby, albeit a chubby-faced one. Perhaps I would see a difference when we saw him face to face. I've never been the biggest fan of babies. I haven't had a great deal to do with them. I visited and brought gifts to celebrate their birth, but nothing more than that.

Not many in my circle of friends have become parents over the years. Still, my human employees have families, and I ensure I welcome their safe arrival into this world with a monetary gift for their future.

I wouldn't need to do that with Alex's son, so I'll have to be more inventive with little Rory's gift. On the other hand, Julia will be given sapphire and diamond earrings to show how special she is to me—for loving one of my best friends and making him a father. Two very precious things.

I brought Chloe a gift, too, and it's one of many that I

have stored away at my favourite jewellers in Russia. It is a gold bracelet with floral charms made from various coloured precious gems. Flowers for my little flower girl. It's a nickname I gave her during the time we spent together on my last visit to the UK.

I was ever the gentleman with her those few short weeks ago. With how I was feeling now, I wouldn't stay that way much longer.

During my last stay, I took her out to dinner several times. We also went to the cinema, which I detested due to the number of noisy people who kept insisting on getting up and squeezing past us. I should have hired the whole cinema that night, and if Chloe wanted to go again, that's just what I would do.

I was hoping, however, that she would be agreeable to becoming so much more than just my friend. I could not wait to explore more of the witty and intelligent Chloe, who'd become such an obsession to me. I wanted to touch her constantly, even if it was just holding her hand, and while I wasn't sure at first that I would be attracted to someone as full-figured as Chloe, I found myself lusting after her ample curves.

Usually, the subs I take in my club are a little lither, which helps them hold a position easier and for much longer. But I long to see Chloe and her generous curves strapped to the St Andrew's Cross in my cellar at the manor. Her breasts have also appeared in many of my fantasies, bound in leather and sporting clamps on what I guess will be rosy-brown nipples.

I turned to look at Keeley and realised she had been speaking to me. We had walked to the SUV I'd bought her a few months ago, and I felt a little ignorant in not paying her my full attention.

"I am sorry, Keeley. It has been a long day with a particularly gruelling flight, and I wasn't giving you my full attention. So what were you saying, my dear?" I asked, stroking her hair back from her face affectionately. We got into the vehicle and started the drive to Barrowfield.

"I was saying that Aunt Maggie's niece, Chelsee, is moving into the bungalow that Josh is renting her tomorrow. I know she's looking forward to having lunch with you next week. Sergei and Yuri have offered to help her move in, along with Josh and Nik."

"I offered her a cottage on my land, but she wouldn't take it," I told her, still a little put out that Chelsee hadn't wanted me to help her. She's Maggie's—Alex's PA—sister's girl. Although, she's not a little girl anymore.

Chelsee is twenty-eight now, but when she was nine, she came down with an autoimmune illness called pars planitis, which was caused by sarcoidosis. This attacks the eye, and sadly, in Chelsee's case, she lost her sight. She's been so brave in her short lifetime, and it doesn't look as if that's about to change anytime soon, even after her sixty-five operations since being diagnosed. I offered her a home on the Rothley Manor Estate that I own, but the stubborn girl turned me down.

"Gregor, Chelsee said that she appreciated you offering her a home, but she wanted to be in the village so she could use public transport and have easy access to the shops," Keeley said.

"I would have provided transport to anywhere she wanted to go. She knew that."

"That's not being independent, though, Gregor, and it's what Chelsee has strived to be above anything else. It would have helped if she'd stuck it out on the two-week *Guide Dog*

Matching Course, but she came home after just one day," Keeley muttered.

"Why didn't she stay the full two weeks?" asked Sergei.

"Chelsee said she didn't stay because they treated her like a blind person, which she objected to," I answered, shaking my head in bewilderment. I knew it would have been a real boost to her independence. I told her this, but she told me to *"butt out"* because I didn't know what she went through on a daily basis, which was right, I know, but I only ever wanted the best for her.

When she was first diagnosed, we tried our best to heal her, but unfortunately, our blood didn't have any effect on the autoimmune disease that ravaged her sight.

We had seen her grow from a determined young girl into an exceptionally tenacious and strong-willed young woman. She had her mother and aunt's beauty, but with stunningly silky, long dark hair: the kind you want to run your fingers through. I was surprised she hadn't got herself a husband already, but Chelsee has concentrated on building her career and recently qualified as a counsellor. She's secured two positions of part-time work: one at Rothley Medical Centre and one in a private practice in Barnsley. I am immensely proud of her achievements, even if she doesn't let me help and spoil her anymore.

Traffic had been minimal due to the time of day, which I appreciated. I felt quite weary, and I was anxious to get back to my new home—amongst other things.

My mind wandered yet again back to the delectable Chloe. I hoped she wasn't busy tonight. She was always a little vague on our phone calls and messages; perhaps that's why I found her so appealing. Maybe it's the chase? It's the first time I've ever had to do it. I have to keep guessing as to her moods and feelings and find her so hard to read.

I long to take her under my command and have her obey me, naked and wanting. I would be a gentleman no more where Chloe was concerned. But how do I approach the fact that I am immortal? And that I would like to take her blood as I take control of every inch of her body?

I took out my phone to send her a text message, but as we pulled up to Alex's home, I saw her little white van with Chloe's Flowers and Gifts written on the side. Josh was helping her carry large floral arrangements into the cottage.

Chloe glanced at our vehicle and smiled when she noticed me in the front passenger seat. That one thing lifted my spirits higher than they had been since I last held her hand in mine.

We all got out of the vehicle and said hello to Josh and Chloe. I took the floral arrangement from her as I leant to kiss her cheek. Before I pulled away, I whispered in her ear, "Come and see me at the manor later, Chloe. I have missed you."

"I've missed you too, Gregor, but you'll have to wait until after nine o'clock for me to join you. There've been so many orders for Julia today that we're running behind with the rest of our work. I have Pam doing some overtime, but I'll have to finish up, get a shower, and have something to eat before I come over," she said as she followed me into the cottage.

"I will order something from the Italian restaurant in Rothley," I told her, my eyes scanning over her full hips and bottom as she walked in front of me. Chloe and I had been to that restaurant a few times on my last visit. I knew her favourite dish because she would never order anything else.

"Gregor, that restaurant doesn't do food to take away," she stated.

"My darling Chloe, for the right price, I am sure they

will," I said as I winked at her. Chloe huffed and shook her head.

Alex stood beside the fireplace, smiling broadly, his son in his arms. Something hit me deep in my gut when he looked at me and found my gaze. Like he was communicating without words that this is what life was all about. And if I wanted to see true happiness, I should look no further than the baby in his arms and the woman sitting on the sofa looking radiant, wearing the same expression as her husband.

Sergei and Yuri went straight to Alex to take the baby, so I crossed to Julia and sat beside her.

"Congratulations to you both," I said as I kissed Julia's cheek and shook Alex's hand.

"My darling Julia, you look more beautiful today than ever, although a little tired, so we won't stay long. I couldn't resist buying you a gift to celebrate the birth of your son. I hope you like them."

I handed her the sapphire earrings and said, "Blue, for a boy," as she opened the box.

"Thank you, Gregor," Julia said as she wiped a tear from her eye. "They're beautiful. While you're here, there's something we wanted to ask you. Alex and I have discussed it, and we would love it if you'd be Rory's godfather."

I was taken aback for a moment. I looked from Alex to Julia and then to the baby, who was currently in Yuri's arms.

"If you don't want to, that's okay," said Julia quickly, taking my lack of speech to mean that I wasn't interested. But that couldn't be further from the truth.

"I would be honoured to be his godfather," I declared,

swallowing hard to dislodge the lump that had suddenly appeared in my throat.

Yuri came over and handed me the baby. It took a few moments to get him cradled correctly in the crook of my arm because holding babies didn't come naturally to me. But when I looked down at him—my precious little godson —I was overwhelmed with emotion.

He stared at me, unblinking. His eyes were a mixture of his mother's blue and his father's grey, and his little rosebud mouth pursed as he studied my face.

I smiled down at him and said, "Hello, little Rory. You have my love, my protection, and anything else you will ever need."

He wore a blue sleepsuit and was loosely swathed in a blue and white blanket. He raised his arm, opening and closing his tiny fist. I dipped my head and kissed it before lifting him a little and kissing his forehead. I saw a couple of flashes and looked up to see Keeley and Chloe taking photos of us on their phones. I smiled and turned Rory slightly so they could get a better picture.

"I want a photo of him on my desk, and we will get a professional in to take some for the walls and cabinets in the sitting room," I told Julia. Chloe took a few more photographs and told me she had the perfect frame in her shop.

"Would you like to hold him, Chloe?" Julia asked.

"Oh, I would love to," she said, taking him from my arms gently.

I inhaled both Chloe's and the baby's scent, and it stirred something inside me. I looked at her, gazing down at him so sweetly as she cradled him. She was doing a half-bounce, half-rock sort of thing while singing the Judy Garland song "Over the Rainbow."

Chloe has a beautiful singing voice, more so than any professional female singer I'd ever heard. Everyone in the room stopped what they were doing and stared at her in awe.

"Wow, Chloe!" exclaimed Josh as he looked at her admiringly. "I didn't know you could sing like that. How come you aren't singing professionally or even doing the odd gig around the local clubs?"

Chloe looked embarrassed at Josh's question and avoided everyone's smiling faces when she spoke.

"I used to sing when I was younger. I've done a few open mic sessions in a bar where my mum and dad live, but I'm not good enough to sing professionally, and I wouldn't be confident enough to do it either."

"I beg to differ," said Josh. "I think you're a brilliant singer, and I'll be doing a duet with you on the next karaoke night at the Red Lion now I've heard you sing."

Everyone joined in with the compliments, but Chloe was clearly uncomfortable under all their scrutiny. I stood and took my beautiful godson back from her arms and kissed her cheek, whispering in her ear that she should accept their compliments because they were well deserved.

She blushed before making her excuses to leave. She told Alex and Julia that their little boy was beautiful, and if they needed a babysitter, they should give her a call. Julia smiled and said she would. Then Chloe left, waving goodbye to everyone as she did so. I missed her presence immediately, and so did little Rory. He began to cry and turn his head towards me.

"I think he's hungry again," said Alex as he took him from me and carried him over to Julia. She unbuttoned her blouse and removed her left breast from her bra as discretely as she could, and after a couple of attempts, the baby latched on.

"A woman's body is a marvellous thing," said Sergei. "To carry and birth a child, then give them nourishment… Women are far superior to men in so many ways." We all nodded and watched as Rory fed from his mother's breast greedily.

"Well, come on, fellas, let's leave Mummy and Daddy to get some rest. If you need us at all, either of you," Keeley said to Alex and Julia, "we'll be around. But try to get some rest when he falls asleep."

Turning to me, Keeley added, "Freya's taken Daisy to stay at my dad's for the night with her and Dan, so she said she'll see you in the morning, Gregor."

I nodded in acknowledgement and followed Keeley to the door. We all said our goodbyes and left the cottage feeling lighter than we had before we arrived.

Chapter Four

Gregor

Keeley dropped Yuri off at the Red Lion pub in Barrowfield village. He'd recently become the new owner after buying the business from Josh, so he opted to stay there instead of with me. I think he was eager to see how the renovations to the living quarters were going, and to see Mel, the bar manager.

Sergei was staying with Nik and Gina, as per usual, so it was just Keeley and me in the vehicle as we made our way to Rothley.

She asked me about my staff in Russia and a few business matters that we'd spoken about previously on the phone. I missed Keeley when I was back home. We had become very close after Maxim attacked her and she was turned.

The blame for that, as far as I was concerned, lay heavily on my shoulders, but Keeley denied that fact. She said that Maxim had a choice, and he was the one who attacked her, but I couldn't help those guilty thoughts. I was very protective of her, even though I knew she was to be Bonded to Josh. He would always defend her when necessary. Although, from what I have seen, Keeley is a force to be reckoned with in her own right.

After a few minutes, we pulled up outside Rothley Manor—my home while in Yorkshire. I'd renovated the almost derelict old mansion to bring it back to how it would have looked when first built.

"I made sure your blood store was replenished, and the wine cellar's been restocked as per your request," said Keeley.

"Did you give Mrs Timmins the champagne, chocolate and flowers I ordered for her birthday?" I asked.

My other housekeeper had left suddenly, saying she'd found me too intimidating to work for, although I cannot understand why. Mrs Timmins, on the other hand, treated me like a long-lost son and tried to mother me, which I found quite amusing.

She was sixty-three years old last week, so I made sure she had the best champagne, Belgian chocolates and a large floral display to celebrate. Her husband, John, had taken the job as head gardener on the estate. When my other housekeeper left, he suggested his wife for the position.

Both John and his wife had previously worked for the Night Movers company. They'd left the village for a short time to go on an extended holiday and stay with their son, who works in New Zealand. So both of them knew about the vampires who lived and worked in their village, and it made my life a little easier when I didn't have to hide the fact that I was immortal.

"Yes, she got them, and the mobile phone you insisted she carry. Although, I can't seem to get through to her that the concept of having a mobile phone is that you take it with you and not leave it in the kitchen drawer," said Keeley in a huff.

She'd instructed Mrs Timmins on how to use the smartphone, which had taken my housekeeper a number of days to master, only for her to keep forgetting it. I chuckled at Keeley's frustration but resolved to speak to Mrs Timmins about it. Maybe she needed a much simpler phone.

"She's left you some sandwiches and a homemade apple and strawberry pie. She also lit you a fire in the sitting room about half an hour ago. That room always seems cooler, even on a late summer evening like this."

"I will thank her when I see her tomorrow, and I promise I will speak to her about the phone."

"Thank you. Will Chloe be joining you tonight?"

"That, my darling Keeley, is my business," I said, placing a kiss on her cheek before I opened the door.

"Gregor, will you give it a chance to be something more instead of just being about, well, you know what?"

"Keeley, don't! We've had this conversation before, and I said I would try. It might surprise you to know that I find myself wanting more from Chloe than any other female I have ever been attracted to. The bigger question is, what will Chloe do when she finds out I am immortal? She may go running for the hills."

Keeley knew about my cellar here, the range of furniture it held, and the purpose for it. She'd made it her mission to teach me that women could enjoy the type of sexual behaviour and needs that I craved, yet still be in a *normal* loving relationship.

Of course, I knew that anyway. There were many Dom/sub married members in my club who enjoyed the same sexual proclivities as I did. The issue was with me.

Once I had taken a woman into my club and had her body and blood, I no longer found myself wanting to spend time with her outside of a sexual encounter.

Keeley wanted to change that, and because I'd spent time with Chloe, she assumed that Chloe would be the one to change me. I wasn't so sure at first. I knew I was attracted to her, but when I went back to Russia, that attraction had morphed into something else entirely.

I'd been happy with my life the way it was. I didn't need a regular relationship. I was too busy with my many and varied business ventures to settle down with anyone on a long-term basis. And yet, there was something about Chloe that appealed to me.

As I waved goodbye to Keeley and made my way through the doors of Rothley Manor, I decided that tonight, I would reveal my true self to my little flower girl. After I'd lost myself in her generous curves, of course.

Chapter Five

Chloe

Gregor opened the door looking as suave as usual. His short brown hair was damp at the ends, so he must have had a shower.

Instead of throwing on something casual—like jeans and a T-shirt—he wore smart grey trousers that showcased his very sexy arse, and a plain white shirt with the top two buttons undone. I suddenly felt underdressed in my gypsy top and skirt.

Gregor complimented me on my outfit as he guided me into the dining room and pulled out a chair for me to sit on. After pouring me a glass of red wine, he served me my favourite dish from the Italian restaurant we dined at during his last visit. Their carbonara was the best I'd ever tasted, and my mouth watered at the tempting aroma.

I had been so busy I hadn't eaten all day, so I welcomed the tasty dish, along with the sides of home-baked garlic bread and the polenta chips that the restaurant did so well.

In between bites, I asked Gregor about his business before he could focus on the goings-on in my world. He was evasive, as always, only telling me about stocks and shares in oil and gas. I was sure he made it sound boring so that I wouldn't ask anymore.

Since Gregor had flown back to Russia, I'd had so many problems with my little shop and the flat above it, and I'd begun to wonder if it was all worth it. I told him about the first issue I'd had, which was a leak from the water tank up in the attic. Then two weeks after that, all the electrics fused and nearly caused a fire. Last week, during the night, my oven had somehow switched itself on and I'd had a small kitchen fire. Luckily, my smoke alarms had gone off and I was able to put the fire out quickly before it got out of hand.

"Why didn't you call me and tell me about all of this?" asked Gregor angrily.

"Why, what could you do? You were in Russia, remember? I took care of it myself, Gregor. Although I pray to God, nothing else happens. I went through the insurance company for the damage caused by the leak. But the other stuff I paid for out of my savings, so there's very little left for the holiday I planned on taking. I was going to take some time off and visit my parents in Spain, but that will have to wait until Christmas now," I told him. I couldn't hide the disappointment in my voice.

"I would have organised and paid for tradespeople to fix everything for you. I have many contacts from the renovation of this place. Keeley has a list of all of them in her office," he said.

"Gregor, I can take care of myself. You are just my friend. Friends don't pay for home repairs; they pay for dinner, a bottle of wine or a taxi."

I'd never felt nervous or scared in Gregor's presence

before, but right now, his expression was hard as stone, and I could swear I'd seen a flash of red in his eyes. It must have been a trick of the light and reflection from the wine bottle or something, because it was gone as soon as it appeared.

Gregor stood abruptly and made his way towards me. Holding out his hand, he said, "Come with me."

I placed my hand in his, and he almost dragged me to his sitting room. There were embers from a fire burning low in the grate. It made the room feel homely and was currently providing the only light in the room.

Gregor's sudden mood made me question my presence here tonight. It wasn't the first time I'd faced an angry man when I'd done nothing wrong, and each time it hadn't gone well for me. I'd taken a taxi to the manor because I knew we'd have wine with our meal, and I'd never drink and drive. But I wondered if I'd made the right choice.

"Gregor, I think it's time I went home," I told him, hoping he couldn't hear the nerves in my voice when I tried to extract my hand from his. His grip held firm as he turned and pulled me flush to his body, chest to chest.

I chanced a look into his eyes to determine his mood. Gone was the anger, and in its place was something that looked a lot like lust.

"You need never fear me, Chloe," Gregor whispered, running his hands down my back until they cupped my bottom. "I was angry because you said we were just friends, and I don't see you that way."

He ran his nose from my shoulder up to my ear, licking the pulse point at my neck, groaning as if he'd tasted the best dessert ever.

"Gregor, you're normally such a gentleman in my presence; you scared me a little when you became angry and almost dragged me in here," I admitted.

My knees nearly gave way when he licked a path up and down the other side of my neck, stopping again at my pulse point.

"Well, if it's a gentleman you want, Chloe, you are out of luck tonight," he said before kissing me.

His kiss was soft to begin with, but within seconds became fiercely passionate. He fused our mouths together by holding the back of my head; I couldn't have pulled away even if I'd wanted to. His tongue seemed to duel with mine for supremacy, and I moaned my pleasure into his mouth. Lust and longing had taken over my senses, replacing the uncertainty and fear. His erection throbbed against my belly, and my body responded instinctively to his need. I felt myself getting wet between my legs, my nipples hard against the fabric of my bra.

Gregor lifted his face from mine for a few seconds and commanded, "Tell me you want this as much as I do. Tell me I get to be inside you tonight."

It wasn't just his words that made my recently neglected places throb with anticipation, but also the feeling behind them. His desire for me was genuine, something I hadn't considered possible, although I'd fantasised about it since the day we met.

"I do want this, Gregor, more than you know," I told him sincerely.

He nodded his head and pulled the tie strings at the neck of my gypsy top. As soon as they were undone, he lifted the top over my head slowly. My strapless bra was quite new, with a pale cream floral-lace design. He ran his hands over my lace-covered bust before reaching around and unhooking my bra. My heavy breasts sprung loose from the slightly too small cups, and I felt embarrassed about their size, which made them much less pert than I would like.

"Beautiful," whispered Gregor while stroking his thumbs over my nipples. They puckered even more from his touch, and once again, I moaned my response to the exquisite feeling that radiated south to my core.

Gregor was much taller than my five-foot-four height. He stooped low to take my nipples into his mouth, one after the other. My knees suddenly became boneless as waves of pleasure flowed over me, steadily taking me under. I had to lean against him to keep myself upright.

He kissed his way down my quivering tummy before dropping to his knees in front of me, then he pressed his face into my sex through my clothes and inhaled deeply. That was something I hadn't expected, but for some reason, I found it highly arousing.

When Gregor tilted his head back and looked up at me, I once again caught a glimpse of red in his eyes. A glowing ember from the fire, maybe? I didn't question it further because Gregor began pulling down my elastic-waisted gypsy skirt, along with my knickers.

I was suddenly very grateful that the glow from the fireplace was the only light in the room, so he couldn't see the cellulite that graced my hips and thighs. Again, Gregor pressed his nose against my sex and inhaled before making a sort of growling noise, flicking out his tongue and lapping at my slit.

This time, my knees did buckle, and I heard myself moan deeply. Gregor lifted me up and then lowered me gently onto a heavily patterned rug in front of the fireplace. He stood and removed his shirt, not once taking his eyes away from me. He unbuttoned, then unzipped his trousers and slid them

down along with his boxers. His erection sprang forth, and...
WOW! I knew he'd felt big when he was pressed against me,
but this was something else. I'd had three previous sexual
partners, and I can tell you that none were as big as Gregor. I
should have felt nervous but instead, my mouth watered,
eager to taste the cock he was stroking rhythmically.

I tried to sit up, but he dropped to his knees and shook
his head. To placate me a little, he swiped his thumb over
the head of his erection, coating it with the glistening fluid
that had gathered there before running it over my lips and
onto my tongue, teasing me with the taste of him. I ran my
tongue around his thumb, and when he pulled the digit
away from my mouth, I licked the rest of his essence from
my lips.

Gregor hitched in a breath and stared down at me in
silence. Then a slow smile appeared on his face, and I
smiled at him in return.

He was so good-looking, and I wondered yet again why
he wanted me. Before I could open my mouth and ask him,
he grasped my ankles, pushed them towards my bottom,
then placed his palms on the inside of my thighs and
opened my legs.

Seconds later, his face was buried in my sex as he thrust
his tongue inside me repeatedly. My back bowed and rose
off the rug as pleasure spread through every nerve ending
from my sex outwards. I panted and pushed against him like
a woman possessed, and when he replaced his tongue with
two fingers, fastened his mouth around my clit and sucked, I
screamed in utter ecstasy. My orgasm felt stronger than any
I'd ever experienced, and before I could come down from it,
Gregor lapped at my clit with firm, rapid strokes. I came
again, harder this time, crying out his name while pleading
for him to get inside me.

I realised I'd grabbed his hair and pulled it firmly when I'd ground myself against his face. I felt embarrassed by my actions and began to apologise.

"Shh, Chloe. You should never need to apologise for giving yourself so fully to sexual pleasure. It gave *me* great pleasure to experience your reaction, and I hope I get a similar reaction when I am deep inside you," he said, raising his eyebrows suggestively.

He kissed me from my belly to my breasts, teasing my nipples with his tongue. Grabbing his cock, he ran it slowly from my clit to the mouth of my sex. A sudden thought sprang to mind, and I placed my hand on his chest to stop him while I still had a coherent thought.

"Gregor, we need protection. I'm clean...I mean...I haven't had sex for years, but I'm not on the pill, and I don't know your sexual history and—"

"You need not worry about me, Chloe. I don't have any diseases, of that I can assure you, and I cannot get you pregnant. So relax, my darling, and let me have you. I have waited so long to feel you wrapped around my cock."

And with that, he pushed himself inside me, almost to the hilt.

I cried out as his thickness invaded my sex. At first, I thought he was just too big for me to take all of him. Gregor groaned and squeezed his eyes closed while slowly stretching me with each thrust.

Seeing him so affected by the feel of being inside my body made me even wetter, which eased the way for the deeper, harder thrusts he gave. I was lost in the rhythm of our lovemaking, and make no mistake, this *was* making love. I thrust my pelvis up to meet his, and my clit ground against him, creating the most delicious sensation that spread upwards from my sex to my head. After less than a minute, I experienced my first-ever orgasm through penetrative sex.

Again, Gregor didn't let me come down from the bliss that consumed me, and with his hands now on my bottom, he once again brought my pelvis up to meet his thrusts. This time, when I came, I swear I almost lost consciousness, and when Gregor pounded his release into me, I was more content and sated than I had ever been in my life.

Gregor placed his forehead against mine and whispered, "What have you done to me, my little flower girl?"

Before I could answer with some witty comeback about what he had just done to me, he said the words that everyone hates to hear.

"Chloe, we need to talk."

And just like that, my heart dropped to my feet, and I suddenly felt cold.

Chapter Six

Gregor

Chloe placed both hands on my chest and pushed me. I lifted myself up and away from her quickly, afraid I was crushing her breasts. But she carried on pushing me away and rolled over onto her side, grabbing her clothing from where I'd dropped it earlier.

I grabbed her arm to still her, but Chloe shook me away, saying, "Just let me get dressed, Gregor. I think this type of conversation should only be had when fully clothed."

What was she talking about? Did she already know? I wrestled the clothing away from her before pinning her back down on the floor, her hands above her head.

"What type of conversation are you talking about, Chloe?" I asked while pressing my erection against her struggling body.

"The one where you tell me this shouldn't have happened; that it meant nothing and you regret it," she said, her eyes widening at the feel of my hard cock as it pressed against her belly.

"Does it feel like I regret what happened, Chloe? Do you think what we just shared meant nothing to me?"

She shook her head and looked at me curiously. Perhaps she could see some confusion in my eyes, too. Normally, her first instinct would have been the correct one. Although it was usually delivered when I'd given a sub some much-needed aftercare. But never in a setting like this: in my home with only the glow of firelight surrounding us after we'd just made love. Because Gregor Antonov never made love. Ever!

For some reason, this woman made me want to cherish her, to give more of myself than I have ever given before. The thought was slightly disturbing, but I shook it off. Her reaction to what I was about to tell her would decide our fate, no matter how I felt.

I kissed Chloe softly until I felt her relax and become pliant against me. Letting go of her arms, I knelt up and lifted her while readjusting my position, then I cradled her on my lap.

My strength surprised Chloe because I'd lifted her with no effort required. Good. That was one thing out of the way.

"Well, go on, then, Gregor. Spit it out. Why do we *'need to talk'*?"

I took a deep breath and began with, "Do you sense that there is something different about me, Chloe?"

She raised one eyebrow. "Do you mean because you're Russian? Or that you're a billionaire? Or because you have to dress like you're attending a business meeting when we have a takeaway in your home?"

"No, none of those. And for your information, I did not

dress like I was attending a business meeting tonight. I merely put on trousers and a shirt. If I were attending a business meeting, I would have also worn a jacket and tie, possibly a waistcoat."

"Gregor, you could have thrown on jeans and a T-shirt and been casual. Do you even own jeans?" she asked.

"Yes," I replied hesitantly. I was sure I owned at least one pair, maybe?

"Good. It would be nice to see you a little more chilled. We could go for a walk around the estate and collect chestnuts from the woods out back. I used to do that with my aunt in the late October holidays when I was a young girl. You can't do that in late autumn in a business suit."

"Wait. We are getting off track here. I need you to listen to what I'm saying, Chloe. It's very important," I told her.

"Umm, it's kind of hard to do that when your cock is poking me in the bum," she said, wriggling against me.

"Chloe, if you'd just keep still, then it wouldn't be poking you in the bum," I replied, shifting her position.

But the words were out there now, and all I could think of for the moment was bending her over the specially designed furniture in my cellar, shackling her hands in front of her and fucking her in the ass. She wriggled again, and I felt a sticky wetness against my leg as my come left her body.

"Gregor, I need to get cleaned up," she said, trying to hide her embarrassment.

"No," I answered harshly, leaning her back and opening her legs so I could see my come as it left her body. I'd give her more of it later, of course, if she accepted what I was about to tell her. To make Chloe feel better, I took my boxer shorts and wiped the evidence of our tryst from both my leg and her glistening sex.

She kept her pubic hair trimmed yet naturally shaped, which I found appealing, although different from what the women in my club sported.

I threw my boxers to the side of us and turned her to face me.

"Chloe, there's no easy way to say this. I am what's known as a Born Immortal. I'm a vampire, Chloe. I have been on this earth for over five hundred years, and I plan on living for many more."

She was quiet for a time, then started laughing nervously.

"Gregor, is it like a Russian Halloween night or something? Or have you been drinking strange wine before I came over?"

"Chloe, I'm being serious," I said as I held the back of her neck to keep her gaze on mine. "Watch me, Chloe," I commanded.

She stopped giggling, then gasped when she first noticed the change in my eyes, when my irises took on a red rim. Then she lowered her gaze and watched as my fangs descended. Chloe held her breath and didn't move.

Although her heartbeat raced, Chloe's gaze never left my face, her eyes climbing slowly upwards to meet my own.

"Are you going to hurt me, Gregor?" she asked boldly, although I could also scent her fear.

"No, my darling. I could never hurt you. On that, you have my word."

I kept my eyes and fangs for a few moments longer, then changed them back to their regular human appearance.

"So, are you Dracula or something?" she asked.

"Or something," I answered.

"How did you become this way? And do your friends know?"

"Yes, most of my friends know. Many of them are immortal, like me." I waited while she absorbed that bit of information.

"You mean Sergei and Yuri?" she asked.

"Also Alex, Joshua, and Nik. And now Keeley, too."

"No. Alex has just become a father. Vampires can't reproduce, can they? I mean, I've watched a few vampire films in my time, and none of them has ever had children—until the last one with the sparkly vamps, that is. Will Rory age quickly like that?"

"I don't have the faintest idea what you are talking about, and no, my godson will not age quickly. Rory will grow like any other normal human baby. He is, however, a Born Immortal child—meaning a child born to an immortal father and human mother. He can remain human, yet with better healing abilities, greater strength and a longer lifespan, or he could opt to take human blood when he is an adult and become a Born Immortal vampire."

"Wow, so is that all you have to do? Just decide one day that you want to be immortal, drink human blood, and then magically live forever? I mean, I know you eat regular human food and drink normal, if not ridiculously expensive, wine."

"We also drink blood, Chloe, but our need for it lessens with time. I only need to drink blood maybe three times a week. More if I need to heal or if I'm tired or under stress."

"I've seen you go out in the daylight, too, so vampires burning in the sun is a myth, I suppose?"

"No, that's not a myth for Made vampires, and even Born Immortals tend to tire more easily in strong sunlight."

"What's a Made vampire?"

"A Made vampire is a normal human that's been

drained to the point of death or is already dying, who's then fed the blood of an immortal. Made vampires will hunger for blood more than a Born Immortal, and it can take months or even years to control that craving. A Made vampire cannot tolerate daylight like a Born Immortal, and it would take centuries before they could safely go out in sunlight without burning from the inside out."

"So you and everyone else you mentioned is a Born Immortal because you can all go out in the sun?"

"Josh is a Made vampire, or Made Immortal, if I'm being politically correct. But he was turned over two hundred and seventy years ago, so can tolerate a few hours of sunlight. Although, I imagine he must tire extremely easily."

"You said earlier, 'and now Keeley.' Does that mean she changed quite recently?"

"I'm afraid that will have to be Keeley's story to tell, my inquisitive little flower girl," I said as I kissed her on the tip of her nose. To my great relief, she didn't pull away from me, and I was happy to know she didn't fear my kiss.

"You said I didn't have to worry about diseases when I mentioned protection. But what about getting pregnant? I mean, Julia has just had a baby, and you told me that an immortal male can get a human female pregnant. Gregor, I'm not on the pill, so should I be worried?"

"No. The immortal male and human female have to be Bonded by blood for that to happen. To do that, the couple would need to drink blood from each other at the same time, which normally happens during sex. When an immortal feeds from someone during a sexual act, their feelings increase tenfold and will induce an immediate and powerful orgasm."

Chloe's eyes widened at that statement. I carried on explaining the Bonding process.

"When a couple drinks enough of each other's blood at the same time during sex, they become Bonded to the other for eternity—as long as the human keeps taking small amounts of the immortal's blood, that is. In fact, if a human regularly takes a small amount of immortal blood, they will never age or get ill. And our blood can heal most things, although there are some diseases that cannot be cured, despite its medicinal properties."

"So Alex and Julia will be together for eternity?" she queried.

I nodded and smiled, remembering their wedding day, standing as best man at the altar with Alex.

"Did you know that both their rings have the inscription *My Love Forever* on them?" I asked.

"Yes. Julia told me the story of how they'd both asked Alex's sister to help with the rings, and they ended up surprising each other with the same inscription. But now I know that forever means just that, the sentiment seems more heartfelt and true."

I watched Chloe's eyes glisten with that emotional statement. It seems my practical little flower girl is romantic at heart!

I remembered the gift I'd bought for her, so I leant back to switch on a table lamp and grab the blue velvet box I'd placed beside it before she arrived.

As soon as the light came on, Chloe tried to cover herself by placing an arm across her chest and one over her abdomen.

"What are you doing, Chloe?" I asked while using my free hand to uncover her breasts.

"I'm not comfortable being naked with the light on,"

she replied, once again reaching over to grab her clothing. "I'd feel happier wearing something just now." I could hear what sounded like panic in her voice.

"Well, I'm hoping you'll wear this gift I brought you—if you like it."

I held out the gift box so she would have to uncover herself to grasp it. After a few seconds of hesitation, she took the box from my hand and opened it. The gold stood out against the deep blue silk it was cushioned against, and the various coloured gems that were set like flowers sparkled when they caught the light.

Chloe was silent as she tilted the box one way and then the other—either admiring the bracelet or trying to find something she liked about it. I couldn't quite tell what she thought, and that just didn't sit well with me. Gregor Antonov always bought the very best, from the very best, and to my knowledge, my gifts were always appreciated.

"Do you not like the bracelet, Chloe?" I asked with trepidation.

"Gregor, it's beautiful, thank you. But it must have been so expensive. I mean…are these real gems?"

"Of course. Those are emeralds, and these are pink sapphires. Then here we have yellow diamonds, and this one is blue sapphire, followed by rubies." I looked up at her face, trying my best to judge what the problem was.

"Why did you buy it for me, Gregor? What made you spend so much money on someone who, until tonight, you only had a platonic friendship with?" She held my gaze while asking this question, clearly trying to figure out if I had an ulterior motive. But anyone who knew me would tell you I had not.

"Chloe, I am a very wealthy man, and the cost of this item is nothing to me. I like to spoil the people I care for. I do it often and offer no apology for it. It is something you will need to get used to because I'll shower you with gifts whenever I get the chance. So are you going to put it on, or just keep it in the box? Either way, the bracelet is yours," I informed her gruffly. Then I watched as she took it out of the box gently and was secretly thrilled to hear the near-silent gasp when she placed the pretty item over her wrist.

I helped her fasten it, and then kissed the inside of her wrist before turning it over and admiring how the bracelet looked against her lightly tanned, freckled skin.

Before I could say anything, Chloe surprised me by moving position and straddling me. She grabbed my head and kissed me with an open-mouthed, hot, wet kiss while she ground herself against me. This was a much better reaction to my gift. I lifted her until I could position my cock against the entrance to her wet sex, then thrust myself deep inside her.

Chloe cried out as her muscles clenched around my cock, and I groaned out loud. I let her get used to this immediate, deep penetration for about thirty seconds, just kissing her hungrily. When Chloe rocked herself against me, I started to move again, lifting her up and slamming her back down; her passionate cries fuelling my desire to hear her come apart for me.

I had another desire, too. I desired her blood flowing through my veins, and Chloe knew it somehow without me even saying it. Maybe she had caught me staring at the rapid throb of the pulse at her neck. Whatever it was that gave me away, I wasn't about to question her while she tilted her head and cried out, "Do it."

My fangs dropped a second after she uttered those two words, and I sank them into her neck in an instinctive move that vampires perfect almost immediately. She gasped and tried to pull away at that first bite of pain, but once I had taken the first swallow of her blood and sucked back the next, her orgasm ran through her body, making her almost convulse with pleasure. I had to hold Chloe still so that I didn't tear her delicate skin.

I was only going to take a little, but she tasted better than anything or anyone I'd had before. She was perfection.

Some strange emotion came over me, which caused me to hold her tighter against my body. I fed longer than I ever had from another human since the day I became immortal.

One climax turned into another, then another for my beautiful flower girl, and I had to stop myself before I took more blood than her body could healthily cope with. As it was, she appeared a little shaken and dizzy, although that could have been from all the orgasms that feeding from her during sex had caused.

I held her still for a while, just content to hold her against my body and touch her wherever I could. Chloe gifted me with the softest of kisses, and I closed my eyes, letting myself enjoy the closeness and whatever else we were sharing in this moment.

I lifted her slightly and laid her back down on the rug. When I slipped inside her again, I kept my pace steady and gentle, just adding a slight grind of my pelvis against hers. This time, when she came, I came with her, crying out her name as I filled her with my seed. I had a sudden thought, a vision if you will, of my seed taking root and Chloe carrying my child. Instead of finding the thought disagreeable, it actually warmed my cold immortal heart.

Chapter Seven

Chloe

Wow! Just…wow!

I didn't know it was possible to feel this good. Gregor was still pressed against me, his cock still semi-hard inside me and his kisses softly skimming my jawline up to my ear.

"Stay with me tonight," he whispered.

I was tempted to say yes, really tempted, in fact, but I had a 5 a.m. start in the morning so I could get to the flower market early.

"I can't tonight, Gregor. I have to be up by four thirty at the latest, and I'll need a shower before I go to bed."

"That's a great idea, Chloe. Let's shower together," he said as he slipped out of me and quickly stood. He held out his hand to help me stand, but I had to end the night here, no matter how delicious a hot shower with the super sexy Gregor sounded.

"No, I'm sorry, I can't. I really do need to go home. I

can't miss tomorrow's flower market, and I feel quite tired after all that activity."

I wasn't kidding, either. I did feel sleepy, so much so that I stumbled when putting on my skirt.

"Let me help you, *moya malen'kaya tsvetochnitsa*," said Gregor as he took my bra and top and helped me get dressed.

"What does that mean?" I asked.

"It means my little flower girl. It is how we say it in Russian. And now my flower girl is wearing the flowers I brought over from my country," he said, turning my hand and kissing the inside of my wrist behind my new bracelet.

"Thanks again for this bracelet, Gregor. I don't have much jewellery, and certainly nothing as pretty and feminine as this."

"You are more than welcome, my darling. I'll buy you a pair of earrings next. Something to match your eyes. Such a beautiful shade, neither blue nor green, but a perfect mix of both."

"You don't have to buy me anything, Gregor. And I couldn't ever afford to get you anything as nice as this."

He stopped dressing as soon as I said that and pulled me towards him. His trousers were still unbuttoned, and his shirtless, muscular chest seemed to beckon my lips towards it. I couldn't help kissing him there, the light brown hair on his chest tickling my nose as I did so.

"Chloe, I do not buy gifts because I expect something in return. I do it because I want to. It makes me happy to know I can show my appreciation for someone with a gift, and happier still to know I've brought joy into someone's life by doing so."

Oh, I could seriously fall for this man, or vampire, or whatever I should call him. Right now, he was just a man, albeit a very attractive, sexy man. He looked and smelled so good as I placed more kisses on his chest.

"Chloe," Gregor groaned before he took my mouth in a passionate kiss. My breathing quickened in response, and I knew that if I didn't move soon, I would certainly not be leaving here tonight.

I pulled away while I still could and made my excuses about using the bathroom in the hallway. The hallway in the old manor house felt cool after the warmth of the fire in the sitting room. It made me feel slightly less tired, which I was grateful for.

After using the bathroom, I came out to find Gregor in the hallway, waiting for me.

"Are you still intent on going home?" he asked.

"I have to, Gregor. I need the fresh stock to replace what I used today for Julia. We haven't been as busy as this at such short notice in quite a while. That's probably why I feel so tired and a little dizzy," I said, placing my hand on the wall to steady myself. For a moment, I thought I was going to pass out.

"This is my fault; I took too much of your blood. I am so sorry, Chloe. Please forgive me and let me give you some of my blood. It will help your body replace all the blood I've taken."

Gregor was at my side in an instant, concern and guilt on his handsome face. He pressed me back against the wall, gazing into my sleepy eyes. After unbuttoning his shirt sleeve, he rolled it back a little before lifting his wrist to his mouth.

It was then that I noticed Gregor's fangs had lengthened. He bit deeply into his wrist and lowered it to my mouth. I hesitated, but when I looked into his beautiful blue eyes, I became a little bolder, flicking my tongue out to meet the thick red blood as it made its way down his arm. After the first metallic tang, the taste changed to something sweet, a little like honey, and I found myself closing my mouth over his wrist and sucking. Gregor closed his eyes and threw his head back, letting out a sexy breathless groan that went straight to my core. When he brought his head up and opened his eyes, they had red rims around the irises. I wasn't sure if this was a good or bad thing, but when I felt him rub his erection against my belly, I knew to carry on.

He growled in my ear while using his free hand to unbutton his trousers and pull them down. Gregor wasn't wearing any underwear after using them to clean me up earlier, so his cock sprang free onto my waiting fingers. Running his hand under my skirt, he found my underwear, tearing through them quickly. I let go of his throbbing cock and pulled my skirt up out of the way as he lifted my leg to his backside. I felt him bending at the knees before lifting me slightly.

I tried to pull my mouth away from his wrist but he growled out a loud "No," so I carried on sucking steadily. Gregor's thick cock probed the entrance to my sex before thrusting inside me, hard and deep. He was breathing harshly in my ear as he carried on with his hard, deep thrusts. This wasn't lovemaking, this was fucking, and I loved it.

Pretty soon, the feelings became too much, and I felt an orgasm hit me deep and hot in my core, spiralling outwards throughout every inch of my body. I was still moaning out my release over Gregor's wrist when I felt the sharp bite of his fangs as they sank into my neck.

For the second time tonight, as soon as Gregor sucked my blood from that fresh bite, I hit a breathtaking climax. After swallowing another mouthful of his blood, I let go of his wrist and screamed out his name like I was trying to call on the gods, throwing my head back and gazing at some unseen force from above.

Gregor roared his release, holding me tightly as our breathing slowed. He removed his mouth from my neck and licked the wounds he'd made, then his lips met mine, giving me the type of kiss they write stories about. The kind that makes you hold on to that person forever so you can relive the kiss over and over every day.

"Please stay, Chloe," Gregor said before kissing me again.

I knew I needed to get home, but I just couldn't leave him. Not now, not when I felt so utterly connected to him. Like I belonged with him, or to him. The thoughts were confusing, but something in me told me they were right. I did belong to Gregor, but he also belonged to me.

Chapter Eight

Gregor

I awoke to the sound of the alarm on Chloe's phone. She was asleep in my arms, her head resting on my chest and her right leg wrapped around my thigh. I had to let go of her to roll slightly for her phone, which was on the bedside table. She stirred as I hit the button that was highlighted to make the buzzing sound stop.

I put my arms around her again before stroking down her side and onto her hip. There were still smudges of blood left there from my wrist before it healed when I'd lifted her higher to get inside her last night. Just thinking about it had my cock throbbing against her belly.

There were things about last night that I needed to address, and on the top of that list was the fact that I very nearly Bonded with Chloe without her consent.

I saw her stumble because she was dizzy, and I knew it was because I'd taken more blood from her than I should have. So I bit into my wrist to offer her my healing blood, helping her replenish what she'd lost.

As soon as Chloe took her first swallow, I was lost. Thoughts of what was right and wrong simply vanished. All I knew right then was that I had to be inside my flower girl, and I needed to make her mine in the most permanent way.

I know we took each other's blood at the same time, although not enough to trigger full Bonding. But if Chloe hadn't let go of my wrist, I wouldn't have stopped the process. And that would have been wrong.

In our circles, it can involve the most severe punishment, and rightly so. But something in me told me that Bonding with Chloe was right. And hours later, with her wrapped around my body, I still felt the same.

Chloe had meant to leave me and head home, which had surprised me. Usually, it was me who left after I'd taken the blood and sex that was offered. But she outright told me no. It wasn't a word I was used to hearing from a woman.

I knew her reasons were valid; I just had a hard time accepting them. However, after I'd had her again, there was no way she was leaving my side. I'd asked her to stay once more, although I don't think I would have accepted no as an answer if she'd said it. But she didn't deny me that time, and I hoped beyond all hopes it was because she felt the same as I did.

I'd told Chloe I was getting up with her to go to the flower market, so when her alarm went off again, I lowered my head towards hers and kissed her awake.

"Come on, sleepyhead," I murmured against her lips. "Don't you have a flower market to go to?"

"Mmm," she murmured back as she snuggled up closer. Then I felt her freeze when she realised she wasn't alone.

"Gregor, what time is it? I need to have a shower and change my clothes. I need to go home and get my van, or I'm going to be late."

"We can shower here, and then we can go and get your van or take my SUV. Your choice."

Chloe pulled away from my embrace and climbed out of bed, putting an arm over her breasts and one over her belly and sex. I knelt up and reached for her, pulling her arms away from her body.

"Don't, Chloe. Don't hide your body from me. I think we are well past any shyness after last night, don't you?"

Chloe blushed from just above her breasts to her hairline before once again leaving my embrace. She walked into the en-suite bathroom and closed the door. There were no locks on it, but I didn't follow her straight away, not until I heard the water running.

When I stepped into the shower, she turned away from me, picking up a bottle of shampoo.

"Gregor, I don't have time for any more sex, so if you don't mind leaving the shower, I'll be out as soon as I finish washing my hair."

I took the shampoo out of her hands and poured some over her hair. The length was short and cut in a pixie style around her ears, which really suited her.

I was used to seeing long hair on the women I normally spent time with, both in and out of my club. But I found I liked the pretty pixie style. It brought out her bone structure and those blue-green eyes that had haunted my thoughts and dreams since I'd met her.

As I massaged the shampoo into her hair, I looked down her back to the plump cheeks of her bottom and the sexy flare of her hips. Now that was a sight I wanted to see.

I'd pictured it many times in my head—imagining what

her larger-than-average hips and bottom would look like when she was bent over naked before me. But I knew if I touched any part of her other than her hair, we would never get to the market. So, using all the control I could muster, I got on with the job of getting her hair rinsed, turning to hide my erection while she washed her body.

Chapter Nine

Chloe

I felt like I was in some sort of alternate universe.

Last night, this gorgeous, way-too-sexy-for-his-own-good billionaire had wanted to have sex with me. Of course, what should have made the night even more interesting was the fact that he was a vampire and had drunk my blood, something I offered willingly.

And yet, what had thrown me for a loop—more than any other occurrence last night—was Gregor hadn't wanted me to leave. He almost begged me to stay with him after we'd had sex in his hallway. But he hadn't needed to beg. I wanted to stay with him. Needed to, even.

It was as if he'd flipped some internal switch that left me open to thoughts of loving him. But that was just ridiculous.

I'd spent a lot of time with him when he was here in England a couple of months ago, and we had a wonderful friendship. He'd flirted with me constantly, but he was always a gentleman.

Gregor had only ever kissed my hand and my cheek before last night, but he would always linger around my neck, saying he liked my perfume, although I never wore any. It would attract too many bees and wasps, which is never a good idea when you're around flowers all day. So I have to say that I didn't see any of this coming at all.

The man in question was driving us to collect my van, which was parked at the back of my shop. He'd insisted he was coming to the market with me because he was curious to see how I chose my stock. Gregor offered the use of his vehicle, which was a Volvo XC90. Although it was really nice, I'd been surprised when I found out that this was the car he drove.

I'd expected him to drive some ridiculously expensive Italian sports car, but Gregor said he only ever had the best, and as far as he was concerned, nothing could rival the pure luxury of driving while sitting in something that feels as comfortable as your favourite armchair.

I agreed with him in that respect. The comfort level of this vehicle was superb. So he'd certainly feel like he was slumming it when he sat inside my little van.

I wondered what the market sellers would think when they saw Gregor. He didn't look like he belonged at the flower market. He was wearing tailored mid-grey trousers that fit his long legs and sexy arse perfectly, and a pale blue shirt with the sleeves rolled up in an attempt to look casual. But Gregor had a hard time with casual, of that I could tell. I, on the other hand, had quickly changed into my old jeans and a T-shirt, so we couldn't have looked more different if we tried.

It didn't take us too long to get to the market. There was little traffic on the roads at this time in the morning, but I was concerned by the car park being so full. It could mean that the better deals had already been snapped up.

I took my cross-body bag out of the back of the van, along with the list I'd compiled after I finished work yesterday. There was always room for manoeuvre as long as I could get the basics. So I grabbed a large cart and began my journey through the market with Gregor by my side.

The main floral best sellers in my shop were carnations, roses, lilies, gerberas and gypsophila. I looked around to find my regular suppliers and started there.

Gregor was great, never once getting in my way, and not afraid to pitch in and carry anything I needed.

I missed out on a good deal on some red miniature roses but more than made up for it with some late summer hanging baskets.

On the way back out of the market, I stopped for more wreath and floral display foam before grabbing us a cup of tea and a bacon and egg sandwich from the café on the corner. I could tell from the look he gave the food before taking a bite that Gregor wasn't impressed, but he didn't complain. The tea, however, was a different matter.

"Chloe, how can you drink this? It is disgusting. There is too much milk, and it comes in a polystyrene cup. This liquid cannot be called tea," he said with a grimace.

"Gregor, once I get back to my shop, I'll be so busy that this may be the last hot drink I get before any of my staff arrive."

"That will not happen today. I will carry everything in from the van while you make tea. Everyone should start the day with a decent cup of tea or coffee. I find my staff are much more amenable after their first cup."

We chatted away on the journey back to Barrowfield. I told him more about my upbringing and what it was like living in Germany and the various other places my father was stationed during his time in the army.

Gregor told me about his home in Moscow and how much his country had changed over the last fifty years. I couldn't decide whether he sounded happy about it or not, but secretly, I wanted him to be more at home here. I missed his friendship when he was away, and I had a feeling that when he went back to Russia again, I would feel so much worse.

He also told me how important it was to keep the fact that he and his friends were vampires to myself. Of course, he didn't need to tell me that, as I would never tell anyone. And who would believe me if I did?

Gregor mentioned the extra strength he had as an immortal and the way he could manipulate someone using mind control. I asked him never to use that on me, and he promised me he wouldn't. The idea of another man trying to control me again was totally unacceptable, whether they were a sexy vampire or not.

Gregor was as good as his word and carried everything into the back room while I made us a pot of tea. He watched while I put together a dozen bouquets that I could price up quite cheaply. I made up three more expensive ones and placed gold-coloured hearts on sticks inside each one. The cheaper ones would always sell, but the more expensive ones rarely do—unless it was Valentine's or Mother's Day.

More often than not, it was the scented candles I stocked that people chose as gifts instead of the more traditional flowers. We had customers who came in regularly for their favourites and also for the novelty candle holders, ornaments and photo frames we stocked.

I'd set aside a beautiful photo frame in oak that had the word *"Godson"* written on a small brass plaque on the bottom of it. I'd wanted to print off a photograph of Gregor and little Rory to put in it and take to Gregor's last night, but my printer had run out of coloured ink, so I needed to get new cartridges.

Gregor had been in my shop before, but as the shop was still closed, he was able to relax and browse more. He selected a few scented candles as gifts for Keeley, Gina, his new housekeeper, as well as one for Maggie Saunders, the office manager at the Night Movers depot.

Gregor was such a thoughtful man. Well, he was a vampire, actually—from what I'd found out last night. But from where I stood watching his incredible physique move around my store, he looked all man to me.

When Pam arrived, Gregor said good morning, then he came towards me, telling me he had to leave and get on with some work. He placed both hands on my face and gave me a panty-melting kiss that I really wasn't expecting him to do in front of anyone else. We hadn't discussed our relationship after his admission that he thought of us as more than friends.

"I can pick you up after you finish work, Chloe," he told me. "What time will you be done?"

"I… Oh, I can't tonight, Gregor. I'm going to a meeting at the community hall in Rothley; it's about the supermarket you and the Night Movers company are building. I thought you'd be attending."

"Of course. You kept me distracted, my flower girl. I am attending the meeting. Tell me, Chloe, should I be ready for the local shopkeepers storming the meeting and wielding weapons?"

"What? No, at least, I don't think so," I giggled, picturing him being chased away by Kenny from the bakery. "Isn't the meeting being held so you can calm our fears when you tell us that the supermarket won't impede on our businesses?"

"Do not worry about your shop, Chloe. We have proposals to put to all the local shopkeepers and market traders tonight, and I think that many will be pleasantly surprised."

"I hope so, Gregor. It would be a shame to see anyone go out of business because of it," I said with all seriousness. Many of these little shops had been here since long before the war, and it would be such a shame to see those local places close.

"If I recall, the meeting starts at seven thirty tonight. I could pick you up at six thirty and feed you first," he offered.

That would have been lovely, but I'd already made plans with Dave from the butcher's next door. He was picking me up just after seven so that we could get there early and meet with Kenny and Jill from the bakery, as well as Mr Singh and Easha, his wife.

Afterwards, a few of us were going to the Red Lion to discuss the meeting further—or to drown our sorrows in despair. I wasn't quite sure about everyone's motives yet. But it was good to know that we were all trying to support each other in what could be a difficult and costly time when the supermarket opened.

"I'm sorry, Gregor. I've already made arrangements with Dave Higgins, the butcher, so I'll be going to the meeting with him," I said. Gregor's eyes flashed red when I told him about my plans for the evening, and I became quite nervous.

Gregor bent close to my ear. "You can have your time of shopkeeper solidarity, Chloe," he whispered, "but at the end of the night, you will be bound and at my mercy. I plan on feasting on your pussy until I am satisfied I've tasted enough of your come to keep me sated until morning. And when tomorrow dawns, I will do it all over again. Is that clear, my little flower girl?"

I nodded my head, unable to speak. With his breath against my ear and his words painting pictures in my mind that made my heart beat faster and my sex throb in anticipation, I had no hope of denying him.

"Until tonight, my darling," whispered Gregor with a slow, sexy smile and a wink. Then he turned and said, "It has been good to see you again, Pamela. I missed your beautiful smile when I was away."

"It's good to see you too, Gregor," said Pam, blushing profusely. "And I hope we get to see more of you from now on."

"My dear Pamela, I can guarantee you will see more of me. I find I am increasingly drawn to the tempting delights that this little village has to offer," Gregor stated while staring straight at me. Then he winked at me before saying goodbye.

Once the door had closed, I heard a loud *"Oh. My. God,"* as Pam dashed from behind the counter and hugged me.

"Pam, what's got into you?" I asked as she squeezed me tightly.

"Well, from that kiss and the look he gave you before he left, I can guess what part of him got into you last night."

"I can't believe you just said that, Pam," I told her, trying to sound all innocent and disgusted. But I couldn't help the smile that tugged at the corners of my mouth.

"Come on, spill the beans, Chloe. Was it as good as my imagination is telling me it was?"

"Better," I sighed, then laughed out loud at the dreamy look on Pam's face.

"So, are you two an item now?" she asked.

"I think so. I mean, he's just asked to see me again, and we did...you know... But neither of us has actually come out and said anything. Maybe we can discuss it tonight after the shopkeepers' get-together."

"Don't tell me you've given up time with that sexy Russian billionaire for a night at the Red Lion with sausage-fingered Dave from next door? The man is a pest, Chloe. He was the same with your auntie Joyce. Always interfering and making it look like he was helping her. She put up with it because she'd been good friends with his parents and had known him since he was a baby. But I could see she got fed up with him. Now he's trying to do the same with you."

"He can be a bit much, I agree. But he was so good when I had the water leak, and he helped out when I had the fire, too."

"Yes, wasn't it so convenient that he was around when they happened?" she added with an edge to her voice.

It was clear she didn't like Dave that much. She was friends with Jill from the bakery, who was unhappy when Dave had bought the empty wool shop next door. He extended his shop to include ovens, in which he baked various meat pies, sausage rolls, quiches, pasties, and a small selection of sweet treats.

Dave once told me that Aunt Joyce had promised him

her shop because she'd wanted him to open a small café in which he could sell his freshly baked goods. She never once mentioned it to me, and Pam vehemently denied any knowledge of it. I'd been the sole heir in Auntie Joyce's will; there was no mention of Dave Higgins, the butcher.

Chapter Ten

Gregor

I drove home from Chloe's shop in a foul mood. Who the fuck did this Dave the Butcher think he was escorting my Chloe anywhere? Obviously, I should give the butcher some leeway; he did not know that Chloe was mine. After tonight, however, he would have no doubt whatsoever that Chloe belonged to me.

When I arrived at the manor, Keeley was in my office sorting through mail. I asked to be brought up to speed about previous meetings held with the council and shop-keepers regarding any objections against the supermarket build.

As always, the ever-efficient Keeley showed me her detailed, no-nonsense findings, which she presented both digitally and in print. There were graphs to show the different objections, where possible we could overcome these, and also where we couldn't.

Keeley had been adding to her previous idea that we

stock some of the local shops' best-selling produce. There were items such as the bakery's scones and apple pie, as well as seasonal delights like parkin: the traditional Yorkshire cake made with oatmeal, treacle, and ginger—usually sold around bonfire night.

She also recommended that we stock bouquets of flowers from Chloe's shop, which I heartily approved of. There was no mention of the butcher who'd be escorting my Chloe to the meeting.

"What about the butcher? Surely it would be good to get the meat man on our side?" I queried.

"Dave Higgins has been a royal pain in the arse, Gregor. Out of everyone at the last meeting, he was the most vocal, and he was extremely patronising when I tried to placate him. I tried to speak to him alone regarding stocking some of his pies, but he started raising his voice, saying I was trying to bribe him.

"I could have slapped him at that meeting, but I remained calm and used mind control—both to shut him up *and* to get him to apologise to me publicly. Then later that night, I punctured all his tyres and painted the word dickhead across his car windscreen."

"You did well, Keeley. Thank you for all your efforts and the way you managed what must have been an awkward situation at the meeting," I said, trying to hide the grin that was slowly spreading across my face.

While some acts of retribution can be deemed irresponsible and risky where business is concerned, in this instance, I was proud of my PA. She had shown the cleaver-wielding fucker that she was no pushover, and I was only disappointed that I had not seen the result of her revenge. I made a mental note to give her a bonus in her next wage.

So, Higgins the butcher had shown by his treatment of

Keeley at the meeting that he had no respect for women. This made me even less happy about him escorting my Chloe anywhere.

We broke for tea and biscuits, and Keeley filled me in on all the other developments that had happened while I was away. Nik and Gina were planning their wedding and honeymoon for when Alex came back to work. Maggie had once again been talked out of part-time work and retirement, and Joshua and Keeley had decided to Blood Bond in two weeks' time. Daisy's grandparents were taking her away for five days, so it made sense to wait until she left.

During the early days after Bonding, couples find it hard to be apart and often need to have sex and share blood more frequently. So it was better for Keeley's daughter to be away when the couple Bonded.

Keeley was gracious enough not to ask me about Chloe, even though I could tell it was on the tip of her tongue. Although I adored Keeley, there was one other person who I felt I needed to discuss this with. One who knew me better than any other. Luckily, I had just heard her car pull into the driveway.

Keeley and I walked to the door and greeted Freya with a hug. Keeley's brother, Daniel, was with her, and I shook his hand before guiding them both back towards the kitchen. Mrs Timmins had made another pot of tea and produced a lemon drizzle cake from a tin on the counter before she left on her lunch break.

We each took a slice and proceeded to eat it while Freya told me about her morning visit with Julia and my little godson. Apparently, the midwife had visited, and all was as it should be. But Julia was quite tired today, so she was having a nap while Alex took care of Rory.

Freya had stayed a while but could see that Alex wanted

to spend time alone with his son. I could understand that. He'd waited over 900 years to become a father, so he'd treasure those moments with his child.

Daniel had proved to be a talented artist, though he'd only used pencil and pastels so far. Freya had discovered just how good he was when he'd drawn a likeness of her daughter from Freya's own description. It was a beautiful thing to do and a precious gift for Freya.

Both Freya and Alex had openly wept when they'd seen it because the likeness had been uncannily accurate, from what Alex had told me.

I wondered whether Rory had a look of Freya's daughter. If he did, Freya had not let herself give in to any melancholy and was staying here to support her brother and his wife in these early days of parenthood.

I had asked previously if Daniel had any objections to doing some sketches of the manor and the grounds. He said he would be happy to do it, so I asked if Keeley could show him the areas I thought would make good spots to sketch.

I informed Daniel I would leave it up to him to decide which areas he finally selected, as long as he included the front aspect of the house and the secret garden.

"Come on, then, Gregor, spit it out. What is it that's bothering you?" Freya demanded when Daniel and Keeley left the room.

"How do you know I have something bothering me?" I asked curiously.

"Because I know you better than you know yourself, Gregor Antonov. Also, you get a line appearing in between your eyebrows, and you have a small muscle twitch in your jawline," Freya said as she poked at the areas she'd mentioned. I smiled and threatened to bite her finger, which she laughed at before taking my hand in hers.

"Freya, I did something last night that I should be very ashamed of, but I find that I am not. I do not wish to discuss my sex life with you in detail, but as you appear to be the oracle of all that is immortal, I know you will speak with me both as a friend and advisor on this matter," I said.

"Go on," she prompted.

"Last night, Chloe and I made love for the first time. It was beautiful and special and meant even more to me than I thought it would!"

Freya was quiet for a moment, so I looked into her beautiful grey eyes to try to determine what she thought about my statement. First and foremost, she seemed surprised, but then she broke into a huge smile before jumping up and hugging me.

"Oh, Gregor. Chloe must be it for you; the one you are destined to Bond with. I've known you for centuries, and that's the only time I've ever heard of you making love with a woman, instead of simply fucking or having sex."

"Freya, we have rarely discussed my sexual preferences, but obviously, you are aware of where they lie. I used to think that if you were more submissive, maybe we could have had something. And that, although we were never *in love*, in time, we could have learned to love each other in that way. But you are a very dominant woman, so that would never have worked," I admitted.

Freya was a strong female who would find it hard to let a man dominate in any aspect of her life. It just wasn't who she was.

"I used to think so too, but then Daniel came along.

Even though he works for me, he's most definitely the dominant force in our relationship—especially in the bedroom."

That was something I never expected to hear. Freya had made it clear we would be incompatible in that respect, so we'd remained the best of friends instead.

"What changed?" I asked, not sure how I felt about this entire conversation.

"Nothing changed, Gregor. I just found the one for me, and I was happy for him to take the lead. I like not having to be in control all the time. If I'm honest, it was just so tiring to maintain over the years. But I trust that Daniel loves and respects me enough to give me what I need, both in the bedroom and in life in general. Whether that be control *or* submission. In fact, I don't like to call it submission. I prefer to see it as handing over the reins and letting the other person lead for a while. A good relationship requires give and take on both sides. Be it friendship or love, a partnership has to be equal.

"Think about your night with Chloe. You said you made love. There was a reason that this happened on your first time with this woman, Gregor. I think you recognised that she's the one, and you wanted to show her this by making her feel loved and special when you first took her body, something you would have never done otherwise."

Freya was right. What happened between Chloe and me by the fireside last night was truly beautiful, and something I hoped to have again. But it was the third time I was inside my little flower girl that my once-famed control had slipped.

I did not want to see the judgement in Freya's eyes when I told her I'd almost Bonded with Chloe without her consent, so I recounted all that had happened without looking at her. When I finished telling her last night's story, I did not hear a gasp of shock or a tut. Instead, Freya squeezed my hand and asked me to look at her. As I raised my blue eyes to her pale grey ones, I did not see any judgement. Only understanding and love.

I should have known my best friend would not find me lacking integrity or moral code, despite what I had done. But the guilt I felt over what had happened still came from within.

"Gregor, I think you should tell Chloe what nearly happened, and what made you act this way. I think that when our vampire side—which can be quite animalistic in its focus—recognises its mate, it instinctively wants to claim that mate by Bonding. Obviously, at this particular time, your vampire side took over from your human side and you lost control of the situation. Something else I've also never known happen to you. I think if you can explain your feelings to Chloe, it will help."

"But that's just it, Freya. I don't know what my feelings are exactly. They don't have a name that I can identify."

"Not love, then?" Freya queried.

I shook my head. "Love is something pure and gentle. What I feel for Chloe is anything but. She has become an obsession for me. She is in my thoughts constantly. I want to protect her and see her smile, and I'd give anything to make her happy. But I also want to possess her and bind her to me so she can't escape. I want to hurt anyone who has ever hurt her, and I would kill anyone who tries to take her from me. The only time since meeting her that I have felt truly whole was when I was buried deep inside her and when I awoke with her in my arms. Does that sound like love to you, Freya?"

"Well, yes, it does, actually. Love isn't always pure and gentle, Gregor. And it doesn't always make us act that way, either. Love can twist our hearts and minds just as much as it can soothe our spirits.

"I loved my father. But his heinous actions—brought about by his own twisted version of love—caused me to lose my daughter, son, and husband. The people I loved most in this world.

"My father had lost the woman he loved and thought he would lose Alex and me because we rejected immortality. His push for us to do so became his obsession. He had no balance in his love for us. What you just explained to me has balance.

"You said she was your obsession, and you wanted to possess her and bind her to you so she couldn't escape. But you also said you wanted to protect her and see her smile, that you'd give anything to make her happy. You told me you had moments with her that made you feel whole. That's balance, Gregor, and that's what keeps love healthy. That and respect."

"So, I'm in love with her, then?" I asked, not only Freya but also myself.

Is that what had happened? Had I fallen madly in love with my flower girl, as well as recognising she was the one I should Bond with?

The two don't always come hand in hand, but I was glad in my case that they had. I was always quick to tell both Freya and Keeley that I loved them. It seemed easier to accept that I loved in that way: a deep friendship and almost familial. Yet, in over five hundred years on this earth, I had never truly fallen in love with a woman until now.

Chapter Eleven

Gregor

I visited Chelsee later that afternoon to see if she needed any help with moving her furniture, but it appeared that Josh, Nik, and Sergei had organised everything earlier. So I took her out to the Italian restaurant that Chloe favoured, and we chatted about her upcoming job.

Chelsee was an extremely witty young woman, and despite the fact that she was blind, she had an uncanny ability to read someone's character. I asked her if she would accompany Nik, Keeley and me to the meeting about the supermarket, so she could give her thoughts about the main objectors to the proposal. She agreed to do so, and at seven fifteen, we took our seats next to Keeley and Nik on a platform at the front of the community hall while the room began to fill.

I felt her presence before I even saw her. Turning towards the door, I watched my little flower girl being guided into the room by a tall, blond, red-faced fellow who had his hand resting on her back.

The ends of my fingers throbbed as my claws threatened to emerge, but I managed to keep them hidden. Despite how laid-back the people of Yorkshire appeared, I'm sure they would take objection to me slicing the local butcher in half. I smirked at the irony, imagining the man trussed up and hung from one of his butchering hooks.

Chloe looked radiant in a pale lemon sweater and beige linen trousers. I wanted to walk over and kiss her full lips in front of everyone here, but then I saw that fucking butcher move to brush something from her cheek, and anger swept over me once again.

Chelsee took my hand and asked if I was okay. She must have felt me stiffen in my seat when I noticed his hand return to Chloe's back. I instinctively turned to Chelsee and smiled, for the moment forgetting her blindness. On realising my mistake, I raised the back of her hand to my lips and kissed it before reassuring her I was okay.

I turned back to look at Chloe and found she was scowling at me. It wasn't until I noticed her look down to where my hand was still joined with Chelsee's that I could see why. She was jealous.

As far as I was concerned, this could only be a good thing. Although, in the past, I would have never encouraged such behaviour in a woman. Indeed, if any sub I had in my club ever became jealous or possessive, I made a hasty retreat, and she would not be invited to sub for me again. Of course, it rarely got that far. I would lose interest before anything could develop on her part. But I found I liked the fact that my Chloe was jealous and possessive. They were the same feelings that were flying through my mind when the meat man leant closer to my woman.

I let go of Chelsee's hand and took a pen and paper out of my pocket to make notes about the meeting. I did not need to do this because Keeley was already waiting with a pencil and notepad, but holding on to them gave me a purpose. They kept me from crossing the room and punching the man by my flower girl's side into the next county.

Ten minutes had passed since what should have been the start of the meeting, and I was even more irritated than I had been earlier. Tardiness was something I found hard to tolerate.

There were about forty or so people in the room facing me, Chelsee, Keeley, Nik, and councillor Sherman. A woman taking notes for the council sat by the side of the stage.

It did not surprise me—from what Keeley had told me earlier—that Higgins the butcher seemed to feel it was his sole responsibility to lead the meeting. Unfortunately for him, I was born to be a leader.

I shot him down with every objection he sent our way, from car parking and traffic increase to job creation and the effect on local businesses. I outlined the same proposals that Keeley had put forward, and I offered concession space for local businesses, so they could keep a presence in the store and recoup any lost revenue.

Nik had stayed silent so far, but I could feel he was about to explode when once again, Dave Higgins sounded off about us only offering help in the short term, saying that we would increase rent on the concessional stands within a few weeks of opening.

A man who identified himself as Ken Fearn from the bakery asked about the concession stands we were offering. This angered Higgins, who called Ken a Judas.

Nik stood and said, "Mr Higgins, clearly you came to this meeting to hurl insults at us and our proposals. After the last few meetings, we already expected this type of behaviour from you. However, I do object to hearing you call someone who is asking a perfectly reasonable question a Judas. I would ask that the wonderful lady from the council, who's been working so hard to take notes on the meeting so far," he said, turning to face her with a smile—one that always used to get women to drop their panties whenever he was around, "if the lovely note taker, Selena, could highlight Mr Higgins' rude behaviour towards other business owners, I think it would be a great help to whoever reads them."

Apparently, all the ladies in the first three rows had also been blessed with Nik Harding's smile, as most were looking at him with adoring gazes. Higgins blustered a little, but after being glared at by several attendees, he closed his mouth and was quiet for once.

"To answer your question, Mr Fearn, we would be willing to offer a six-month rent-free concession stand or stall. I feel that six months would give you enough time to know whether it's worth it to you as a business to have a presence in the store. If you do not feel it's worthwhile, we could go with our original plan to purchase items from your best-selling ranges and sell them as part of our local produce range," I told him. I continued with some of the ideas that Keeley and I had discussed earlier.

"If the stall seems financially profitable for you, we could look at providing you with an affordable rent agreement that we can guarantee will be less than market value. We are not building this supermarket to close down local businesses but to enhance the lives of people in the community who have to travel so far outside their local area to buy things they need on a weekly basis. Public transport is so unreliable, and not everyone drives. The supermarket is just outside of Rothley town, and there are at least half a dozen business owners from Barrowfield village. This could mean that whoever signs up for a concession would benefit from getting trade from people in Rothley who would not normally travel to your shop to buy something."

"I'd be happy to read more into these terms," replied Mr Fearn. Many more followed, angering the huffing, red-faced Higgins even further.

Chelsee leant towards me and whispered, "I would love to see the look on his face right now, Gregor. Describe it to me and make my week."

"I would like to ask a question," fumed Higgins. "What relevance does *she* have to this meeting—other than to sit up there lording it over everyone and whispering things about us?" he yelled, pointing at Chelsee.

Nik and I jumped up so fast that our chairs fell over. Keeley placed herself in front of us with a hand on each of our chests. I was seething, and I could feel the force of Nik's barely restrained anger.

To my surprise, Chelsee stood and took a step forward.

"I assume, Mr Higgins, that the *'she'* you referred to was me?" she questioned.

Higgins glanced at me and Nik warily before nodding his head.

"I'm sorry, Mr Higgins, I didn't hear your answer," Chelsee said calmly.

"It was," replied Higgins, sounding much braver than he looked.

"Mr Antonov stated at the beginning of this meeting that I was here to give advice as a mediator. Did you not hear that in the introduction, Mr Higgins?"

"I did hear that, but you—"

Chelsee interrupted his blabbering. "So you heard and accepted my presence here as a mediator at that time, but now you have a problem with it?"

Once again, Higgins tried to speak, but Chelsee cut him off mid-sentence.

"Now, I have to wonder, Mr Higgins, if you have a problem with me because I'm sitting up on this stage with whom you clearly see as the enemy—from your behaviour this evening. Or do you just have a problem with blind women in an authoritative position?"

Everyone in the room gasped at that statement, then turned to glare at the now scarlet-faced Higgins.

I heard Keeley whisper, "Oh my God! I can't believe you just said that, Chelsee!"

"Did it work?" whispered Chelsee, trying to suppress a smile.

"If you meant, does everyone look like they want to chase Higgins out of the meeting with pitchforks and blazing torches, then yes, it worked."

Chelsee coughed before raising her voice and speaking to the crowd.

"Well, I think as a mediator, I should call a short break to this meeting to let everyone cool down a little. I believe there's tea and coffee being served in the next room by the wonderful women of the Barrowfield and Rothley Ladies Group," said Chelsee with a beaming smile.

The room seemed to heave a collective sigh of relief.

"In a professional capacity, I normally wouldn't have done that," said Chelsee as she turned to retrieve her bag from the arm of the chair. "But that awkward bastard wasn't going to shut up, so I threw something non-PC into the mix. Works every time, so I've been told. Now come on,

Keeley, lead me to the coffee. I think I'm going to need it if I have to sit and listen to Dave *the-huff-and-puff* Higgins again."

Keeley led Chelsee towards the back of the room, stopping to talk to a couple of people on their way. I turned to see Nik picking up his chair before coming to stand next to me.

"I feel sorry for Alex and Keeley having to deal with that prick over the last few months," he said, nodding his head towards where Dave was standing. I was pleased to see Chloe shrug her arm out of his grasp as she walked away from him. Good. I would have ripped his hand off if he'd touched her a moment longer.

I told Nik about Keeley's run-in with the prick at the last meeting, and her subsequent revenge. Nik was as pleased as I was, and I thought he might be plotting something similar. Nik had always been like a dog with a bone when it came to things like this, and I dreaded to think what would happen when he inevitably involved Sergei.

I excused myself from Nik and watched him smirk at me a little as I made my way towards where I'd seen Chloe disappear. I followed her down a short corridor to the left and watched as Chloe made her way out of the ladies' bathroom. I grabbed her around the waist and pulled her towards me.

"Gregor, what are you doing?" she asked as I turned the handle on the door next to the bathroom. It was locked. The next door I tried opened up to a supply cupboard, so I bundled us both inside and closed the door behind me.

I brought my mouth down on hers and kissed her hard. I wanted to be gentle, but in my head, I could still see that fucker's hand on her back and the way he'd grabbed her before she walked away. She had the scent of him on her skin and clothes, and I needed it gone. In truth, I wanted to fuck her hard and deep and fill her with my come, so I could scent myself on her in the most obvious way. But now was not the time *or* the place. Although I could give her something to think about as she sat next to the butcher.

Chloe pulled away from me and frowned. "You kissed the woman next to you," she grumbled angrily.

"On the hand," I said, defending myself. "You let the butcher touch you," I countered.

"I did not."

"He had his hand on your back when you walked in. I wanted to tear it off," I admitted.

"Gregor, that was nothing. And please don't talk like that," she half-whispered.

She seemed scared, and it bothered me that she flinched a little when I put my hands on her cheeks.

"Don't, Chloe. Don't ever be scared of me. I will never hurt you, ever."

"I just... I don't know, Gregor. Sometimes you can be a little intimidating, especially recently. It's like something has come over you."

"Something will come over me in a few minutes, Chloe, and that something will be you," I told her while removing my tie. Spinning her around, I leant her against a broom handle next to the wall. Chloe gasped but didn't complain, so I made short work of tying her hands around the handle before unbuttoning her trousers, kissing and nibbling her neck as I did so.

"Gregor, we can't have sex in here," Chloe said with a groan.

"Shh, Chloe. We are not having sex. I'm going to make you come with my fingers before licking them clean. Are you ready?" I asked as I pulled her panties down below her bottom.

I could tell she was about to object, even though the scent of her arousal was thick in the air. So before she could speak, I opened her folds, sought out her swollen nub, and stroked it firmly. She let out a soft moan, and I pressed my straining erection against her bottom, trying to gain even the slightest relief.

Kissing from her neck to her shoulder had me desperate to sink my fangs into her pulsing vein. On hearing her breath quicken, I moved my hand to slip two fingers inside her tight, wet sheath while I strummed her clit with my thumb.

"Oh God, Gregor, I'm going to come. Please," Chloe begged.

She came seconds later with a low cry and several deep panting breaths. She was truly exquisite, my little flower girl, and I told her so while kissing and nibbling on her ear. Reluctantly, I removed my fingers from her dripping sex and brought them to her mouth. "Lick them," I commanded, and to my utter delight, she obeyed without argument.

"Good little flower girl," I praised. "I'm so glad you like the taste of yourself, my darling; you will be sucking it off my cock later."

I removed my fingers from her lips and licked them clean. Then I took a silk hanky out of my pocket and dabbed her sex before pulling up her panties and trousers.

"Um, Gregor. I'm still tied up."

"You need to get used to it, Chloe. You'll be spending hours that way later," I told her as I loosened my tie and removed it from her wrists, rubbing them gently as I did so.

This time, when I kissed her, it was soft, sensuously

gentle, and filled with all the love I felt for this amazing woman.

"So you like a little kink, then, Gregor," Chloe quipped, and I felt her smile against my mouth.

"Oh, my darling Chloe, you have no idea," I replied, giving her one last toe-curling kiss before I opened the door.

As the door swung open, I came face to face with the woman who'd been sitting next to the baker. I assumed, from how she'd held his hand during the meeting, that she was his wife.

"Oh!" she said as I walked out of the cupboard with an extremely red-faced Chloe behind me.

I looked the woman directly in the eyes and told her that she did not see either myself or Chloe in the supply cupboard, and she'd just spotted Chloe coming out of the ladies' room. When Chloe realised I was using mind control to make the woman forget she had seen us, she gave me a scowl. But even with the scowl, I could see she was relieved.

Chloe took her leave and walked away with the woman without giving me a backward glance. I would show her later how I felt about that little act of defiance with a well-delivered spanking. The thought appealed to me, bringing my erection back to life.

I stayed in the small corridor until I could see people working their way back to their seats. Just as I was about to step back into the room, Nik came into the corridor.

"There you are," he declared as he stepped towards me. I saw his nostrils flare before a huge grin spread across his face.

"If you'd told me what you were planning, Gregor, I would have directed you to the office next to the kitchen. It has more room than the cupboard," he said with a wink.

"Fuck off, Nik," I replied, trying to act as though I

didn't know what he was talking about. I was in no doubt that he could scent Chloe on me. Our sense of smell was one of the strongest senses we had; our hearing followed a close second.

"Well, here's the thing, Gregor. The scent I'm picking up is from Chloe, not you, so although I commend you for proving you're not a selfish lover, I can also sympathise with your plight. So what do you say to us getting out of this building and into our women as quickly as possible?"

"I would say that sounds like the best idea I've heard in a long time," I replied.

"Good," said Nik as he slapped me on the back. "Now follow my lead...."

While walking out of the corridor, I noticed Nik stop and speak to a portly-looking gentleman.

"Dougie, you can smell gas. You'd better tell someone."

It took a few seconds to figure out what Nik was up to. He stood in front of a woman I seemed to recognise, saying, "Moira, is it just me, or can *you* smell gas in here too?"

The woman stood still and inhaled through her nose, looking a bit confused. Nik held her gaze and followed with, "You *can* smell gas, Moira, and you think you should tell everyone from your ladies' group."

Moira nodded her head and said, "You're right, Nik; I can smell gas. I'd better tell the ladies' group so we can evacuate everyone and get the emergency gas team out."

"Good thinking, Moira," replied Nik as he leant down to place a kiss on the top of her head.

I followed his lead and used mind control on three

unsuspecting business owners. Soon, the noise level in the room had risen as rumours of a gas leak spread.

Keeley walked up to Nik, and I watched him whisper a few words in her ear. She then approached the confused council spokesman, who'd been sniffing the air suspiciously. Within ten seconds, he seemed to panic before announcing, "I can smell gas, so can everyone please leave the building as quickly as possible and do not use the light switch or mobile phones. Oh, and please, can anyone who smokes avoid lighting a cigarette until they are well away from the vicinity of the building?"

Keeley took hold of Chelsee's arm and led her safely out of the hall. I watched as Higgins tried to guide Chloe towards the door, but she shook him off and turned to look for me. She smiled in relief when she saw I was making my way towards her.

Nik followed Chloe and me out of the door, and as a few people were already making their way to the car park across the road, I heard the councillor shout, "We'll reschedule tonight's meeting. I'll let everyone know by email and will include the matters discussed earlier tonight. Have a safe journey home, everyone."

"I feel a bit sorry for him, Gregor," said Keeley. "He'll have to stay here until the gas board comes out and deems it safe."

I walked up to the man and told him, "I couldn't smell gas, and you couldn't smell it either. But after that man Higgins approached you and said he could smell it, you became worried. You think he started a rumour to get people out of the building because the meeting wasn't going his way. You are so angry with him that you wish you could ban him from the next meeting."

Nik and Keeley quickly caught on and used their

natural vampiric skill of mind control to get everyone to think on the same lines. Unfortunately, Chloe had witnessed this and looked mightily pissed off.

"I don't like it when you do that, Gregor. I worry that you could be doing it to me, and I wouldn't even know," she grumbled.

"I do not need to use mind control to get you to do anything, Chloe," I whispered. "I have other skills I prefer to use to make you more compliant."

Chloe was just about to rebuke my statement when Higgins approached us.

"Chloe, everyone has decided not to go to the pub tonight, so if you want, we can grab a bottle of wine and—"

The low growling sound I made was enough to cut off whatever proposition Higgins was about to make.

Keeley announced that she was taking Chelsee back so they could have a catch-up, which left me free to take Chloe home. Higgins didn't seem to like the sound of that and once again put his hand on Chloe's arm. Before I could reach the slimy fucker, Nik stepped in front of me and blocked my way.

"Not here, Gregor; he's not worth it," Nik said as he used his chest to shield him.

"Get the fuck away from my woman!" I yelled at Higgins. Obviously, the man had a death wish, as he once again tried to touch her.

"She's not your woman, you stuck-up Russian bastard," he countered.

We had quite an audience by now, so although I felt like picking the irritating man up by his throat and squeezing the life out of him, I kept what little I had left of my control and turned to look at Chloe instead.

"Come home with me, Chloe," I commanded. I thought for a moment she would deny me when I saw her bristle at my high-handed order. But I followed it by softly adding, "I need you."

Chloe pushed Nik to the side and stepped into my waiting arms. I placed a gentle kiss on her lips and one on the tip of her nose before taking her hand and leading her to my SUV.

Before Higgins could hurl any insults our way, the councillor went over to him and started yelling about all the trouble Higgins had caused by spreading rumours of a gas leak.

I didn't look back. I didn't need to. I knew that Nik, Keeley, and Chelsee had things under control.

No wonder I felt more at home in this place. I had everything here that I hadn't known I needed. It would be even harder this time when I had to go back to Russia. Unless, of course, I could convince my little flower girl to come back with me. But I knew the outcome of that could very well depend on what happened at my home tonight.

Chapter Twelve

Chloe

We made the short journey to Gregor's home in silence. There were so many questions I wanted to ask, but the sexual tension in the vehicle was so high it felt as though someone had removed all the oxygen from the air. My heart was racing, and by the time we pulled up outside the manor, my rapid, shallow breathing had fogged up my window.

Gregor left the vehicle and, as he always did, came around to open my door. He lifted me out of the vehicle but kept me a short distance away from his body. When I tried to pull him closer, he said, "Don't, Chloe. If you touch me, I will fuck you where we stand, and I need to show you something tonight. I need to be sure you can accept me for what I am. And for all my needs."

He sighed heavily, and for all the confidence and cockiness he'd displayed earlier, I could tell he was nervous. Vulnerable even. And it made me want to hold him even more.

Gazing into his beautiful blue eyes, I asked, "What did you mean when you said I was your woman?"

"I meant just that. You are mine, Chloe. My woman. The other half of my soul. I recognise you as such. I pursued you without fully realising what you were to me, but in doing so, I fell madly in love with you, and I want you to be mine in every way possible."

"I don't understand, Gregor," I said, swallowing nervously. I think I more than understood what he meant. But how could he mean it when we hadn't been in a committed relationship, or any sort of relationship, other than being friends?

"You doubt me, Chloe. Why do you doubt me? Have I ever not been honest with you? When an immortal finds the one they recognise as being theirs, there is no mistake. I feel blessed that it is you, *moya malen'kaya tsvetochnitsa*."

Oh wow! With him looking at me with such love in his beautiful blue eyes, then calling me his little flower girl in Russian, I couldn't help but want him. Right here, on this remote tree-covered driveway.

Gregor's eyes grew wider, and his nostrils flared. I knew he could sense how aroused I was, but in this instance, it wasn't a bad thing. It meant I didn't have to let him know how much I craved him.

I expected him to push me up against the SUV or lower me to the hard pebbled surface of his driveway. Instead, he closed his eyes and took a deep breath before looking back at me with a sexy smile. He held out his hand, saying, "Come with me, my darling. There is something I want to show you."

I may have pouted a little, as well as letting out a disappointed sigh. Gregor laughed, tugging me with him through the huge oak door of the manor.

After less than a minute, Gregor lost his playfulness, becoming tense when we approached a door I hadn't noticed before. He took out a key from a pocket in his jacket and the door opened with a slight creak. "After you," Gregor instructed as he motioned me inside, onto what appeared to be a stone stairway.

He closed the door behind him, and after pressing a couple of light switches, he followed me down the steps. I thought we were going to look at his wine cellar, but when I got to the bottom step, I stilled in shock.

I wanted to say something, but I found myself suddenly mute. All around the room were exquisitely carved oak… well, I wasn't sure what to call them. I noticed the St Andrew's Cross first of all, but as my eyes slowly wandered around the room, I could see more pieces of what I could only describe as sex furniture, and all had leather straps and cuffs.

"Say something, Chloe," Gregor said anxiously.

"It's sex furniture," I almost whispered.

Gregor nodded, then held out his hand to me. I placed my hand in his and looked down at them as he wove his fingers through mine. I don't know what I was looking for. It was the same hand that touched me in the cupboard at the community centre earlier. The very same hand that had caressed me so gently last night when we made love. But I began to see his hand being used for different purposes in this room, and although I wanted to appear strong and confident, I couldn't stop myself from trembling.

Gregor pulled me towards him, then cradled my face in his hands as he tilted my head up so I would look at him.

"Don't be scared, Chloe; you know I won't hurt you," he whispered as if trying to calm a scared animal.

"But you will hurt me, Gregor. You want to strap me to

some of that sex stuff, and as soon as I can't move, you'll hit me with something. Well, I'm sorry, Gregor, that's not going to happen. Not to me. Not again."

Brow furrowing, he asked, "What do you mean, Chloe? Have you experienced something like this before?"

"No, nothing like this. I…I need to go," I said, trying to pull out of his arms. But he held me tight to his body, preventing me from leaving.

"You need to tell me who hurt you, Chloe?" Gregor demanded. "Was it your ex-husband?"

"No, it wasn't Craig. He was as gentle as a lamb," I told him truthfully.

"Then tell me who put this fear in your eyes because I know it wasn't me. I have never caused a woman pain unless it was in a room like this with her full consent. You must believe that, Chloe."

I could tell deep down that Gregor was being sincere, but I was too scared to listen. I kept staring at the wooden contraptions, visualising being held—unable to move so I couldn't defend myself.

I felt clammy and lightheaded as memories I tried to keep suppressed began to surface. Gregor caught me as my knees gave way. He picked me up and carried me to a large grey chaise, which was placed against a wall at the side of the room.

Turning me slightly in his arms, he cradled me like a baby. I shivered slightly, so Gregor took a silver-grey fleece from the back of the chaise and wrapped it around me before holding me close. He placed gentle kisses on my forehead, eyes, the tip of my nose, as well as on my lips. I could tell he was desperate to ask me questions, but I didn't want to talk about it. I didn't want to relive the horror that had once been my life.

"I know you don't want to tell me about it, Chloe, not just yet. But you can trust me. You know this. I would never hurt you. You are more precious to me than anything on this earth. If anyone ever harmed you, I would kill them without a second thought. You are mine, my love, for always."

"You speak about me like I'm a possession. That's what he did, and I don't like it. I won't be anyone's possession ever again," I told him as defiantly as I could while wrapped in a blanket being cradled like a baby.

"And you are talking as though possession only goes one way, my love." Gregor ran the tip of his nose down the side of my face. "But you would also possess me, Chloe. I would be yours. You would own me, heart and soul, as well as everything else I possess. We would share eternity together, and raise a family if you wished it. But throughout it all, I would never hurt you. I could never raise a hand to you or any woman in anger. That type of behaviour is abhorrent to me and most everyone I know."

"I believe you, Gregor. I just...I didn't expect this." I gestured around the room. "I don't think I would like to be strapped onto one of those contraptions. Earlier, in my shop, you said I would be bound and at your mercy. I thought you meant you wanted to tie me up during sex with your tie—like you did at the meeting. Not one of these contraptions you have down here with the built-in wrist and ankle restraints."

"But what's the difference, Chloe? You are just being bound by different materials. A silk tie. Leather cuffs. They all serve the same purpose. Why would one scare you above the other?"

"Because I've read the books, Gregor. I know what goes on once you have someone bound against something like that. You hit them or whip them, and they can't get away."

"You keep mentioning hitting, Chloe. So someone hit you? What with?" he demanded.

"He didn't need anything more than what God gave him. But I don't want to talk about it anymore, Gregor. I just...I don't know what I need right now," I said with a tearful sigh.

"What if I said that the purpose of these machines was for pleasure only? That there would be no contact other than kissing, caressing and the sexual act itself?" Gregor enquired.

"So you wouldn't want to hit me with anything?" I asked hesitantly.

"Do you see anything I could hit you with?"

I looked around again and shook my head. I expected to see whips and floggers somewhere in the room, but there wasn't anything of the sort.

"I won't lie to you, Chloe. There are several implements hidden away here that can be used to cause both pain and pleasure, but they will stay hidden if you wish. Your pleasure is all I want to experience tonight and every night. And most mornings, too. Plus a quick tumble whenever we can throughout the day. Certainly something naughty during meetings at the community hall," he said with a laugh.

He was so handsome, yet even more so when he laughed. Gregor had a strong jawline and perfectly sculpted cheekbones. Although he was gorgeous, he could look quite hard and intimidating. But when he laughed or even gave a smile, his features captivated you. His blue eyes sparkled and crinkled slightly at the corners, and it seemed as though he'd cast a spell over me, my fears, and my senses.

"You can say no to me, Chloe. I will never make you do something against your will. But would you allow me to give you pleasure in this room tonight? I will not bind you down without your consent, and you can say no to anything I suggest. Allow me to dispel some of the fear you have shown about the contents of this room. Please."

I looked around the room one last time and tried to view its contents differently. Now that I didn't have fear keeping my chest in such a tight grip, I could relax in Gregor's arms and fully appreciate the workmanship in the furniture. The wood appeared to be highly polished oak with intricate carvings around some of the edges. They looked like letters of some sort.

"What does the writing say, Gregor?" I asked. He stood and let the blanket fall from my arms.

"Come, my curious little flower girl. Let me show you."

I took his hand while he led me to the St Andrew's Cross. I could see close-up that the letters were in Russian.

"It's written in Cyrillic," he said as he placed my hand over the carvings and ran it down along the edge. "This says, *with trust comes pleasure.*"

Taking my hand again, he led me over to what looked like my school gym horse.

"Are those wires?" I asked, as once again Gregor ran my fingers over Cyrillic letters.

"This says, *to give pleasure is to receive pleasure*, and yes, those are wires. Most of this furniture can be altered mechanically to suit the Dom and the sub. I have them made to my own specifications."

"How many women have you had down here, Gregor?" I asked sharply, feeling a slight pang in my chest at the thought of Gregor placing other women in them.

"Keeley and Freya have seen this room when their inquisitiveness won out, but I've not had any women in here for sexual purposes. You would be the first and only one if you decide you would like to try it. But there will never be any pressure from me, Chloe. The decision is yours."

I looked around at the other items in the room, carefully taking in what looked like the least threatening pieces.

"I don't think I would ever want to use the stocks," I said, pointing towards them. "And that thing next to them looks way too complicated."

"Ah, you mean the swing. I assure you, Chloe, once you get the hang of that particular item, the pleasure you feel will be out of this world," Gregor whispered against the back of my ear before running his tongue down the side of my neck.

"What about this one? It looks like something we used at school for gymnastics." Of all the furniture in this room, I thought it appeared the least threatening.

"You made an excellent choice for your first time in an environment like this, my darling," Gregor praised. "I'm sure we can do something special here without using the restraints. For the moment, anyway."

He lifted the hem of the lightweight lemon sweater I wore, so I raised my arms to aid its removal. I expected him to go for my bra next; instead, he chose to remove my linen trousers, tossing them on the floor to join my sweater. I couldn't help but think how badly creased they'd be later. Ridiculous, really, to be considering my poor clothing choices when I was standing in my undies in what, for all intents and purposes, was Gregor's sex dungeon.

"Chloe, you need to let go of whatever thoughts are distracting you at this moment. Don't think, just feel. Feel the reaction on your skin when my hands trace over the edges of the pretty white lace of your bra and panties," Gregor said as he traced every inch of skin around my underwear, leaving goosebumps wherever he touched.

"Tell me, Chloe, did you wear this see-through lacy underwear to entice me? Because you are so enticing right now, my darling."

I watched as Gregor walked around my body until he was once again in front of me. He reached out with both hands, tugging at my nipples through the lace of my bra, before lowering his right hand and tugging gently on my pubic hair through my knickers.

"I think you wanted me to see how tempting your rosy-brown nipples look when they're confined in your bra, and the brown hair covering this moist, warm heaven as it pokes through the lace of your panties."

Gregor's voice sounded soft and melodic. He stepped forward and closed the distance between us, pulling me in for a passionate kiss. It wasn't hard and punishing; it wasn't gentle either. It was a perfect combination of both, and when his tongue flicked against mine, I felt my body becoming weak and pliant against his.

But that didn't stop him. If anything, it made him take the kiss one step further. Gregor ran his hand down my spine, pausing around my bra before reaching down to grab my bottom in a firm grip. I felt him slip his hand inside my knickers before lowering them down my legs so I could step out of them.

When I moved, I felt my bra slip forward and realised he must have undone it as he caressed my back. I now stood naked in front of him, but as I took a glance at the wooden and leather furniture, I realised some of my nerves had been replaced by anticipation.

Gregor stood, picked me up, and then set me down on

top of the gym horse. There were wooden handles next to the cuffs over the back of the horse, and Gregor whispered, "Lean back and grab the handles." Once I had done so, he lifted my legs and opened them wide, exposing everything I had to him.

For a moment, he just stroked my inner thighs with both hands, running them up and down without letting them meet in the middle, the place I was so desperate to feel them.

Gregor had made me so wet, and I could feel it cooling slightly against my opening. He dropped to his knees and placed his hands under my bottom, lifting me to his face before burying his tongue deep inside me. I moaned in pleasure and tried to push against his tongue, but Gregor stilled, controlling me with his firm grip.

When I was just about to beg for him to move, he seemed to curl his tongue slightly, rubbing it against the sensitive spot inside me, making me pant and moan. I could feel an orgasm starting to build, but Gregor removed his tongue before I could climb any higher to reach that desired peak.

"No, please," I groaned when he sat back on his heels.

"Patience, my beautiful flower girl. You will get what you need tonight, and so will I. There is no hurry; we have all the time in the world."

Before I could process his words, he leant forward again and fastened his mouth around my clit, flicking his tongue in hard, rapid strokes until I felt the build-up to orgasm race through my core. Just as I was about to hit my peak once again, Gregor sat back on his heels.

"Oh, God, Gregor, you have to let me come, please," I yelled, both horny and angry at the same time.

"Do I, my darling?" he questioned with a smirk. Before I could yell anything more, he leant forward and seemed to bury his face in my whole sex.

He licked and sucked on every part like a starving man eating his first meal in days. This time, the orgasm came speeding towards me like a high-speed train, but Gregor tore his face away from my body before that train could reach its destination.

"No," I screamed, so frustrated that tears escaped me. Before I could do anything, Gregor commanded, "Let go of the handles, Chloe."

As soon as I did so, Gregor flipped me over, placing my arms and upper body across the leather top. My legs were pressed against the wooden structure, and once again, Gregor demanded that I hold on to the handles. My knees rested on padded leather that was cool at first before warming to the same temperature as my skin.

While my orgasm-starved body was relatively comfortable, my mind was not. I imagined how bad my dimpled thighs looked and how huge my bottom must appear from this position. Before I could protest, I felt Gregor's tongue trace those exposed cheeks.

"I have fantasised so many times about seeing you naked and bound to this machine. But the true vision I have before me appears even more satisfying than I had imagined," Gregor said, as though he was awed by what he saw.

Impossible. Cellulite did not inspire awe.

"Gregor, my arse and thighs are too fat to fantasise about."

"My darling Chloe, I know that physical discipline is not on the agenda tonight, but I could spank your ass so hard for doubting me, and for doubting how fucking sexy you look right now. If you only knew how many times I had to take myself in hand to get some relief after imagining you like this. Since meeting you, I haven't been able to look at another woman in a sexual way. You have ruined me for any other."

He sounded so sincere when he said that. His lips were moving softly against my ear as he leant over my body, his erection a hard pulsing rod against the cleft of my bottom.

Gregor turned my head to the side so he could kiss me, melting away the last semblance of fear and self-doubt I'd harboured for many years.

Oh, how this man could kiss. If there was ever a kissing manual, I'm sure Gregor Antonov wrote it—being the expert that he was. There was no doubt in my mind I had fallen in love with him. Yet the thought didn't scare me. Instead, it felt freeing, which is strange because love ties you to the very person or thing that holds your affection. Nonetheless, I still felt free and ready to place my trust in the man I loved.

"Gregor, would you still like to bind my hands?" I asked when I freed my lips from his. Gregor stroked my cheek while looking into my eyes.

"If you would like me to use the cuffs next to the handles you are currently holding, then I will. But I will apply them loosely so you don't feel so restricted."

I nodded my head. Gregor kissed me again before getting to his feet and coming to stand in front of me. He ran his hands up and down my arms before taking each of my wrists and fastening them loosely inside the cuffs, just as he said he would.

I raised my head and looked into his eyes. The smouldering look I saw in them made me even wetter.

He slowly unbuttoned his shirt, revealing the hard set of

abs covered by a trail of dark hair. After throwing his shirt to the side, he unbuttoned and unzipped his trousers, keeping his eyes locked with mine the whole time. When he began to remove his trousers and boxers, I chanced a look down so I could admire his erection, licking my lips in anticipation.

Gregor stepped forward, took his granite-hard cock in his left hand and tapped me on the cheek with it, commanding in a raspy voice, "Open."

I opened my mouth, and he slid inside repeatedly, going slightly deeper each time until I felt myself gag as he hit the back of my throat. He stilled for a moment, telling me how utterly beautiful I looked just now, how much he adored me and the strength I possessed to be able to overcome my fears, and how much it meant to him that I had given him my trust.

More saliva gathered in my mouth when Gregor started moving again, quicker this time.

It felt so different this way, without the use of my hands. I couldn't control the act, yet for some strange reason I didn't fully understand, I found the whole thing so empowering. Maybe it was because I had this powerful man/vampire panting and throwing his head back in utter ecstasy because of what I was doing to him? Or maybe it was because, as Gregor had said before, I didn't have to think; I just needed to feel and allow someone else to control what happened.

I thought I'd never be able to do that again, but here I was, surrendering to a man who was deserving of my faith and trust.

Gregor's breath hitched, and I felt his balls draw up under my chin. I thought he would come, but he stopped and withdrew from my mouth. He knelt in front of me, kissing me hard, thrusting his tongue in and out of my mouth as his cock had been earlier. I tried grinding my clit against the wood of the furniture, my hard nipples pressing into the leather my upper body was spread over. I was so desperate for sexual release right now that I didn't care what I did as long as I could come.

"I want to bind you tighter so you can keep in position when I fuck you hard. Do you want that, Chloe?"

I nodded my head as I tried once again to build up the friction against my clit.

"That won't do, Chloe. I need to hear you tell me exactly what you want."

I knew what he was trying to do but, God help me, I just didn't care in my sexual frenzy. So I gave in willingly.

"Bind me tighter, Gregor. Do whatever you want as long as you make me come."

"I love you, Chloe," he said as he tightened the leather cuffs. Then he stood and picked up what looked like a little box before walking behind me and kneeling. I was just about to try and push back against him when I felt the padded leather beneath my knees begin to lift, raising my body higher.

I realised the box was a remote control that Gregor was using to get my body to a height that made it easier for him to fuck me. What I didn't expect was that after he was done lifting me, he would use the remote to spread the knee rests wide apart, baring my sex to him completely.

"I'm going to bind your legs to the knee rests so you don't slip as I thrust. This is for your safety and enjoyment, Chloe, so you can orgasm without the fear of falling. Do you understand?"

"Yes," I said expectantly. The words *"thrust"* and

"orgasm" seemed more important than *"bind"* at that moment.

Gregor worked quickly to secure my legs, then pressed his body against mine. I expected him to push inside me immediately and wanted him to do so with everything I had. Instead, he placed soft kisses all over the back of my neck and shoulders and ran his hands all over my body.

My sex felt heavy and was throbbing with need; I was on the verge of orgasm without even being touched there.

Because my knees were bound and separated, I couldn't even get relief by closing my legs when I clenched my internal muscles. When Gregor finally placed the head of his cock where I needed it most and thrust inside, I immediately spiralled into an orgasm so strong I sobbed with relief.

Gregor stayed still inside me while my body came down from the endorphin high and the tremors abated. When my breathing had returned to a near normal state, I heard a faint humming sound, then felt something touch my pubic hair and carry on—pressing into my sex. I tensed at the unknown.

"This vibrating panel is a clitoral stimulator, my love. I'm going to fuck you now, hard and deep. I want you to feel pleasure like you've never known before, and when you begin to orgasm, I'm going to taste that pleasure in your blood and make you come all over again from my bite."

Before I could nod or reply, the vibrations on the panel increased. Gregor fucked me hard and deep, just like he'd said, and the build to orgasm took a matter of seconds. When I started to come, I heard Gregor cry out before sinking his teeth into where my neck met my shoulder. The orgasm didn't have time to abate before another slammed into me and took my breath in a silent scream.

Gregor grabbed my hips even harder and thrust into me

one last time before loudly proclaiming his love for me, then collapsing onto my back. The vibrating panel was too much for my sensitive tissues to handle at that moment, so I was grateful when Gregor switched it off.

He pulled out of me slowly, then walked over to some drawers next to the chaise, opening the top one and pulling out a small towel. He came back and knelt on the floor beside me, cleaning between my legs before using the towel on himself. Then he undid the straps at the back of my knees before standing up and leaning over to remove my cuffs.

"Don't move for a moment," he ordered, rubbing me firmly from my wrists to my shoulders. He massaged my back in a kneading motion, moving over my buttocks and down my legs. With my back to his chest, he stood up behind me and helped me up from the kneeling position I'd held for so long. I wobbled unsteadily, my knees still weak.

"Keep still, Chloe, and let me take care of you," Gregor admonished.

Placing an arm under my knees and across my back, he picked me up and carried me all the way from his cellar to his bedroom.

After laying me gently on his bed, Gregor opened the door of a small, inconspicuous drinks cooler and took out a bottle of water. He poured it into a cut crystal glass and brought it to me. I didn't realise how thirsty I was until I took my first sip, drinking it down within seconds. Gregor took the glass from my hand, and I lay down and closed my eyes, smiling when I felt him lie beside me and throw an arm and leg over me.

"I've fallen in love with you, Gregor," I whispered, glancing across at him to gauge his response.

Gregor gazed at me and smiled. "You don't know how much it means to hear you say that, Chloe. I will spend the rest of our very long lives together making you happy and showing you just how much I love you in return. But we can talk about that later. For now, let's sleep."

Chapter Thirteen

Gregor

I woke from a sleep that was less than restful. I'd dreamed of the fearful look that appeared in my flower girl's eyes when I'd shown her my cellar and its contents. I knew she had overcome it, but I felt so angry that she'd known that type of fear in the first place.

She seemed reluctant to tell me what had happened and who it was that had caused her so much distress, but I needed to know. Both the human and vampire sides of me needed to know, so I could deal with that person accordingly.

I'd not killed a human for many years. Not since the last of the vampire hunters came to murder my kind. But that would change when I found the man responsible for hurting my Chloe.

She stirred beside me before getting up and making her way to the bathroom. I did not like the feel of my bed without her in it, so after a few seconds, I followed her.

Chloe had just set the bath running when I opened the door. She apologised for waking me, but I cut off that apology with a sensual kiss as I pinned her to the wall and ground my cock against her cleft.

"It doesn't matter how many times I have you, Chloe; it's just never enough. Tell me I can have you and love you every day, forever. Tell me you will Bond with me."

"I need to know more, Gregor, starting with, why me? So as much as your kisses take me to that special place I love so much, let's just get in this huge bath you have and talk about our expectations."

I knew she was right: we needed to talk about our future. But Chloe had looked so sexy when she was bending over the bath, and she smelled divine—of her and me and sex—and it was hard not to let my throbbing erection find its way into her body.

I kissed her once more. How could I not? Her lips were full and tempting, feeling soft and supple as they moved against my own.

"Gregor, you have to stop turning me on," she groaned. I smiled against her cheek. "Never, my love. I will devote my life to keeping you in a perpetual state of arousal."

"I can believe it, too," Chloe said with a giggle, as if I had been joking. I had not.

My slipper-style, claw-foot bath was larger than average, which made it easy for me to slide in behind Chloe and lie against the sloping backrest. I pulled her down towards me and used some of my body wash to soap up Chloe's larger-than-average breasts.

"Gregor," Chloe sighed as she stopped my fingers from tugging at her nipples.

"I can't help it, my darling. Your breasts are a perfect

distraction. It is your fault that I cannot keep my hands to myself."

"Well, you have to try, Gregor, at least while we talk. I want to know why you want us to be permanent. You've only known me a matter of months."

"My darling Chloe, from the moment we met when you came to my home delivering flowers for Keeley, I knew I wanted you. At first, I thought it was just a sexual thing. I was attracted to you, and I wanted your body and your blood. But I also fell for your intelligence and wit the more I got to know you.

"I should have known in the beginning that you were mine. I remember thinking I recognised your fragrance. It captivated my senses, yet you insisted you wore no perfume. That was my immortal side recognising you. But I know that not every woman responds well to my sexual demands and tastes.

"I own a private club in Moscow where people who share my tastes can go. But even though I'd not even kissed you on the lips before I left, I could not visit my club. It felt as though I'd betray you if I did so. I could only think of you and how you looked when you smiled, the sexy flare of your hips in those tight jeans you wear, and the blue-green colour of your eyes that was so deeply ingrained in my memory. I became obsessed.

"So many times I wanted to fly back to Yorkshire. It made my day when I spoke to you on the phone or you sent me a text. I lived for any updates about how your day had gone, and hearing that husky, sleepy voice you have when you are tired did more for me than I would like to admit. I haven't masturbated so much since I was a teenager.

"When I came back to Yorkshire, I was so desperate to see you, and I knew I would have you that night. But you said we were just friends. It made me so unhappy to hear you say that. I knew then that I wanted a relationship with you. But I didn't know I was in love with you because I thought love was pure and sweet and inspired happiness, so surely, what I felt couldn't be love.

"I wanted to possess you and have you acknowledge that you were mine, but then I kissed you, and something hit me deep inside. All the happiness I'd felt during our many conversations seemed to flow over me. I didn't want to fuck as I would normally do; I wanted to make love to you and show with my actions how much you meant to me. I will never forget how I felt the first time we made love. It was perfection."

"It was," Chloe agreed as she linked her fingers through mine. "But then again, every time you've been inside me has been perfect."

I agreed with her and placed a kiss on the top of her head. I had to tell her about nearly Bonding with her without her knowledge, but I was dreading the outcome of that conversation.

"Chloe, I have a confession to make. When I gave you my blood and took you up against the wall in my hallway, I also took your blood at the same time. If you hadn't let go of my wrist and kept on drinking from me, we would have Bonded. I knew this, but at the time, I couldn't seem to stop it.

"I felt so guilty, but I was worried about your reaction if I told you. I've never lost control like that before, in any part of my life. But I wasn't in control of that situation. I spoke to Freya about it. She seemed to think it was because my vampire side—which can often seem animalistic—recognised you as his and acted instinctively."

"You spoke to Alex's sister about it?" Chloe clarified. "About us having sex?" I felt her shoulders tense.

"I didn't go into detail, Chloe. Freya is my best friend. Alex, Freya and I have been friends for centuries. But Freya has always been special to me. I'm glad she's found love and has Bonded with Dan. He is a good man and so obviously adores her."

Chloe sighed heavily. "The fact that you were out of control scares me a little, Gregor. But you didn't force me to keep drinking from you when I finally let go. You accept what you did was wrong, and you do feel guilty about it. You still want to Bond, but you are asking me now, just like you did in the cellar, although denying me a much-needed orgasm helped you achieve the desired response in there."

"So, are you saying that you forgive me, Chloe?" I held a cautionary breath while awaiting her answer.

"Yes."

"Thank you, my darling." With that one word, my anxiousness lifted, and almost all was right with my world. Until I found out who'd hurt the woman in my arms, I could never fully rest.

"Chloe, will you tell me who hurt you and how? I need to understand what provoked that reaction from you."

She shook her head. "No, Gregor. I'm sorry, I can't. Not tonight. Our relationship is new, and I want you to see me as the woman I am now, not the helpless victim I was."

"I see you as the woman I love, and that won't change, no matter what you tell me. But I need to know what happened so I can avoid doing anything that could trigger your fear again. Please, Chloe, let me protect you."

"Not tonight, Gregor. I promise I will tell you soon, but let me do it in my own time. Please."

Her voice cracked a little, and I didn't want to see her

cry again, so I turned her around to straddle me and kissed her tenderly. I held her in my arms for a few minutes more, enjoying the feeling of being this close to the woman I loved.

"Thank you, Gregor. It means so much that you're giving me time to open up to you. I love you, and it would make me happy to call you mine. I don't think we should rush into Bonding, but it's something I will consider in the future—if you still want me, that is."

"I will always want you, my little flower girl. That will never change. Meeting you has not only given me a reason to wake up every day, but also to smile, to look forward to a happy future, and to love. You are the reason I exist now, Chloe. It has taken me over five hundred years to find my reason, and to be part of a Bonded pair with you is everything I could ever want."

We held one another until the water began to cool. After washing, we got out of the bath and dried each other off, sneaking a kiss or two here and there. To me, these simple acts seemed more intimate than sex.

The hour was late, so we retired to bed, where soft sweet kisses turned to gentle lovemaking. Even without the Bond, I felt more connected to this woman than I ever thought possible. This was the purity in love I'd been looking for, and I knew I'd do everything I possibly could to make this woman happy.

Chapter Fourteen

Gregor

Chloe left at seven-thirty this morning to open up her shop, though we were both reluctant to leave each other's arms. I couldn't wait until the day she made the manor her home, and I hoped that would happen very soon. The only thing marring my happiness was the constant need to find out who'd hurt my little flower girl and how they had done so.

Five minutes after Chloe left, I sat at my desk debating what to do. I wanted to see her open up to me in her own time about the traumatic occurrence. But the not knowing had my mind in turmoil, and I knew I could not go about my daily life without having my questions answered. Feeling on edge, I found myself going to my blood store and taking out two bags of blood.

The feeding calmed me slightly, and I was able to think clearly enough to compile a list of details I knew about my flower girl. As soon as this was done, I emailed the list to

Viktor—my friend and longtime business associate back home in Russia.

I must admit, my finger hovered over the send button for a moment before I pressed it. However, I reasoned that by doing it this way, I could support Chloe more effectively when she did open up to me.

Her reactions yesterday told me she would find the whole process emotionally draining and would need me to stay calm and offer as much support as I could. Unfortunately, for a vampire, staying calm and focused when a loved one is hurting is not an easy task.

I called one of the secure numbers that Viktor had provided me with before I left Russia, and he answered, as always, on the second ring.

"Good morning, Gregor. How are you, my friend? And how is Alex's son? I might come over to see him next week. Tell me, are there still as many sheep in that village?"

"I am good, Viktor, as I hope are you. My godson is perfect. You really must come and see him, no matter how many farm animals there are in Yorkshire."

After a night out drinking some ridiculous concoction with Nik and Sergei, somehow Viktor ended up waking in a field surrounded by sheep. He now detests them with a passion and uses this as an excuse not to visit the village. But the real reason is that Viktor hates to travel, and he's more at home behind a computer screen than in the company of others. However, he's great friends with Alex, Nik, and Josh, so he does visit on occasion. But as Viktor is a master hacker and often works for high-ranking government agencies, he likes to keep the whereabouts of any friends and family under wraps so that no one can use them as a bargaining chip to force him to work for them.

"So, Gregor, I am a busy man. For what reason have you contacted me today?"

"I have sent an email to your secure address with details of someone I would like information on. It is important that I know about her past relationships, as well as anyone who might have caused her any harm."

"Ahh, so this Chloe Davies in your email is the flower girl you talked about in every conversation before you left for England?"

"Yes, that is her. I found out yesterday that there is something from her past that causes her fear and much sadness. I need to know what that is."

"You could always ask her, Gregor. Or does she not want you to know?"

"She says she will tell me, but in her own time."

"So, am I right in thinking that your vampire side is as disapproving of this as your human one, and you find yourself fighting to keep the control you are so famous for?"

"Viktor, my friend, around this woman, control is something I have to work harder than ever to achieve."

"Gregor, if I do this for you, you must never let her find out. She will not appreciate you ignoring her request to give her time," Viktor cautioned.

"She will not find out. Call me as soon as you have something."

"Do svidaniya, Gregor."

"Do svidaniya."

Keeley arrived about ten minutes after I ended my phone call with Viktor and headed to the kitchen to make a pot of tea. My housekeeper arrived a few minutes after Keeley, and she set about her daily chores after I gave her yet another demonstration of how to work her smartphone.

Keeley said that Yuri and Sergei were taking her daughter out for the day. They'd promised her a special treat, and although Daisy had been excited to go with her honorary uncles, Keeley was a little anxious about what this special treat was. She had no doubt in her mind that her daughter would love whatever new way Sergei and Yuri had come up with to spoil her, but she was worried about what that would entail.

We worked through the notes that Keeley had taken during the meeting at the community hall last night, making a rough draft of the proposals we wanted to put together for local businesses who'd expressed an interest in the concessionary stands we offered.

I left Keeley to make copies to send to everyone at Night Movers, so they could agree to everything in principle before we proceeded. Then I went down to my cellar to clean the furniture that Chloe and I used last night.

Although I had Mrs Timmins, the housekeeper, I considered this part of my life here very personal, especially since I had shared the experience with Chloe. Also, I wasn't sure whether the contents of this room would disturb the normally laid-back Mrs Timmins, and I wanted to retain her as a housekeeper. Although, who knew what she got up to with her husband on those chilly Yorkshire nights? For all I knew, the contents of this room may be a little on the mild side for them.

I could still smell the scent of sex and my delightful little flower girl, and it took all I had not to go to her and demand she give me her body again. But I didn't want to overwhelm her, so I ignored the throbbing hardness inside my boxers and made sure the equipment was cleaned and put in order before leaving and locking the cellar door behind me.

Keeley gathered her paperwork together and took Mrs Timmins out shopping for the day. My gardener had been working on cultivating an area behind the derelict hothouse, and hopefully, next year, the old Rothley Manor Estate would once again produce its own fresh vegetables.

———

Thirty minutes after Keeley left, I received a call from Viktor.

"Gregor, I have the information you were referring to. I just need to ask… Are you alone?"

"Yes, I am alone. Why? What have you found?"

"I will stay on the phone with you, Gregor, but I need to know before I reveal what I have found—have you taken blood today?"

Viktor sounded so grave and worried for me; I knew whatever information he had would not be something I would find easy to digest.

"Viktor, just tell me what you know," I demanded. After putting the phone on hands-free, I poured myself a large whisky. It wouldn't calm my nerves, get me drunk, or do anything that would normally benefit a human in such a situation, but it gave my hands something to do as I sat at my desk, dreading the next few minutes.

"Very well, Gregor, I am sending you an email. Before you open it, I will give you a short, mostly undetailed rundown of my findings.

"Before Chloe met her ex-husband, she was involved with a man called Peter Finch. This man—Finch—was three years older than Chloe, and at the time of their relationship, he worked as a builder. Finch had no previous criminal record prior to them becoming involved."

I heard Viktor sigh and take in a deep breath before carrying on.

"During their eighteen-month relationship, Chloe visited the emergency department of the hospital where she worked on two separate occasions before the night of the twenty-fifth of January, 2005. The first injury was a broken wrist, which she said had happened when she fell after being drunk on a night out. The second was a suspected broken nose that also came with a black eye and busted lip. This was explained as falling down the stairs. Luckily, her nose wasn't broken, and though her notes say she was questioned further about the incident, she once again stated it happened when she fell downstairs."

Viktor paused for a few moments, then carried on speaking as I heard my email alert ping.

"On the night of the twenty-fifth of January, 2005, Chloe Davies was admitted to hospital with the following injuries you see in the email. The photographs above the hospital statement were taken by the police as evidence, which led to the arrest of Peter Finch—the man pictured below all of Chloe's injury photographs.

"As you can see from those photographs, Chloe's face and neck are heavily bruised and so swollen she was unrecognisable. She had two bald patches where clumps of hair were ripped out from the side and back of her head. Her right cheekbone was fractured, and one of her upper back teeth was knocked out. She suffered three broken ribs on her left side and a fracture on her right.

"Thankfully, there was no haemothorax involved, although looking at the photographs, I am surprised this did not occur. I will let you look at the rest of the reports and photographs in silence, but I will stay on the line for any other questions you have, although I already know what will be the first."

I felt sick, which rarely happens to a vampire, but nonetheless, the images I saw on the screen of my laptop made my gut clench tight. My fangs descended, and it was hard to keep the red from my eyes.

As I read on and viewed even more terrible photographs of my beautiful Chloe's bruised and broken body, I felt the wetness of tears sliding down my cheeks.

The next photographs I viewed showed boot prints around her stomach, hips and thighs, where the despicable human had kicked and stamped on as much of her body as he could. There was also grazing and small cuts on various parts of her delicate skin, possibly due to her being dragged along the floor.

I had seen enough. There was only one other question I needed answering now.

"Where do I find him, Viktor?" I asked, in a voice hoarse with tears and anger I was desperate to unleash.

"You don't!" Viktor stated. He paused before adding, *"Because someone else has already done so."*

I hadn't expected to hear that piece of information, and if I was honest, I didn't want to hear it. I needed to feel this man's bones crush in my grip. I needed to see his facial features become unrecognisable as I beat him to death.

Viktor carried on speaking. *"Finch was arrested, charged, and remanded in custody, originally for eight months, but was let out after only serving six because of an earlier trial date."*

"Which fucking judge decided on that?" I shouted as my claws extended and dug into the leather armrests of my chair.

"The British justice system is known for its leniency in such matters, Gregor. As a matter of fact, there are many truly terrible crimes that are not given the punishment they deserve. But I digress. Peter Finch was tried for assault occasioning actual bodily harm at a crown court six months after the date of the offence. But on the day of the trial, Chloe and her family did not attend court."

"Why? I cannot understand why she would not want this man punished."

"I checked on it a little further, and it appears that on their way to court, Chloe's father suffered a massive heart attack, which resulted in a cardiac arrest. Luckily, they were able to restart his heart at the scene, and he later received a triple heart bypass. However, in court that day, Peter Finch only received a twelve-month suspended sentence. He'd already served six months, so the judge didn't see fit to give him a custodial sentence."

"It's a fucking joke, surely?" I questioned, stunned that anyone in authority could see those photographs and written evidence of injuries sustained and dismiss them as if they were nothing. What about the victim? My poor Chloe must have felt that the law was certainly not on her side.

"Ten weeks after being released with a suspended sentence, Peter Finch was knocked down by someone driving a black SUV with blacked-out windows. Not only did the driver of the SUV run over him, they also reversed the vehicle and backed over his body while he lay broken and bleeding on the road. Unfortunately, the incident didn't kill him. However, his back and neck were broken, and his pelvis shattered along with both legs and an arm. He also had a major head injury, which resulted in some brain damage.

"The injuries have left him a quadriplegic, with total loss of sensation in all four limbs. His head injury was severe and causes regular fits and slurring of speech. Finch now resides in a residential nursing home on the outskirts of Nottingham, where his care is paid for by the state. He is visited once a week by his mother, Audrey Finch."

I let this information sink in for the moment to see if it pleased the raging beast inside me. It didn't.

"Viktor, this man Finch is breathing good air, and the people who contribute national insurance in this country are paying for him to have that privilege. I want him dead."

"Would you not prefer to see him face what has to be a living hell every day, incapable of even wiping his own ass?" Viktor questioned.

"Frankly, no. I would rather his existence be removed from this world altogether. Send me the address of the nursing home so I can look him in the eyes when he takes his last breath."

"No, I cannot do that, Gregor. If you want him dead, I can see it done in a way that will not lead back to any of us. Give me two days to make it happen."

"Viktor, I want—" I was cut off mid-sentence as I tried to plead my case to be the one who killed the man.

"Gregor, you would do well to spend your time with your woman. Let me take care of this matter, and you can owe me one, my friend. And bring your flower girl to Russia. I need to see the woman she is today, so I can put these photographs out of my mind. As do you, Gregor. Do not let what you have seen today cause you to treat her differently. From other information I have gathered about her, she appears to be a strong, beautiful, capable businesswoman. A good fit for you, I think."

"She is remarkable, Viktor. I am blessed to have found her."

"Do svidaniya, Gregor."

"Do svidaniya, Viktor, and thank you."

Chapter Fifteen

Gregor

When I ended the call, the silence of this old house descended all around, and for a few minutes I let the numbness that was creeping through my limbs take over. I needed to do something, anything to make this feeling of helplessness go away, but looking at the evidence photographs of Chloe on my laptop wasn't helping.

She must have been in absolute agony, and being human, it would have probably taken her weeks, if not months to heal fully from this. But emotional healing would have taken much longer, and I cursed myself for causing her fear last night when revealing the contents of my cellar.

I remembered her mentioning hitting, assuming I had wanted to restrain and hit her. As I thought more about her words, the fantasies I'd had of Chloe over the past few weeks played in my mind. The one that appeared in my subconscious most frequently was of Chloe naked and bound as she was last night, her ass in the air as I spanked

113

her repeatedly, leaving hot red handprints every time my hand impacted against her soft skin.

I felt disgusted with myself for having this thought, and I began to examine my past behaviour, comparing myself to that man, Finch.

Maxim, my old bodyguard who'd attacked Keeley, had thought I hated women because of my activities in my club. To me, my actions were a normal, acceptable part of being a Dom.

Many women were more than happy to sub for me. Men, too, although I never participated as it wasn't my thing. But would my thing be as acceptable in today's society as Keeley had said? Or did my need for this behaviour mean I had more in common with Peter Finch than I cared to accept?

The more I thought about it, the more sickened I felt with both myself and the contents of my cellar. I could feel the key almost burn its way through my pocket, begging me to remove it.

I found myself moving with vampire speed towards my cellar, and after opening the door, I leapt down the steps. The lights were still on from when I'd cleaned up earlier, and the St Andrew's Cross I had once thought to be an exquisitely carved work of art, seemed to taunt me from its illuminated position.

Gone were the fantasy images of Chloe's ankles and wrists cuffed to each corner, of her writhing in pleasure against the thick, polished oak. Instead, I had a vision of Chloe screaming in fear as I approached her bloodied and bruised body. Rage consumed me, and my prized furniture became the target.

My first kick to the middle of the cross made little impact, which caused my anger to grow even further. The second kick caused a split that fractured deeper when I kicked it again. Then I let go with a series of kicks and punches, only stopping to tear away the electrical cords and steel rods from the back.

When the cross became a jagged, splintered mess, I moved on to the stocks that Chloe had insisted she would never want to use. Wrecking those was much easier than destroying the four-by-six-inch-thick beams of the cross, yet was just as satisfying.

I thought I heard a noise upstairs, although it wasn't enough to stop me from using my claws to tear the leather off the furniture I'd bound Chloe to last night. But this piece had created a wonderful memory for me, and it felt wrong to destroy it.

Indecision caused me to pause for a moment, and in doing so, I heard footsteps running down the hallway before my heavy wooden door slammed shut.

Chapter Sixteen

Chloe

Throughout this morning I'd been lost in my own world, the events of last night playing over and over in my mind. I'd been shocked and scared when I'd first seen the contents of Gregor's cellar, more so than when I discovered he was a vampire, which made no sense at all.

But when I'd finally been able to let go of my fears and give Gregor my trust, I had the most thrilling sexual experience of my life. I would never have thought that being naked and cuffed to something could feel so empowering and liberating, but amazingly enough, that's how it felt.

I certainly wouldn't be opposed to doing that again, although I still didn't think I could deal with the stocks. Pam had been begging me to tell her what it was that Gregor had done to put the huge smile on my face and the twinkle in my eyes, but I wouldn't tell her. I think the contents of Gregor's cellar just might be enough to shock the normally unshockable Pam.

I was on my way to surprise Gregor with the photo frame I'd finally managed to fill. Looking at the smile on Gregor's face as he held baby Rory made me feel so broody. I thought about him saying he wanted to Bond with me and what that would mean. Instead of finding it much too early to be thinking about a permanent relationship, I found myself wanting it more than I ever thought possible.

I'd fallen madly in love with him, and I knew he was telling the truth when he said he loved me too. I could feel that love, sense how real it was, and knowing I'd get to experience that forever made me one hell of a lucky woman.

When I finally got to the manor, I rang the doorbell a couple of times, but there was no answer. I tried the handle and found that the door wasn't locked, so I let myself in and quickly made my way down the hallway to Gregor's study.

I couldn't wait for him to come home and see the gift I'd brought him. Okay, it wasn't much compared to the gifts he normally bought everyone, but I knew he'd appreciate it.

Looking around the study, I found his laptop open on the desk. I decided to place the photo in front of the keyboard so he'd see it when he sat down to work. I pushed the laptop back slightly to make enough room to stand the frame, disturbing the screen as I did so.

What appeared before me made my blood run cold. The photograph was of my grotesquely swollen, battered and bruised face from when I was attacked by my ex-boyfriend.

Why did Gregor have it on his laptop? It was part of the official police evidence taken from my hospital bedside after I was admitted. Tentatively, I reached out to scroll down the page. There were more photos and copies of the medical and police reports detailing my injuries and the events leading up to them. There was also the police mug shot and current information about Peter Finch, the bastard who caused my injuries.

Why did Gregor have all this? I looked around the study as if trying to find something that would explain the reason why he held this information. But of course, I knew I'd find nothing in this room that would reveal why the man would need those details.

No.

The reason that Gregor had this information was plain to see. After I'd shown fear last night, it triggered his curiosity and need to put things right. Only, he could never put this right. This event was in my past, or had been. I'd laid it mostly to rest or, at least, I thought I had. But here was a stark reminder that you can never fully leave your past behind. Not when you have an interfering Russian willing to throw money at someone to illegally acquire official police documentation.

Gregor asked me for trust, and I gave it to him willingly. I wanted to tell him about the abuse in my own time, so I asked him for patience. But obviously, that was something he wasn't willing to give.

I'd worked so hard for so long not to be seen as a victim. My ex-husband gave me a safe haven and also confidence for a while—until he wanted to replace me with a man, that is. And Gregor had just become yet another man to give me false hope for a perfect future that included love and respect, as well as passion. The images on his laptop showed just how much Gregor Antonov respected my wishes.

With a heavy heart and eyes full of tears, I left the

manor—slamming the door on a future I thought had lain in front of me.

Chapter Seventeen

Gregor

After hearing the front door slam, I ran up the cellar steps and down the hallway with vampire speed. I nearly tore the door off its hinges in my pursuit to get to who I knew had left my home in such a rush.

I reached the door to Chloe's van before she had time to close it.

"Leave me alone, Gregor," she cried while trying in vain to wrestle my hand away from the door. Then she noticed the blood on my hands and the wood stuck in my flesh.

"Oh my God, Gregor, you're hurt!" she exclaimed while her eyes took in the rest of me.

Was I hurt? In my heart, I was. How could I not be after seeing those photographs? But as I looked down at my shaking hands, I saw they were battered and torn, and my injuries didn't stop there.

There were small pieces of wood sticking out of my flesh over most of my upper body, and my legs had large gashes that would not heal without extra blood. I truly hadn't felt the pain from any of it; my rage had dealt with that. But to Chloe, I must have looked frightening. Both my shirt and trousers were covered in my blood, which was dripping onto the pebbles of my driveway.

"What happened?" she asked, getting out of the vehicle. I saw my bloody handprints smeared across the white door and roof of her van as I backed away.

"I think you know what happened, Chloe. Or what I have seen, anyway. That's why you were running away, isn't it? You wanted to get away from me because you saw what was on my laptop. That's why you were crying...because you knew I had acquired the information you asked me to wait for. But I couldn't wait for you to tell me, Chloe. It was driving me crazy; both the human and vampire side of me felt the same. I couldn't rest until I knew."

"So you went behind my back and got the information. The bare bones of it, anyway. But that's all you'll ever know now, Gregor."

I read the unspoken words in her eyes. She was done with me. I had betrayed her trust, and that was something she vowed never to accept again. I could see it all laid out like a script, but I wasn't going to hear it.

Not today.

Not ever, in fact. I couldn't deal with those words and the meaning behind them.

I stumbled forward, trying to put some distance between us, but Chloe came to my side and took my rapidly healing arm.

"Gregor, let me help you. No matter how angry I am with you, I can't see you hurt and bleeding."

The shallow cuts were already healing, though I didn't tell her that. Instead, I let her scent and her closeness wash over me and take me to a different time—one where she wasn't angry with me and had no tear tracks down her cheeks.

Once inside my home, we entered my study, and she set me down carefully on my high-backed leather reading chair. My thigh throbbed when my leg made contact with the seat.

"Stay here while I clean you up and find something to help me remove the wood. I assume you don't need a hospital?"

"No hospitals for my kind, Chloe."

"Good. Do you have a first aid kit?"

"I think there's one under the sink in the kitchen, but again, it's not necessary."

"Well, I say it is, so sit still until I return," she commanded.

I bit back a smile and nodded. When she left the study, I glanced over at my laptop and saw it was in screensaver mode, with different shapes appearing at random intervals. Sat in front of that was a photo frame with the word *Godson* written on it. Inside was a photo of me and baby Rory that Chloe had taken at Alex's cottage.

So that's what brought her to my home and to my study. She wanted to bring me a gift, and in return, I broke her heart.

I closed my eyes and prayed to any god that would hear me for the chance to earn Chloe's forgiveness.

I heard her footsteps and the sound of water sloshing around. When I opened my eyes again, I found Chloe standing there with a bowl of water and a couple of towels. Under one arm was a small first aid box that I took from her and set on the side table. She placed the bowl on the floor and sat back on her heels to study me.

"You need to remove your shirt and trousers, Gregor, so I can see what I'm dealing with."

I got up from the chair, wincing when I removed my bloodied shirt because doing so also pulled two pieces of wood from my left side. I'd been so numb before, first with rage, then with the realisation I had just fucked up my relationship with Chloe, and I'd somehow blocked the pain. But believe me, I was feeling it now.

Blood poured freely from the deepest wound. Chloe gasped but didn't falter in her attempt to help me. She quickly wrapped one of the towels around her hand, pressing it firmly to my side to stanch the flow. With the other towel, she wiped away the dried blood from the healed wounds, marvelling at how quickly they had done so.

She carefully picked out small splinters of wood and ran her hands down my arms and body, feeling for others. I looked down at her and realised that this could be the last time she touched me. The pain that caused was real and spread throughout my gut and chest, bringing me to my knees in front of her.

"Gregor," Chloe cried out before catching me in her arms. I rested my forehead on her shoulder, taking in the scent of her neck where I had once drunk. I was tempted to sink my fangs into her delicate skin and taste her again, but I couldn't do it. I knew, however, I would need to take blood soon to help heal the deeper wounds.

Chloe unbuttoned my trousers, and despite the pain, my cock twitched expectantly. When she carefully pulled down my trousers to where my knees rested on the wooden floor, I knew the sight disturbed her.

"Gregor, you have a deep wound in your thigh. I think

there's still a chunk of wood inside, but I don't know how best to remove it. There's blood trickling away from it, and I'm worried that if we remove the wood, I won't be able to stop the flow."

The concern she showed brought me both joy and pain to me. Joy that she was worried about my welfare and pain because I knew my Chloe would be trying to help, even if I were a complete stranger, someone who meant nothing at all to her.

I stood and fully removed my trousers, revealing other deep gashes in my shins. What a fucking idiot I had been. I was lucky that none of the pieces of wood had lodged in my heart, although to kill me fully, I would also have to be burned after having my head removed. If Chloe was to deny me a relationship with her, that didn't seem like a bad option, and I knew now how my father must have felt when he lost my mother.

"I'm going to need blood, Chloe. There's a small refrigerator in the walk-in pantry where I keep my blood bags. One should be sufficient, as I've already had two today. It will help when I dig out this piece in my thigh."

"You can't do it, Gregor, and I really think you should see a doctor. It's just too deep," she said with a sob.

"Hush, Chloe. I have dealt with injuries far worse than this. I will pull out the wood, and as long as I feed immediately, the wound will begin to heal. Trust me on this. I know you may find that hard to do after today, but please try. To see you in such distress hurts me more than any injury ever could. Don't let it be the last memory I have of you, my flower girl, because I know that after today you'll want to forget about me and what we had."

Chloe wiped away her tears with her bloodstained hands and then did something that shocked me to my core.

She placed her wrist over my mouth and said, "Take what you need, Gregor."

I kissed her wrist while I dug my fingers into my thigh. The piece was deep, but once I extended my fingernail into a claw, I was able to hook it around the wood and pull it out. As Chloe had predicted, as soon as the piece was removed, blood gushed profusely from the wound that was gaping open.

"Gregor, you have to drink from me; we need to stop this bleeding," she screamed as she panicked and stuffed the towel hard against the mouth-like hole in my thigh.

For a moment, I had black spots in my vision, but they began to clear when my vampire hearing picked up on Chloe's racing heart before registering the sounds of her begging me to take her blood.

Instead of taking the blood from her wrist as she had offered, I grabbed the back of Chloe's neck and pulled her towards me. Like she did the first time, she tilted her head to one side, exposing her rapidly beating pulse…and I was lost.

I lapped at her quickly before my fangs descended, then I took her blood in a deep swallow. I carried on drinking from her, conscious of only taking enough to stop the bleeding. If I were to heal fully, I would need more. But I wouldn't weaken my flower girl. I had done that once before, and I was determined to keep control of the situation this time.

When I tried to pull away after retracting my fangs, she grabbed the back of my head to keep me in place, whispering, "More, Gregor, take more. I know you need it, and you can give me a little of your blood if you have to."

I hesitated—but only for a moment. Then once again, I pierced her neck with my elongated fangs, savouring each drop of her blood that she gave to me so freely. I was in awe of Chloe, and no matter our future, I was determined to prove to her that I was worthy of receiving her love, trust, and everything else that made up the wonderful woman that was my flower girl.

When I had taken enough blood to heal my wounds, I retracted my fangs and then kissed all along Chloe's neck to her jawline, which I peppered with even more soft kisses before moving to her lips. I paused for a moment and looked into her eyes, silently asking if she wanted my kiss. She nodded her head, then closed her eyes as I pressed my lips against hers, softly at first, then with increasing force as passion and need took over.

Within seconds she was underneath me, and I was grinding my hard cock against the zipper of her jeans. To my utmost relief, she was tilting her hips up to meet each grind, and I could feel how hard her nipples were through her bloodstained T-shirt. I extended a nail on my left hand and tore through her T-shirt and bra before pushing her breasts together, licking and sucking on each nipple one after the other.

I could scent her arousal, even through the thick heavy fabric of her jeans. It was fuelling my desire to be buried deep inside her as soon as possible. So once again, I used a claw to tear through the fabric of her jeans and underwear —before shredding my boxer shorts and sinking my cock inside her as deep as I could.

She was hot, tight and wet. I couldn't stop myself from fucking her with hard, deep thrusts, which Chloe countered thrust for thrust. I heard her breathing change as she gripped my back harder, digging her nails in as she chased the orgasm that was ever so slightly out of reach. On the next few thrusts, I pressed and held for a few seconds longer against her mound. Chloe screamed my name when her orgasm hit, and I held still while watching her react to the pleasure it brought, staying that way until her breathing returned to near normal and she opened her eyes.

"Together this time, my love," I whispered, then began to move again—more slowly than before—still deep inside her, pressing the base of my cock against her pelvic bone, making sure it ground against her clit in a regular rhythm.

"Gregor, I'm going to come again...please. Oh," she gasped as she came hard around my cock. The first of her spasms triggered my own release, and I cried out her name as I rode the waves of bittersweet pleasure.

I kissed her before she could say it meant nothing or even sigh with regret because I couldn't stand to see something that was so perfect tainted in that way. I kept on kissing her until I felt dampness on my cheek. When I looked at her, she was crying.

"Don't, Chloe. Whatever happens in the future, don't regret this moment, please. I don't think I could take that."

"I was going to walk away. I needed to walk away. I can't be with someone who doesn't respect my wishes, Gregor. No matter how much I love them."

Her words broke my heart, crippling me with emotional pain. I had to explain myself, though I knew she might still reject me.

"I'm so sorry I went behind your back for the information you saw. But I needed to know what happened, Chloe. Being a vampire, everything we feel becomes heightened. When we love, we love hard and forever. When we hate... well, it's best that whoever we hate disappears before we find them. When we stress out and worry, it's like a driving force takes over to remove whatever is worrying us. And I know that sounds like a human excuse, but I'm not human, Chloe. Today, before I got the information, I had to take two bags of blood just to try to keep calm. Although, it was a good job I fed on the extra bag this morning, or the furniture in my cellar would have caused me even more damage when I tore it apart."

"Why, Gregor? Why did you destroy it? I thought it was your kind of thing."

"Nothing that scares you is my thing, Chloe. And you were scared when I first took you down there. I caused that with my selfish wants. Well, never again, *moya malen'kaya tsvetochnitsa.*"

"But I enjoyed myself once I got into it, Gregor. I mean, really enjoyed myself. There were some things I definitely wouldn't have wanted to use, but the piece that you bound me to; I would have used that again sometime."

"No, Chloe. You were scared because you thought I would hit you when you were bound and defenceless. I couldn't bear to remember that look once I had seen those photographs."

Chloe shook her head, her eyes filled with utter despair.

"So to you, it doesn't matter that I got over my fear? That I trusted you enough to help me do that? No, it doesn't matter because all you'll ever see me as now is a victim. That's why this will never work between us, Gregor—not now you've seen the police report and photographs. So let me get up and leave. I'll need some clothes to drive home in; you've ruined mine."

After pulling out of the warmth of her body, I stood naked in front of her. I held out my hand to help her up, but she declined my offer, preferring to stand on her own. There was a decorative throw rug over the back of my chair, so I wrapped it around her body, not wanting her to become cold. She thanked me without looking at me, then proceeded towards the stairs. At three steps up, she stilled and closed her eyes. The extra blood I'd taken at her request was now showing its effects.

"Gregor," she whispered as she swayed slightly.

"It's all right, Chloe. I'm here," I soothed, picking her up and carrying her the rest of the way upstairs and into my bathroom. Once there, I bit into my wrist and placed it over her mouth. After four big gulps, I could see the colour start to appear again in Chloe's pale cheeks. She let go of my wrist before wiping the back of her hand across her mouth.

"Thank you," she said, looking down at her blood-stained hands and body. "I have to shower, Gregor, so I need you to leave and bring me something to wear for when I'm done."

"You may still be dizzy and will certainly be tired, Chloe. I will leave the bathroom for now, but you mustn't close the door. I need to hear you if you fall."

Chloe nodded her head as she turned around to start the shower. I didn't really need the door open; my vampire hearing would be able to pick up even the slightest stumble.

I went back into my bedroom to find her something to wear, pulling out a pair of boxers and a blue striped shirt. I didn't have anything for her to wear on the bottom half other than my workout shorts, so I collected those and placed them on the chair outside the bathroom. I could hear Chloe crying, but I knew she wouldn't appreciate me going to join her in the shower, so I knocked loudly on the open door.

"Don't cry, Chloe. I can't bear it. Let me come in and comfort you... Please."

She turned off the shower, and I heard her stumble as she stepped out. I ran in to steady her, but she shook me away.

"Gregor, I'm fine. Don't worry," she said, trying not to look down at my naked body.

"I heard you stumble, so you are not fine. Just sit on the bed for a few minutes, Chloe. I think you may need more blood. I knew I shouldn't have taken more from you. It's my fault you feel this way, so please, take a few drops extra," I said while wrapping her in a towel and guiding her to the bed. Chloe shook her head.

"I've left you some clothes on the chair," I informed her. "If you begin to feel dizzy again, I want you to shout for me. But please, my love, you must wait until I get out of the shower before trying to go downstairs. I would hate for you to fall just because you were hurrying to get away from me. Do not let me have that on my conscience, too."

She nodded her head and sat down on the edge of the bed, adjusting her towel as she did so.

Chapter Eighteen

Chloe

I felt so tired. I knew Gregor had taken more blood than he should have, and at my insistence, too. But it was more than that. I was tired of having to fight. Fighting my own feelings just to protect myself was so draining. And despite my better judgment, I'd had sex with Gregor again.

After seeing what was on his laptop, I'd decided to end things with him, and I was leaving his home for good. But when I saw him injured and bleeding, I couldn't in all good conscience leave him like that. So I stayed to help him and, well, I just can't resist the pull that man has on my body. I crave his touch and his love, but in my experience, that can give someone the ultimate power over you—something I never want to give again. Yes, I wanted to find love and passion, but not at the expense of my independence.

I could see the clothes he'd laid out for me on his chair, but sickening exhaustion was sweeping over me. I was too tired to stand and retrieve the clothes, never mind put them on.

I wanted to get dressed and be ready before Gregor left the shower, but that wasn't going to happen. I was just too weak, and although I liked to think I had some pride, I wasn't stupid enough to risk passing out while trying to put on a shirt.

Gregor came out of the bathroom dripping wet with a towel wrapped around his waist.

"Chloe, are you feeling okay? Why are you not dressed?" Gregor asked with concern in his voice as he made his way over to me.

"I feel so tired and a little shaky. I was afraid that if I stood, I'd fall over," I admitted.

He tilted my chin up to look at me closely.

"My darling, I know you don't want my help, but please, let me give you more of my blood to replace what I took from you. Tell me, have you eaten at all today?"

Thinking back through the whole day, I realised that apart from half a biscuit, I hadn't eaten anything since last night. I shook my head and looked down as Gregor tutted loudly.

"I know you are busy at work, Chloe, but you really must find time to eat. Why didn't you have any lunch?"

"I finally had the photo in the frame and I wanted to bring it over to surprise you," I told him.

He shook his head, and I could tell what he was thinking. If I hadn't come over, I wouldn't have found out about him getting the information regarding my assault. I suddenly felt cold, and so angry with myself for trusting him.

"If you can help me get dressed with as much dignity as possible, Gregor, I would like to go home now and rest."

"I will help you, Chloe, but first you must take my blood," he insisted. "Just a few more sips should do it. If you don't do that, then I cannot let you leave. No matter how much the sight and thought of me might repulse you at this moment, you need what only I can give. So drink quickly and we will be done with it," Gregor said before biting into his wrist again and placing it over my mouth.

After four more sips, he pulled his wrist away and turned to get the clothes. I kept the towel around me while Gregor placed the shirt over my shoulders. He watched me closely as I slipped one arm in, then the other, before he buttoned it from the second button down. Then he brought the knee-length shorts over to me, slipped them up my legs and helped me stand to pull them up under the towel. Once they were on, I let the towel fall away and Gregor picked it up from the floor.

"Sit and wait until I get dressed and I will walk downstairs with you. If you wait until I clean up the blood and our clothing from my study, I will take you home," he said rather abruptly.

"I can get a taxi," I told him, but his eyes flashed red with anger at my words. Although I'd seen it before, the sight scared me a little this time.

Gregor backed away from me. "For fuck's sake, Chloe. Isn't it enough that you hurt me by trying to get away from me as soon as we had sex? Like what we did caused you shame? Now you are physically scared of me when I have never raised a hand in anger to you, or any woman, in the 546 years I have been on this earth. If you wanted me to feel this much pain, why didn't you leave me injured?"

I could hear the hurt in his voice but I couldn't comfort him. If I did, I would end up staying, and I needed to leave him. So I turned away, feigning indifference, though it's one of the hardest things I've ever done.

I heard him open drawers, then his wardrobe, as he took out his clothes and put them on. He came to stand by me and offered his hand. I declined, but not for the reason he thought. I knew if I took his hand I would feel that heady pull that made me want so much more of him.

He nodded his head and motioned for me to go first. Ever the gentleman, even in the face of heartbreak.

Gregor stood beside me as I walked down the grand staircase, matching his steps with mine—so he was able to catch me when I stumbled four steps from the bottom. Weariness had taken over again and I had a sudden urge to sit back and close my tear-filled eyes. I knew that not eating anything was a huge factor in this, but I didn't think I'd be able to eat anything now—I was too nauseous.

I was vaguely aware of him picking me up and carrying me somewhere, and was extremely grateful when he laid me down on a comfortable surface and covered me with something soft and warm. I think I recall him calling me his flower girl in Russian, or was it English? I couldn't be sure, but I found the endearment comforting and I fell into a deep and restful sleep.

Chapter Nineteen

Gregor

I looked down at Chloe's sleeping form as she lay on my sofa. She was still so pale, and there was just a hint of shadow appearing under her eyes. I cursed myself for taking so much of her blood, although I knew she could have sustained the loss easily if she'd eaten today.

She'd dashed from my side this morning, promising to eat when she got to her shop, but she hadn't had anything all day. And we were both so consumed with each other last night that neither of us had ventured anywhere near the kitchen.

I'd have words with my Chloe when she awoke, although she wouldn't want to hear them. It would hurt to know she wasn't taking good care of herself, even if I wasn't part of her life. I would still love her long after the day she passed from this earth, whether she accepted that or not.

I heard a vehicle pull up in my driveway and recognised

it to be Nik's, although once my door opened, I scented Sergei, and he was alone.

"What the fuck happened here?" he yelled from what was probably the doorway of my office.

I had forgotten the blood and torn clothing that lay beside my chair. Sergei must have been imagining many things as he looked at the sight and took in the scent. After placing a chaste kiss on Chloe's cheek, I made my way to my office.

"Gregor, why is your blood all over here? And how come I can scent sex in here, too? I'd have thought the sight of all this blood would put any human off, unless... No! I know you wouldn't have hurt her," Sergei said as he shook his head.

"Viktor called and told me to check on you. He said he'd given you upsetting information about your woman. Where is she, Gregor?" Sergei asked.

"She is sleeping in my lounge. Why?" I answered.

"I need to check that she is okay. As I have said, I know you wouldn't hurt her—intentionally, anyway—but I need to see for myself that she is all right."

"What the fuck, Sergei?" I bellowed. "I would sooner die a lasting death than hurt my Chloe. You wound me to think otherwise."

Sergei said nothing as he barged past me to find Chloe asleep. He turned to me and announced, "She reeks of you, Gregor. It's not a full Bond yet, but there is something there."

"There will be no full Bond between us," I sighed. "I have betrayed her trust and lost her love. I only had it for a short time, but it was worth more than all I own."

Shaking his head, Sergei declared, "That is utter nonsense, Gregor. If you had lost her love, then whatever you've done would not have left tear tracks down her cheeks. A woman will not cry over a man she does not love! Now, come, let us clean up the mess you have left in your study, or your housekeeper will have a heart attack. It looks like a massacre happened in there. While we work, Sergei will come up with a plan to get you your woman."

"Sergei," I groaned while following him to my kitchen to get some rubbish bags and a mop and bucket. "None of your silly scheming, please. I need to do this on my own. It was me that caused the problem with Chloe, so I should be the one to put it right or accept it if it cannot be."

As he came to stand in the light of my kitchen window, I noticed blue staining on Sergei's hands and a little on his jeans.

"Sergei, why do you have blue on your hands?" I asked.

"Ahh, so you've noticed. I was hoping it wasn't that obvious," he replied with a deep sigh.

"Your palms and the back of your fingers are blue; how is that not obvious?"

Sergei took off his jacket, and I noticed his T-shirt was also stained blue.

"Well," he began, "Daisy wanted to ride a magic blue unicorn like her favourite book and cartoon character, Queen Ellie, the fairy. So Yuri and I decided to make this happen. The unicorn is coloured the same blue as the fairy's wings, so we got in touch with a few horse-riding schools in Yorkshire to ask if they would make one of their little ponies blue for the day. And somehow have a horn like a unicorn. None of them would do it, even though we offered them two thousand pounds. Eventually, we found someone in Wakefield willing to do it, although we had to double the amount of cash."

Sergei and Yuri considered themselves the little girl's

uncles and liked to spoil her whatever the occasion. But this was something I imagined Daisy would never forget.

"The riding school said they had used child-friendly chalk to colour the pony so that it wouldn't hurt either the animal or Daisy, and it was supposed to brush off. They attached the gold-coloured wooden horn to the bridle somehow, and the colour of the pony was only slightly lighter than that of the wings Daisy wore over her coat. Daisy was thrilled, and she couldn't stop smiling. All was going well, and along with one of the staff from the riding school, we took her into what Yuri said were magic woods.

"Then the heavens opened, and we had a short but heavy rain shower. We got her back as quickly as we could, and it stopped raining only a few minutes after it started. I worried that the chalk could have washed away to show Daisy that it wasn't real, but instead, the colour had become much deeper. I'd been holding on to Daisy but noticed that my stonewashed jeans had deep blue patches on them, and when I steadied the pony, the blue transferred to my hands. I had no worries that the colour would stain; I was assured by the staff it would wash off.

"Daisy was so happy and gave me a big kiss to say thank you for finding Queen Ellie's unicorn. She asked Yuri to pick her up, and then she kissed and hugged the pony before turning quickly and kissing Yuri, too. When she pulled away from Yuri's face, I noticed she had left blue handprints on his cheeks, and his lips and chin were also blue. Yuri hadn't realised because he'd hugged her to his shoulder straight after, so he hadn't had a chance to notice Daisy's face.

"When he set her back down on the floor, we both saw how bad Daisy looked. She had blue in her hair, down her right cheek, her lips, nose and chin, and her hands and the arms of her coat were also blue."

"Has Keeley seen her yet?" I asked, trying not to laugh at Sergei's obvious distress.

"No. We took her back to Nik and Gina's so we could wash all the blue away, but it only lightened slightly. Gina washed Daisy's coat and leggings and then put her in the bath, but as I have said, it has only lightened, not removed it. We rang the riding school, who have no idea how to remove it either, and are worried that the pony will be permanently blue."

Patting him on the shoulder, I said, "Well if Keeley comes, you are on your own, Sergei. She is fiercely protective when it comes to her little girl, and I dread to think what will happen when Josh sees her. Where is Daisy now?"

"She's at Nik and Gina's with Yuri. I was glad that Viktor called me and told me to check on you. It's given me an excuse to be out of the way when Keeley comes to collect Daisy. Gina will put her in the bath again before that happens, but I have washed my hands over and over, and it's still there. My T-shirt is stained from carrying Daisy to the bathtub, and the bathtub is also stained now."

I shook my head and made my way back to my study. Sergei took the mop and bucket, and I picked up the discarded clothing. After checking the pockets and placing my findings from Chloe's jeans onto the side table, I picked up the rest of the torn, bloody clothes and binned them. Then I set to work cleaning the leather armchair while Sergei mopped the floor.

"So, are you going to tell me what information Viktor sent that caused all this mess?" he asked.

I knew I shouldn't tell him, but I also knew he would still

try to fix this if I didn't show him how seriously I'd fucked up.

"Let's get rid of all this, and I will explain," I said, picking up the mop and bucket in one hand and bags in the other. Sergei nodded and made his way towards the front door.

"Where are you going?" I asked.

"I have a feeling this will require much alcohol, Gregor, and it just so happens I have an unopened bottle of Abram's finest vodka."

"I do not like to drink vampire-strength alcohol. You know this," I reminded him.

"Gregor, do not worry about the alcohol. After the events of today, we both need to relax and forget about a few things, my friend, and this will help. Trust in Sergei; he knows what is best for you."

I was about to argue, but he held up his hands to stop me, which of course, were blue, and instead of telling him I wouldn't partake of the high-strength vodka, I laughed as I watched him walk towards Nik's car.

Chapter Twenty

Gregor

"Gregor, where the hell are we?" yelled Chloe through what sounded like a loudspeaker.

Why did she need to use a loudspeaker? I thought as I opened my eyes and tried to lift my head.

Oh, fuck no!

The room was bathed in ultra-bright light that made my eyes water, blurring my vision. I tried to say her name, but it came out sounding raspy. Something was very wrong, but I couldn't figure out what it was.

"Gregor, you need to wake up because I'm really freaked out here. I need to know where we are because it sure as hell isn't the grounds of Rothley Manor I see through this window."

That got my attention, so I tried to open my eyes again. It took a good twenty seconds for them to stop watering, but once they did and I could focus on my surroundings, I groaned and closed them again.

The warm cream tones in this room looked familiar to me, and as the haze began to lift from my mind, I finally realised why. We were in my bedroom in my home in Rublevka, just outside of Moscow. And by the look on Chloe's face, she wasn't at all happy about it. But how the hell had we got here?

My head was pounding hard. I tried to sit up, but a wave of nausea rolled through me. There was a loud knock at the door, and I felt the bed dip as Chloe came to sit beside me.

"Come in," I said as calmly as possible in the circumstances.

"I have brought you breakfast," announced a blue-faced Yuri as he made his way into the room along with Andrei, my cook.

"I also brought something extra to help you sober up," Yuri said. "For the amount you drank, I thought two bags of blood would be good to start with. Sergei said it was Abram's finest vodka, so you will need to eat a belly full of food to feel anywhere near normal. I am surprised at you for drinking his vodka, Gregor; you normally avoid vampire-strength alcohol."

With Yuri's words, it all started to come back to me.

Sergei pouring me a drink as I sat and told him about Chloe's abuse at the hands of Peter Finch… Sergei being angry and upset and wanting to kill him… Me telling him about the man's injuries after the car hit him… Sergei refilling my glass…

Explaining to Sergei how I smashed up the furniture in my cellar, and Sergei telling me he could understand why I did this… Me being so very grateful that he could see my side of things and drinking another glass of vodka…

Me telling Sergei I thought I'd lost Chloe forever… Sergei disagreeing and telling me I should kidnap Chloe and take her back to

Russia… Me saying that would be a stupid thing to do… Sergei pouring me another vodka…

Sergei telling me that spending time with Chloe in Russia would make her fall in love with me, and me seeing merit to his story after I downed the next glass of vodka in one go…

I had one more large glass of vodka that I can remember before things became a little hazy.

Sergei waking Chloe up and asking where she kept her passport while using mind control to keep her compliant… Calling Yuri and then guiding me to the back of my SUV… Placing a smiling Chloe on my lap and…

My mind was a complete blank where the rest of last night was concerned. A couple of things I did know were that I would never again drink vampire-strength alcohol, and Sergei had a lot of explaining to do.

I took the blood bags from Yuri and slowly made my way to the bathroom, my vision creating strange dimensions and abstract shapes in everything around me.

The first bag of blood made little difference, but by the time I'd ingested the second bag, my vision was much clearer, and the heavy, throbbing drumbeat in my head began to subside. I needed a shower, but I wanted to get back to Chloe. I also needed to eat human food.

As I made my way out of the en-suite bathroom, I heard an argument developing between Chloe and Yuri.

"But I never asked to be here," Chloe yelled. So Yuri must have told her where we were.

"I don't know why this bothers you; Moscow has some beautiful sights to see," Yuri replied.

"But I wasn't aware of being brought here. *He* kidnapped me," she almost screamed as she pointed her finger in my direction. I was about to open my mouth and tell her what had happened when Yuri argued back.

"Gregor was in no fit state to kidnap anyone. He was blind drunk and could hardly stand. It was Sergei who organised the trip. He said you were both stubborn and needed time away, and he convinced Gregor to take a drink with him, although I don't know how. That has rarely happened in all the years I have known him," Yuri declared.

"I know that Sergei used mind control to convince you that you wanted to get on a plane—and to tell him where your passport was. I also know that Sergei is working at your shop while you are in Russia. So why should you not enjoy your time here while he is working for you?"

"Because I didn't choose to be here. Why can't you understand that? And why does your face have big blue splodges on it?" Chloe questioned.

"The blue is of no consequence. What is important is your obvious dislike of my country," Yuri replied, a look of hurt appearing on his blue face.

I knew I should have ended their argument there and defended Chloe, but I was so surprised that Yuri was acting this way. He was normally so laid-back—unless my security issues called for more.

"I don't dislike your country; I never said that," Chloe stated.

Yuri turned in my direction and winked before turning back to Chloe.

"So it is Russian people you dislike!" Yuri exclaimed, feigning shock as he took a step back.

"No, I haven't said I dislike any of you either. I just—"

"You are like many others throughout the world. You disagree with our politics…associating Russian citizens with the actions of both past and present leaders. You label us homophobic and racist and think we are obsessed with weaponry and war. Shame on you, Chloe. I thought you were better than that."

"I am...I mean...that's not how I think of Russian people. I hold no prejudice against any race or country. You have this all wrong," Chloe said, clearly distressed.

"So you will stay for a few days? Let us show you around Moscow and visit Gregor's palace in St Petersburg?"

"Yes, I will stay and see the sites of Moscow. And Gregor's palace in St Petersburg," Chloe replied with a disgruntled sigh.

"We don't have to visit my palace," I told her. "I rarely go there, anyway."

"So, Gregor. Are you saying you are refusing to take Chloe to your ancestral home? Why? I thought you loved this woman. Did you lie about that?" asked Yuri with another wink.

"No, of course I did not lie. I love Chloe! I would take her anywhere," I declared.

"Good, so that is settled, then. First, Anna will go shopping to get clothes for Chloe; she cannot visit Moscow in what she is wearing. Here," Yuri said, handing Chloe a pen and a sheet of paper.

"Anna says she needs all your measurements for clothing and shoes so she can bring you some over. She is already on her way to the stores, but Anna can shop for hours, so you can take your time with the breakfast Andrei has prepared. Now, I must go and organise our security detail for your sightseeing tour of the city. Enjoy your breakfast, Chloe."

Yuri and Andrei turned to leave, and I followed them out of the door.

"Yuri, what is the meaning of all this? Why was I not consulted? The last time I checked, you worked for me, not the other way around."

"My orders came from both Viktor and Sergei. I know it is you that employs me, but these men are my friends, as well as yours, and right now, you would do well to remember that, Gregor."

"Sergei…" I yelled. Well, attempted to yell, as my head still couldn't tolerate loud noises. "It is because of Sergei that Chloe is so angry. I mean, really, Yuri, it does look very much like we kidnapped her."

"From what Sergei said, she was angry with you anyway. You always say the first rule of business and women is to listen. So why didn't you take heed of your rule and listen to the woman?"

"I couldn't. I was too wound up to leave it. What has Sergei told you?" I questioned.

"Enough to know you were acting unlike yourself and letting love defeat you. As they say in the movies, *you need to grow some balls, man,*" Yuri said in a poor attempt at an American accent. Then he laughed out loud.

"Yuri, I don't know what has possessed you to speak to me this way, but—"

"Gregor, in this situation, it seems that you must take direction from others for once. Despite how Chloe came to be here, she is in Russia, in your bedroom. She has agreed to stay in Moscow and see the sights before travelling to St Petersburg with you. Take her out today and show her all the beautiful parts of this city, and show her the side of you that listens to everything she has to say. Work on that, and you will have your woman. You have Sergei, Viktor, and me to help you. So how can you fail?" he said confidently.

"Yuri, you have a blue face. You resemble a cartoon character. Looking at you does not inspire confidence that you, or indeed Sergei, can help," I told him, staring at the smudged handprints on his cheeks. "Did Keeley catch up with you?"

Yuri winced. "She chased me out of the cottage and hit me with her umbrella while I was opening the car door. Then she hit me with her bag as I was getting in the car. I did not think a woman could run as fast in high heels, vampire or not. She said she wasn't talking to me ever again, but this morning I sent her all the photographs we had taken of Daisy on the pony before the rain came, and she thanked me for them. So maybe I am forgiven."

"Has she seen Sergei yet?" I asked.

"Sergei is staying in Chloe's flat; he's going to work at her shop while she is here with you. So, no, I don't think Keeley has seen him yet."

"How I would like to be a fly on the wall when she does see him," I muttered.

"He will get out of it; he always does," Yuri said with a shrug of his shoulders. "Now go, Gregor, and stop wasting time talking to me when you have a beautiful woman sitting on your bed."

Chapter Twenty-One

Chloe

The breakfast that Gregor's chef and Yuri brought me was delicious. Who'd have thought I'd get a better full English brekky in Russia than in England? There were also croissants and fruit with a pot of honey I had my eye on for afterwards. I was so desperately hungry, having survived yesterday on tea and a biscuit.

I filled in the piece of paper that Yuri gave me. There were a number of questions about clothing sizes, including underwear and shoe sizes. I didn't like writing those down. The fact that I was a bigger size on the bottom than on top while being five foot four made it awkward when shopping for clothes. My 38DD bra size was something I didn't want to disclose to a stranger, nor was the fact that I was a size sixteen in knickers. They even asked what brands of perfume, make-up and hair products I preferred. I doubted you could get my supermarket's own brand products here, so I left the hair and make-up questions blank.

Looking around the room, I was surprised that it was so modern looking. Gregor's bedroom at the manor was very Georgian in its appearance, and the furniture and fabrics represented that well. But this room was a completely different story. His bed frame was a pale birch-coloured wood, and the bedding was a light cream covered with a dark taupe throw. His furniture was also in pale birch with steel handles, and I counted what I assumed were ten large wardrobe doors. There was also a taupe leather high-backed chair and a round coffee table in front of two tall, narrow windows. The curtains were in the same taupe colour as the throw and matched the luxuriously thick carpet.

The en-suite bathroom was also very modern, with beige marble tiles that covered both the walls and floor. There was an extra-large whirlpool bath next to a double sink and toilet. But the walk-in shower was like something else entirely. It had a huge shower head above, with various jets protruding from different angles, from shoulder to ankle level. I couldn't wait to try it.

Gregor came back into the room looking more than a little worse for wear. His hair was stuck up all over, and he had a day's worth of stubble covering the lower half of his face and chin. It made him look more real than I had ever seen him before. I'd been all set to rip into him about being brought here without my consent, but I could see from the way he'd acted he had nothing to do with bringing me here.

"How are you feeling now?" I asked. His face lit up at my question.

"I never usually drink vampire-strength alcohol, so I fear that this hangover will stay with me the entire morning. But thank you for asking, Chloe."

"Here," I said, handing him the list with my measurements on it.

"Thank you. I will call Anna now so she can get started with her buying. I'm sure this will make her day as she loves to shop. I expect you will have many shoes and handbags; she seems to have a thing for buying those. I am sure she has a handbag for every day of the year," he said with a smile.

"Gregor, I haven't got any money with me. And I can't afford anything expensive after the repairs on my home," I reminded him.

"Nonsense, Chloe, it is my fault you were brought here. I shouldn't have let Sergei talk me into drinking with him. If I had been sober, I wouldn't have let him bring you here against your will. So let me buy you anything you need. I would be happy to do so anyway, you know that."

"I know, but I don't want you to read anything into it, Gregor. Just because you can buy me clothes, it doesn't mean you can buy *me*."

He took a step back at that statement as if I had physically slapped him, and I immediately regretted my words.

"I'm sorry, Gregor. I didn't mean that. I just—"

Gregor held up a hand to stop me. "Don't, Chloe. Don't make excuses to placate me. I will get used to how things are between us now. If you would rather do your sightseeing with Yuri and Anna—my assistant—I can arrange that for you. I will also arrange for you to have your own room, or mine if you prefer. And I'll make sure I stay out of your way whenever you return."

I'd hurt him, and I hated myself for it. I didn't want any of what he said, but I didn't want him to think we had a future together, either.

I made my way across the room to him and took his hand in mine.

"Gregor, I want *you* to show me around Moscow today. I wouldn't want to see it with anyone but you. I'd like to go back to how we were when we were just friends. I miss that —the easiness of just being together and enjoying our days and nights out around Yorkshire. Can we have the same here in Russia?"

"Yes, we can have that, Chloe," he said, giving me a smile that didn't quite reach his eyes. "Just bear in mind that I fell in love with you during those times you just mentioned, and that love will only grow the more time I spend with you. I find I cannot control myself around you—that includes my feelings as well as my actions. But if you wish, I will keep my feelings to myself. It won't be easy, and I think we'll have Yuri playing matchmaker, so that is something else we'll have to contend with."

I nodded my head in agreement. "Yuri was quite cunning with the way he got me to agree to stay. I always get along so well with him, and he knows I've no prejudice towards any nationality. I think I've just been played, Gregor. How about you?"

"My darling, I think my staff and my friends think they are in charge of this little game they are playing. So how about we give them something to think about?" he said.

"What do you have in mind?" I asked.

"I do have something in mind, but let's wait and see what happens. First, I will show you how to use my shower. It may seem complicated, but it's easy once you get the hang of it."

Still keeping my hand in his, he led me into the bathroom and proceeded to show me how the shower worked. He got out a new toothbrush head to apply to his sonic toothbrush, then showed me where the clean towels were kept. He turned to leave and levelled me with a gaze that melted my insides. It would be so easy to ask him to shower with me, but I didn't. I just thanked him for his help and ushered him out of the door before leaning back on it and sighing. How would I ever keep him at arm's length when my body craved his? My head told me to keep my distance, but my heart told me to grab the love he offered and never let go.

After about twenty minutes in the best shower ever, with the gorgeously scented body wash and shampoo that Gregor had, I finally came out and brushed my teeth. Gregor's towels were the most luxurious I had ever used. Even more so than those at his home in Rothley. I'd heard of people stealing towels and bathrobes from hotels before, and after using Gregor's, I could see why they would do so.

I noticed a bathrobe hung up on the back of the bathroom door. I put it on and immediately caught the scent of Gregor's cologne. Rich and spicy, just like him, I mused. I felt like I could stay wrapped up in his plush robe forever, but I knew that Gregor was waiting for the shower, so I made my way out into his bedroom.

I couldn't see him at first, but one of the wardrobe doors was open, so I peered inside. To my surprise, the door opened into another room. A dressing room of sorts, I suppose you could say. As I stepped inside, I caught Gregor looking at the suits and shirts he had hung up on rails all along the back wall.

"The shower's yours if you want it," I told him. He looked at me for a moment, then looked back at his suits.

"What should I wear on a sightseeing trip around Moscow?" he asked.

"I don't know. What would you normally wear?" I replied.

"This." Gregor gestured towards the clothing on display.

"Perhaps you'd feel more comfortable in jeans and a smart T-shirt or sweater, depending on the weather," I suggested.

"I have sweaters, but the only T-shirts I have are what I wear to go running or work out."

"Just wear what you want, Gregor, or more importantly, what you feel comfortable in," I told him.

"My time here is filled with business meetings or nights out at the ballet or the opera, or occasionally, my club. I rarely go out anywhere through the daytime," he said, looking a little lost.

I could tell that Gregor was out of his comfort zone at the moment, but I thought that might be a good thing for him.

"It's good to have new experiences. Wasn't that what you told me when you took me out for sushi in York that night?" I reminded him.

"And if I recall correctly, my little flower girl, you didn't like most of it," he replied with a smirk.

"Exactly," I said, squirming a little as I remembered my first taste. "But at least I tried it, Gregor. I experienced something new that day. Would I want to repeat it? God, no! But I don't regret going and trying it. So how about you put a call through to Anna and get her to buy you a pair of jeans and a couple of smart/casual T-shirts? Let's meander through the touristy areas of the city taking photographs, just like regular sightseers would."

"Okay, I will do this. It will make a change for me to visit the places I have only recommended to my business associates," he said.

"You mean to tell me you've never seen all the touristy sights yourself?" I questioned, surprised by what he'd just revealed.

"Many, many years ago. I've had the odd stroll or two around Red Square and Gorky Park, although again, not for many years. The only time I ever have anything like a day out is when I am in England with Freya, or more recently with you. Freya often asked me to consider wearing more casual attire, and I did purchase a wax jacket and wellingtons for walks along the cliffs with her. But maybe I should move with the times and change the way I dress— become more like Alex and Josh."

I felt a little bad at that. Like I was the reason he was trying to change.

"Gregor, don't change anything for me. If you're going to make a change, then do it for yourself—because it's the right thing to do for you."

"I think it is," he said, nodding his head. "It is time for Gregor Antonov to let go of some of the past. You can help me do that, Chloe. You can show me how to be a little freer and how you say, *move with the times,* yes?"

"Well, I suppose so, but—"

"Good. It is settled, then. I will call Anna back and tell her to carry on shopping. She normally picks up my clothing from my tailor and the stores she orders from, so she knows my measurements and sizes. I know she enjoys spending my money, so I will tell her to buy herself a new bag and shoes. She may make a better choice for me once she does so."

And with that, off Gregor went to make his phone call

before getting in the shower. I didn't feel like putting on the clothes I'd slept in last night, so I searched around in Gregor's drawers until I found his boxer shorts. They were a snug fit around my hips, but at least I was no longer naked underneath the robe. While looking for his underwear, I came across a hairdryer and brush, so I blow-dried my hair. It didn't take long due to the short style I had.

With that done, I took another long look out of the windows. I could see houses in the distance, but this seemed to be in an area on its own, with expansive lawned gardens and a long driveway. Something else I noticed after a while was the many security cameras set around the property. They didn't immediately catch my attention, but now that I'd seen them, I couldn't help but watch the odd movements that came from each one. There must have been at least fifteen on this side of the house. I was so engrossed with their movements I didn't hear Gregor behind me.

"What are you looking at, *moya malen'kaya tsvetochnitsa*?"

"You have so many security cameras, Gregor. Why is that? Don't you feel safe in your home?"

"My country has a very chequered past, and things can change rapidly from peaceful and prosperous to...well, something entirely different I shall not spoil our day talking about. Besides, they are not all cameras; some are infrared motion detectors. Now come, let me show you around my home. You can choose a room you would like to stay in tonight, and I'll have it decorated to your taste for when we return from dinner this evening," Gregor said as if it was no bother at all for him to do so.

"No, you can't decorate just for me! Besides, I like your bathroom. It has that wonderful shower and the softest towels. I might have to steal them," I told him.

Gregor swept his arm out, gesturing around the room.

"Anything you want, my love, it is yours. But I hope you will let me treat you to something other than my towels. I think it would disappoint Pamela to know that you travelled all this way just to get household items."

I gasped and placed my hands on top of my head. "Oh, no. I forgot to phone Pam. Gregor, I need to call and tell her about Sergei. What time is it in England?"

"We are two hours ahead of the UK, so it is now nine-thirty."

"Oh, shit," I muttered anxiously. In truth, I was shocked that I hadn't given much thought to how my business was faring in my absence.

Gregor handed me his phone and stepped away from me while I dialled. Pam answered in her chirpy morning voice.

"Good morning, Chloe's Flowers and Gifts, Pam speaking. How may I help you today?"

"Pam, it's me. I'm so sorry to leave you in the lurch, but—"

"Chloe," Pam almost screamed down the phone. *"I can't believe Gregor spirited you away on a surprise romantic getaway. You are so lucky. And thank you a million times over for getting Sergei to fill in for you. He's so quick at everything he does. It took a few goes to teach him how to arrange the posies, but when he finally got it, he whizzed through them. I'd only just popped out of the back room to serve a customer, and he had all six posies done and wrapped. You should think of employing him full-time. He's a quick healer, too. No messing about looking for plasters with him when rose thorns attack his fingers."*

"Well, erm, okay. It seems like you have everything under control. Can you take down the number I'm calling from and let me know if you have any problems? I'll get back to you as soon as possible, and I'll come home if you need me," I said, both glad that things were going well and a bit sad that I was easily replaceable.

"Oh, don't you worry about a thing. We've got no big wedding or funeral orders coming up, and to be honest, I would much rather spend my day looking at this gorgeous Russian than at you. I mean, honestly, Chloe, are they all as good-looking as Gregor and Sergei? If they are, I wouldn't come back to England. And the way he talks... Oh, wow! He told one customer who asked for help choosing the prettiest flowers for her bouquet that she was the prettiest flower of them all. God, the way he said it was so low and sexy, I thought I was going to have to peel her off him. He's like Johnny Depp, but taller and more built. But that smile... Oh, my! Even the blue hands aren't a turn-off."

"Pam, you're a married woman. Behave yourself." I laughed as she sighed dreamily down the phone.

"A woman can dream, Chloe. My hubby hasn't made my toes curl for years. Sergei's done more for my libido with just a wink and a smile than my other half has done for me in a long time."

"And that's my cue to put the phone down." I laughed again before adding, "Seriously though, Pam, if you need me, just give this number a call."

"I will, and, Chloe... I hope your toes curl many, many times over the next few days."

I hung up the phone, hoping Gregor hadn't heard all of that. If he had, he didn't say anything.

I handed him the phone, and he slipped it into his pocket. Taking my hand, he led me down the hallway, showing me each of the bedrooms as we encountered them. Only three of the seven rooms were furnished apart from his, and he explained that other than Freya, he rarely had any visitors. The bedrooms were similar to Gregor's, having the same modern pale wood design with plain, neutral colours, but the hall and stairway were in oak, resembling the wooden features at the manor.

Making my way down the long, wide staircase, I saw an open-plan room with a roaring log fire in the middle, its narrow chimney breast separating the room. The side nearest to the stairs was set with a large leather sofa and two wingback chairs. From what I could see, the other side of the room boasted a huge pale oak dining table with at least twelve chairs.

As we entered the sitting room area, a tall man with short blond hair and dark brown eyes approached Gregor and spoke to him in Russian. Gregor nodded and had a short conversation with him before introducing us.

"Chloe, this is Dmitry. He is one of my security staff. He speaks very little English, although he is learning quickly."

"Hello, Chloe," Dmitry said with a heavy Russian accent. "I very pleased to meeting you. I see you Moscow this day, no?"

"I am pleased to meet you too, Dmitry," I said, holding out my hand. Dmitry glanced at Gregor—who nodded with a smile—before shaking my hand enthusiastically. "And I am happy to see Moscow today. Please excuse the robe; I have no clothes at the moment," I told him, feeling a little self-conscious about meeting new people while only wearing a bathrobe and Gregor's underwear.

"It is okay. You beautiful with no clothes," he said. Gregor seemed to growl a little, and Dmitry stepped back nervously.

"Thank you, Dmitry," I replied, trying to suppress my laughter.

He nodded. First at me, then nervously at Gregor before turning to walk away. Gregor stared at me for a moment, then put his hand behind my back, guiding me towards the dining area.

"Would you like a cup of tea, coffee, or maybe a cold

drink?" he asked as a young man in tailored black trousers and a burgundy waistcoat stepped out of a doorway.

"A cup of tea, please, but only if you're having one."

Gregor spoke a few words in Russian to the young man, whom I found out was named Stepan. He nodded his head, then disappeared through a doorway I assumed led to the kitchen.

Gregor was then approached by another young man called Daniil, who was Dmitry's cousin. I could see a likeness with the same blond hair and brown eyes, but Daniil seemed shy and blushed when we were introduced.

He spoke English fluently and had even less of an accent than Yuri or Sergei. Gregor said Daniil had studied business at Cambridge University before working for him—overseeing his investments and dealing with day-to-day business demands in his absence. I sensed a real fondness from Gregor towards this young guy and, despite the blushing, when the two men spoke, I could see that Daniil could more than hold his own with Gregor when talking business.

While they discussed work, I wandered over to a wall of glass bricks and looked through them. Through the distorted view, I could see a large swimming pool and an area with padded seating and sun loungers.

"You have a swimming pool," I almost squealed, interrupting Gregor and Daniil's conversation.

"We can talk later, Gregor," said Daniil before turning to me and adding, "It was lovely to meet you, Chloe, but I must leave you now and return to my office. I trust you'll have a wonderful time here in Moscow, as there is plenty to see and do in our capital city. And I hope to see you again soon."

"It was lovely meeting you too, Daniil," I replied, smiling. His blush and subsequent shyness were adorable and seemed only to happen when he spoke to me. Or maybe it was all women?

As soon as he turned to leave, I walked back over to Gregor and grabbed his hand.

"I can't believe you have a pool next to your dining room. Show me," I demanded as I pulled him along to where the glass bricks ended. On one side, leading to a lawned garden, were ten large glass sliding doors that were currently closed. Opposite them were the same amount of doors, but these were in pale greys, like driftwood.

Gregor stepped towards the wooden doors and opened them. Each door was bi-folding, leaving five split doors to each side of the pool room. I walked towards stone steps that graduated down into the water and bent to dip my hand in. It was on the cooler side of lukewarm, just the way our local pool was at the aqua fit class I attended each week.

The walls were a pale cream marble with a hint of sky-blue flecks and veins running through them. A slightly deeper blue covered the bottom and sides of the pool, which matched the cushions and seat pads on pale grey rattan loungers. Altogether, it was like something you would find in the most expensive hotels, and I so desperately wanted to take off my robe and swim.

"It's beautiful, Gregor. I wish I could get in and have a good swim."

"Then why don't you, my love?"

Wasn't it glaringly obvious? "Because I don't have anything to swim in."

"Then swim naked," he said, raising his eyebrows suggestively as he spoke.

"Gregor, your house seems full of people. I couldn't swim naked here—not that I've ever swum naked before," I told him. "It doesn't seem quite right to do it in a pool."

"Nonsense. To swim naked is a wonderfully freeing experience and one I insist you try before you go back to England," he said in all seriousness.

"Do you swim naked in here?" I asked, imagining Gregor's muscular form pushing through the water. Bad idea! Imagining Gregor swimming naked made my heartbeat speed up and certain places tingle. I didn't want him to know that thought had turned me on, but by the look of Gregor's smirk, it was something I hadn't hidden well.

"I often swim naked, *moya malen'kaya tsvetochnitsa*, and I would be happy if you joined me in doing so," he said with a wink.

I stuck my tongue out at him and was about to say *no, thanks*, although my shameless body was saying *yes, please*, but I was interrupted by Stepan bringing us a pot of tea and a selection of biscuits and small cakes.

Gregor motioned for Stepan to set it down on a nearby table, then he walked over and started to pour. He handed me a cup and asked me to sit opposite him. Reaching into his pocket, he pulled out what looked like a phone, although not the one he normally used. Gregor keyed something into it before pointing it at the ceiling. For a few seconds, I wondered what on earth he was trying to do. Then I heard a kind of whirring noise and watched in awe as the ceiling began to part, revealing a glass roof.

Even though the sky was thick with dull grey clouds, the sight was still magnificent. Natural light flooded the room, and the lights around the walls dimmed.

"Gregor, this is amazing," I declared as I glanced around the room.

"Yes, it is…though it is much better when the sun is shining. Unfortunately, we haven't had many sunny days this summer. That is why the fire in the main room has been lit.

Being such a large space, it takes some time to heat up, and I didn't want you to feel the cold and catch a chill, my love."

"Do you use this area often?" I asked. "If this was my house, I think I would use it all the time."

Closing his eyes and leaning back, Gregor replied, "I like to relax in here. Although I can walk in sunlight and enjoy the outdoors, daylight can still be very tiring. The glass in all my homes and offices is specially designed to filter out the harmful effects of daylight on vampires. It means that even made vampires can walk around freely without fear. A lot of my staff in St Petersburg are made vampires, and since I had the glass installed there, they have been able to open those heavy curtains in the daytime. I'm told it has made the atmosphere much more pleasant."

"You said you didn't visit there often. Why is that?"

"Ah, my dear Chloe, that is a long and painful story, and not one I like to share."

"You wanted to know my painful story," I countered.

"You did not want to share that either, *moya malen'kaya tsvetochnitsa.*"

"And look where that got us, Gregor," I reminded him.

But he was right. I could see the hurt in his eyes when he spoke about his home in St Petersburg, and I wanted to know what put it there. What events in Gregor's past caused him to avoid his ancestral home?

I didn't want to pry, so I left it for the moment. I'd give him time over the next day or so to tell me, but I felt that I should know before we went so I knew what conversations to avoid.

Guilt ate away at me when I realised that was why Gregor had wanted me to tell him about the abuse I suffered. So he could avoid saying or doing anything that would upset me. He'd said the same to me, but I hadn't listened. He still shouldn't have gone behind my back, though. That's something I did find hard to swallow.

"Where will you be taking me today?" I asked, changing the subject.

"Where would you like to go, Chloe? Are there any famous landmarks in Moscow you can recall seeing in a book or on TV?"

"Most of the stuff I've seen about Moscow has been on the news, and it's often not that favourable, I'm afraid. But I once saw a building in a film that caught my eye. It was a terracotta red colour and had multicoloured domes on the top that looked like ice cream swirls. It was so different, and I wanted to know what went on there."

"Ah, you mean St Basil's Cathedral in Red Square. It is indeed a beautiful building. And I see what you mean about the ice cream swirls, although there are many other different and colourful domes atop that particular building."

"Isn't Red Square where the Kremlin is?"

"The Kremlin overlooks Red Square and has high walls in the same colour red as the cathedral. It's a government building, so the walls are fortified, as you would expect from such an important place that is centuries old. If you looked down on the city from the sky, you would see Red Square and St Basil's to the east of the Kremlin and the Moskva River to the south. On the west side are the Alexander Gardens, and I am hoping the rain holds off so I can take you there. If not, we can go tomorrow. A lot of the buildings, including St Basil's, are at their most spectacular when the sun is shining down on them. There are also a few sights I have yet to see in this great city, so we can take our time and enjoy them—rather than follow a specific itinerary."

"That sounds perfect, Gregor." Despite not choosing to come here, I couldn't wait to visit Moscow.

Stepan came back to the pool room and said something to Gregor.

"Stepan said that Anna has just arrived; Yuri and Dmitry are bringing her shopping into the main room as we speak. Let us go and see what she has brought for you to wear, then we can get on with our sightseeing."

He held out his hand for me, and I took it gladly. I wasn't sure why I felt more anxious about meeting Anna than I did the male members of his staff. Maybe it was because she now knew my clothes and shoe sizes. Or maybe it was because Gregor spoke of her in such an informal way —like she was more than his employee. But thinking about it, Keeley worked for him, too, and he spoke of her that way. I just hoped she wasn't tall, sexy and pretty like Keeley. The complete opposite of what I would ever be.

When we entered the sitting room there was no longer any seating available. Every available surface was covered in bags and boxes full of clothes, shoes, and make-up. I was surprised to see even more items being brought through the door and placed on the polished wooden floors.

A petite woman, who looked a little younger than me, followed a man in a chauffeur's uniform. She had short, platinum blonde hair, stunning ice-blue eyes, and was dressed in a grey pinstripe skirt suit. She was beautiful and looked effortlessly chic—while I was standing there in Gregor's bathrobe feeling frumpy and fat.

She looked me up and down, and I half expected a scathing remark, but she smiled and grabbed me in a tight hug. She then kissed me on the cheeks and introduced herself.

"Hello, Chloe. My name is Anna, as I'm sure you have guessed. I hope I have made good choices for you. I only went to Ralph Lauren, Armani, Dior, Calvin Klein, Vivienne Westwood and Zara, as I knew you wanted the clothing in a hurry. I called through to the stores as soon as I had your measurements, so they could begin gathering what we needed. Then I made sure to call at Louis Vuitton to pick up some luggage for you, so you could pack everything that you wanted to take to St Petersburg. I have two dresses being delivered from the Vivienne Westwood store later today, and there are a number of items from my favourite Russian designers too. I could have done a better job with more time, but as always, Gregor has me running around with no time to spare."

"I'm sure you bought yourself a few things for all your trouble, Anna," Gregor quipped with a knowing smirk on his face.

"Of course I did. One cannot pass Louis Vuitton without purchasing from their summer range, and every woman needs the new Vivienne Westwood sandals. As the sun came out for a moment, I had to buy an extra pair of sunglasses in Dior. After all, I wouldn't want sore eyes when I sit down to all the paperwork Daniil says he has waiting for me," Anna said with a sigh.

I laughed as I nodded my agreement. Gregor crossed his arms in front of his chest and smiled at the petite little whirlwind, who was now rummaging through boxes and bags.

She handed Gregor several different bags and shoe boxes and ushered him upstairs. He turned to me and told me to take whichever guest room I would like before dutifully climbing the stairs with his newly acquired clothing.

"Thank you for doing all this, Anna," I said as I took in all the boxes and bags.

"You are very welcome, Chloe. I am so glad to meet you at last. Gregor spoke of you often when he returned from

England. I understand that you being here was not planned, but I hope that next time you visit, we can go shopping together and have coffee, yes?"

"Erm, yes. I would like that, Anna. Maybe you could come to England with Gregor," I suggested.

"I am hoping to go to England before Christmas. I didn't get to visit last year because I was so busy, then my husband took me to Paris for a month as a second honeymoon. I would love to meet with Keeley, and I haven't seen Maggie for almost three years now."

"You speak very good English," I remarked.

"I studied English at university and often used to travel with Gregor on business. English is spoken by many nationalities, especially the ones we deal with in the oil and gas area of Gregor's business. It is expected that we are to be fluent in a number of languages," she said.

"In England, we learn French or Spanish, sometimes German, but not enough to be fluent unless we take the subject in further education—such as college or university. I wish I'd paid more attention in language classes."

"I'm sure Gregor would be willing to teach you. He speaks several different languages, although his Mandarin isn't as good as he thinks."

"I heard that, Anna," shouted Gregor from the top of the stairs.

Anna and I turned to watch him walk steadily down each step, and I'm sure my chin must have hit the floor. Gregor in a business suit was gorgeous and sexy. Gregor in black jeans and a fitted black T-shirt was something else entirely.

He walked towards us and turned around. The jeans were Armani and fit him to perfection. The T-shirt was also Armani, and it showcased his muscular upper body. I didn't know what I wanted to grab first; his firm, sexy arse or his...well...everything. How on earth was I supposed to keep my hands off him now? He could grace the cover of a GQ magazine and make all the other models jealous. I turned to look at Anna and saw she had her eyebrows raised.

"Gregor, this look suits you. You should dress like this more often. I think I did well today," Anna remarked. Then she turned to Dmitry and Yuri. "Dmitry, take all this upstairs for Chloe while I try to cover Yuri's cheeks with make-up."

"What? Why would I need to wear make-up?" he spluttered.

"You are supposed to be guarding Gregor and Chloe by staying inconspicuous. How can you do that with a blue face?" she pointed out. "Now sit and be still while I try to work a miracle by making you presentable."

"You will do as she says, Yuri, or stay here. I can take Mikhail instead," Gregor added.

Yuri began to protest, but Gregor raised his eyebrows, quieting his objections. Anna took out from her bag what I assumed to be concealer and gestured for Yuri to sit on the arm of the sofa.

While she went to work on Yuri's blue cheeks, I followed Gregor, Dmitry and Stepan upstairs to the bedroom next to Gregor's. I thought Gregor would stay while I took the clothes out of the bags, but he didn't. He told me to choose something I'd like to wear today, and I could go through the rest later. Before I could protest the amount or even thank him, he left the room with Dmitry and Stepan.

I didn't know which bag to open first, so I started with the smallest. In there were lipsticks, two eye make-up quads, mascara, four different colours of foundation, three blushers, a bronzer, and some sort of pressed powder. As I was taking these out and putting them in the bathroom, I also noticed three eyeliners. All of the make-up was Dior, and I mused that this little lot would probably cover the cost of replacing all four tyres on my work van twice over.

In the next bag—also Dior—was a selection of skincare items, including eye cream, two moisturisers, eye make-up remover, cleanser, and toner. In another Dior bag were shower gels, body cream and perfume. I was shocked. This was just too much.

In a bag that had Russian writing on it, I noticed what I figured out was deodorant, shampoo and conditioner. It looked like a spa brand, but as I couldn't read or speak Russian, I couldn't be sure.

I must have stood and stared at them for at least five minutes before opening the perfume and spraying some on my wrists and throat. Dior Addict. It was a beautiful, floral fragrance that kind of suited me, I thought.

I didn't often wear perfume, especially in the summer. Working with flowers tended to attract wasps and bees, which were also attracted to strong perfumes. I took another sniff at my wrist and smiled.

Wearing perfume meant I really was away from the shop and its demands. As if I was on a real holiday. One that I'd actually chosen and booked.

I dashed into the bedroom and began to root through the bags. There were lots of different-coloured T-shirts from Ralph Lauren, along with jeans and a denim skirt. There was also a deep green jacket that I fell in love with and left out of the bag, just in case I wanted to take it with me.

Next, I rooted through the Zara bags and saw a lovely yellow three-quarter-sleeved boat-neck top that came just below the hip, along with linen trousers in both white and beige. There was also the same top in white, and a nautical striped white and navy cardigan, which I loved.

I looked at everything I'd taken out and thought, *oh, what the hell*, then tipped everything out of the other bags onto the bed. When it came to the boxes on the floor, I found several pairs of shoes from various designers, and bags from Louis Vuitton in different colours, sizes and shapes.

I was glad I didn't know how Russian currency compared with the British pound, as there were so many numbers before the decimal point, I was almost afraid to touch them. This was not my world, and I felt like a fraud sitting in the middle of all this opulence.

After a moment's contemplation, I got up off the floor and decided not to look at the price tag or designer label and just pick what I liked.

I laid out the white boat-neck top, the blue and white striped cardigan, and a pair of white straight-leg jeans. Then I took out a pair of white canvas shoes, which I thought looked a little more comfortable than the toe-post sandals I wanted to wear, and I selected a navy bag and large-framed sunglasses.

Gathering up the toiletries and make-up, I went into the bathroom, and after taking forever to remove all the packaging, I applied eye cream and moisturiser.

I wasn't sure about the make-up. I normally wore very little, even for a night out. In the end, I applied a bit of bronzer and mascara before selecting a nude pink lipstick. Then I re-applied the perfume because, well, I just couldn't help it, and after taking a deep breath and giving myself a once-over, I made my way downstairs.

Gregor came to meet me on the bottom step and held out his hand. He twirled me around and smiled before leaning into my neck and whispering, "You look as beautiful as ever, my love, but you did not need the perfume. Your own scent is much more enticing and makes me want to taste every inch of you."

"Well, I doubt they'd allow that in the middle of Red Square. Now come on," I said as I moved away from his tempting body, "show me all the sights you told me about before it gets too late in the day."

"As you wish, my darling." He picked up a Ralph Lauren windbreaker jacket in French navy that I knew would highlight his pale blue eyes.

Oh my God! Why did Gregor have to be so attractive? And so bloody sweet and generous, too?

I woke up this morning as angry as the devil himself with the situation I found myself in, but now I was fast becoming putty in his hands. I stole a glance at the man in question and looked at his profile from the side. Gregor had sculpted cheekbones and a strong jawline, yet the look was softened somehow by his pale blue eyes and full, kissable lips.

Thinking about the kisses I'd shared with him made my face flush, and my heart ached to think I wouldn't ever experience them again.

I knew it would be my own stubborn fault if that happened.

Chapter Twenty-Two

Gregor

I watched Chloe as we drove into central Moscow. She'd been looking out of the window, barely saying anything as we passed through rich, affluent areas and poor, run-down neighbourhoods. I so desperately wanted to know what she was thinking.

It was so important to me that she had a good time while she was here. Even if she didn't want a permanent loving relationship with me, she would still be my friend, and I hoped she would come back to Russia and spend time with me. It would help to have her by my side, even if it was only for a short amount of time.

Dmitry parked as near to Red Square as possible. Chloe was excited to see the domes of St Basil's, so I handed her my phone to take photographs as we approached. I hadn't been to the cathedral or the square for some time, and I tried to see it through the eyes of a tourist, how Chloe would see it.

Many years ago, the cathedral was known as Vasily the Blessed, and probably still is to the older generation. There were different-shaped coloured domes at various heights, and each dome was topped with a gold cross, which was highlighted by the slight glimmer of sunlight poking through the clouds.

"I think I prefer the dome with the blue and white swirl the most," Chloe said. "The others are pretty, but that one stands out against the terracotta colour of the building itself."

"Would you like to go inside?" I asked. She nodded her head and clasped my hand in hers as we climbed the steps into the cathedral.

"It's so narrow," Chloe exclaimed as we entered. "It looks so big from the outside; I wouldn't have thought it would be so small inside."

Being so narrow with very few windows, the interior was quite dark. This wasn't helped by the cloudy day and the lights belonging to centuries-old chandeliers above us. I explained that the cathedral had two floors and was made up of eight smaller churches, with a larger church that was dedicated to the Holy Virgin.

Chloe was oohing and aahing at all the religious artwork displayed along the walls and ceilings, asking me to translate for her when needed. She began listening to a Canadian couple who were reading out information about the history of the cathedral from a tourist guide. Some of it I knew to be incorrect because I'd lived through it, but I kept my mouth shut and glanced at Yuri and Dmitry, who rolled their eyes and shook their heads.

After seeing everything we could with the limited light available, we made our way outside into much-needed warmth. Chloe took a few more photographs, then we strolled over to the other cathedrals that had their home in Red Square.

The Cathedral of the Annunciation's white walls and golden dome blended perfectly against the Grand Kremlin Palace. Even though the colours matched those of the Cathedral of the Archangel and Ivan the Great Bell Tower, Chloe didn't just walk on by them without taking much notice, like many of the other tourists did. No, my Chloe noticed the differences in style and architecture and appreciated the little things that those who just meandered by failed to see.

Because it was summer, Red Square was full of tourists. This made my security nervous, I could tell, but Chloe seemed to enjoy being one of the many people experiencing the famous landmark. The red fortified walls of the Kremlin stood out against the cloudy grey sky, and I prayed that the sun would emerge for our walk through the Alexander Garden.

The gates to the garden were tall and impressive and reminded me of the gates to my palace back in St Petersburg—being the same black and gold.

Chloe was silent as we approached the Tomb of the Unknown Soldier. His body had been brought back from the Great War, and the front of the monument held the eternal flame, which was transported from the Field of Mars.

Chloe closed her eyes and uttered a silent prayer for the fallen soldier. It occurred to me that her father had been in the army, so she must have associated this poor, unknown soldier with her father and his comrades.

I began to understand my Chloe a little more at that moment. I already knew she was an extremely kind and thoughtful woman, but she also had a sensitive, vulnerable side buried under that assured, resilient exterior.

I thought back to this morning and how she'd quickly given in to Yuri when she thought she was offending him and our country. And to how she was clearly uncomfortable with the amount of clothing and obvious expense that had come with Anna's shopping spree on her behalf—yet she hadn't mentioned it to her. She hadn't wanted Anna to think she didn't appreciate her efforts.

My Chloe is a people pleaser who puts others first. That's why she's still on good terms with her ex-husband, even though he dissolved their marriage so he could pursue men—the real object of his desires.

Since what had transpired yesterday, she'd been insisting we couldn't be together—even when we'd both declared our love. Was she still disappointed and upset with me? Or was she trying to prove a point to herself? Like when it came to matters of the heart, she wasn't going to give in as easily, keeping herself safe from any hurt that might come her way....

Wanting to take Chloe away from the sadness she so obviously felt at this memorial, I tugged gently on her hand and guided her around all the fountains and statues throughout the park.

To my great relief, the sun emerged as we made our way out of the park, and the grey clouds began to disappear. Chloe was keen to get more photographs of the cathedrals, the walls of the square, and the Kremlin Palace in the sunlight.

Although we had many more things to see, I indulged

her request. How could I not when her eyes were so alight with wonder and happiness?

After taking more photographs from different angles, we went back to the car and took the short drive to the Fallen Monument Park. As we walked through the grounds, I told her about its history, which was not one of my country's finest moments, in my opinion. Not that I wanted to go back to the dire way things were before that. In my mind, such wilful destruction of our heritage buildings and artwork served no purpose whatsoever—no matter what political agenda you supported. But, as is often said of myself and others from a privileged background, I do not live in the real world, and it is different for those from a less prosperous way of life. What those people do not realise is that we all have our crosses to bear. Although admittedly, money makes them appear lighter when you can afford people to help you carry them.

The Fallen Monument Park came about when the Soviet Union collapsed. A number of Moscow's statues and monuments were pulled from their pedestals during that time. I'd taken a stroll through this area once before, disliking the graveyard-like feel. But I was informed recently by Anna that it was much changed from the early days. It now included modern artworks and sculptures and continued along the banks of the river.

Looking at some of the city's old statues in their new resting place gave me a sense of anger. Yuri, too, I noted, even though he was keeping a short distance from us. Chloe seemed to sense this and squeezed my hand when she encouraged me to venture further into the park. She also called on Yuri and Dmitry, asking if they were okay and not too bored with escorting us through the city.

As we progressed further along, I noted many of the

new artworks and was pleasantly surprised. How the old and the new came together so easily was a credit to those who'd updated the design of this area. I felt my mood lift further as we walked along the riverside, taking in all the paintings displayed along its bank.

After at least an hour of meandering through the eclectic displays, I heard Chloe's stomach growl. I was about to ring through to one of my favourite restaurants in the city when Chloe asked if we could eat at one of the pavement cafés alongside Gorky Park.

She asked Yuri and Dmitry if they had any preference, but they both shook their heads. I'd wanted Chloe to experience the best that Moscow had to offer regarding fine dining, but yet again, I would not get my way with this woman. In the end, we settled on a table that was covered by a large green and white striped awning, and instead of an intimate table for two, she pulled out chairs for Yuri and Dmitry.

Chloe asked if Dmitry would mind explaining what was on the menu, as she obviously couldn't read Russian. I felt my frustration and jealousy rise before I realised what she was doing. Chloe listened patiently while Dmitry explained in somewhat broken English what was listed. It thrilled my guard to know he'd successfully translated the menu for my flower girl.

Yuri caught my eye and gave me a smile and a nod. One that confirmed that this beautiful woman—who took the time to think of others when the day should have been all about her—was not one I should let get away. Any anger I felt at not being able to spoil my flower girl quickly withered away, being replaced by determination.

Chloe was mine! She belonged to me as much as I belonged to her, and I would take what was mine and keep it for all eternity. I nodded back at Yuri, giving him the same knowing smile.

There would be no more of this *"only friends"* talk that my Chloe was so fond of. No, I would hear no more of that nonsense. Tonight she'd know I intended to keep her by my side and never let her go.

Chapter Twenty-Three

Chloe

After a light lunch, we made our way into Gorky Park, enjoying more of the afternoon sunshine. I was awestruck by the eclectic sights and unique atmosphere in this amazing city. Popular media doesn't do the place any favours regarding how it's often portrayed. There was so much more I'd yet to see, and I couldn't wait to share all the photographs I'd taken.

After twenty minutes of relaxing on a bench, Gregor said it was time we returned home. The sun had been uninterrupted by clouds for some time, and both he and Yuri would start to feel tired soon.

I must admit, I'd forgotten that Gregor and Yuri were vampires. Our day out had been so normal, with no restrictions placed on the places we visited. Even cathedrals. So it appeared that even God accepted their immortality and need for human blood, just as I did.

As we were driving back to Gregor's home, he asked

Dmitry to make one last stop. I didn't know where we were going because he spoke in Russian, but only ten minutes after placing a call on his mobile phone, we pulled up in front of a small jewellery shop.

On entering the quaint, brightly lit premises, a short, grey-haired gentleman came out from behind the counter and shook Gregor's hand.

Gregor introduced me to the jeweller, Boris Yanev, who took my hand and said, "Chloe, it is so good to meet you. Gregor has told me so much about you." He then turned to Gregor, saying, "You were so right about the colour of her eyes, my friend. I think you will be happy with the stone I have chosen. Although it will never be as stunning and individual a colour as her beautiful eyes, I believe it is the best match."

Mr Yanev gestured for us to follow him through a doorway behind the counter while Dmitry and Yuri kept an eye on the car.

We were told to sit and make ourselves comfortable while the old jeweller turned to a set of drawers behind him. Gregor pulled out my chair, and I looked to him for information about why we were there. He said nothing, just sat beside me and turned to watch Mr Yanev unfold a black velvet cloth. Inside were a pair of earrings and what I assumed to be two pendants in the most beautiful blue-green shade I'd ever seen. Both matched the flower design on the bracelet Gregor had given me back at the manor.

"This stone is called apatite. It's not considered to be as precious as other gemstones, and the colour can vary so much between blue and green. But I was able to find a good match for the colour Gregor described your eyes to be," said Mr Yanev.

"You have done well, Boris. This is a perfect match," Gregor told him.

"Gregor, each time you came to see me, you were so animated when describing Chloe and the design you wanted. Your enthusiasm inspired me, and I searched for the stones immediately. They arrived two days after you collected the bracelet, and I began working on them straight away. *'The colour of a small cove around Fig Tree Bay in Cyprus,'* you said, and you were right. Would you like to try them on, Chloe?" Mr Yanev asked as he removed the earrings from the cloth.

I nodded my head, made speechless because Gregor had put so much thought into this gift. I took out my plain silver hoops and put in the pretty floral studs. The gems were set in a gold casing, the same as the pendants. Although, from a second look, it appeared that one of the pendants was actually a charm.

"Thank you," I said in a shaky voice to both Gregor and the smiling Mr Yanev.

"What length chain would you prefer for your pendant, Chloe?" Mr Yanev asked. "Now that you are here, I can show you different styles so you can make the choice yourself."

He selected two velvet mats holding various lengths and designs of necklaces and bracelets. "I will leave you to try them on and make your choice. You know where I am if you need anything, Gregor."

When the jeweller closed the door behind him, I turned to Gregor and threw my arms around his neck, catching him totally off guard and nearly toppling our chairs over.

"Thank you," I said once again while trying to keep tears out of my eyes.

"You are most welcome, my love. Now come, let us see which chain you prefer."

Gregor slid the pendant onto three different chains before choosing one that sat just above my cleavage. Then he chose a matching bracelet and attached the charm.

"I can't believe you did this, Gregor. I'm so touched by your thoughtfulness," I sobbed.

"Do not cry, my darling; I cannot bear your tears," he implored, hugging me tightly. "It hurts me deep in my chest, like an arrow twisting."

Wiping my eyes, I told him, "I can't help it. I've had such a lovely day in Moscow, and now this. Knowing that you planned this gift for me, that it wasn't just an afterthought or an expensive gift that was given to ease your guilt at bringing me here... It means the world to me."

"Chloe, there is something you need to understand. You could never, ever be an afterthought to me. From the moment we met, you were at the forefront of my mind. From waking in the morning to closing my eyes at night. You haunted my dreams in so many ways, and I couldn't wait to get back to you. It didn't seem altogether healthy to crave someone as much as I craved you, and that's why I didn't recognise it for what it was. Love. Deep, powerful, obsessive, and always with a need to keep you safe and well.

"I messed up back in England. I hurt you, and for that, I am truly sorry. But I refuse to let my love...*our* love, go to waste. I'm warning you now, my darling; I will have you as mine. You will share my life, my love, and my name, along with everything I own. And I'll spend eternity proving just how deserving you are of things such as this," he said, taking hold of the pendant that lay above my breasts.

I rested my forehead against his and sighed. "I don't know what to say to all that, Gregor."

"That's because there is nothing *to* say, my love. Now let us speak to Mr Yanev, and then we'll continue our journey home. Perhaps we'll have time for a swim before I take you out for the evening."

"A swim sounds nice, but I am quite tired," I admitted. "Maybe we could just relax by the pool?"

Gregor gave me a lazy, seductive smile. "As you wish, my love."

Chapter Twenty-Four

Gregor

As soon as we arrived back home, Chloe hurried upstairs to put on one of the new bikinis Anna had purchased for her.

I readied the pool area by opening up the ceiling and placed a selection of cold drinks, sandwiches, and fruit on the table for when she joined me. I told my staff not to disturb us and waited for my flower girl to arrive.

As soon as Chloe entered—wearing my bathrobe again —I closed all the doors to the pool, hiding us away from the rest of my house.

"So, my love, will you show me how enticing you look in swimwear? Or am I to imagine how sexy you look in what I'm hoping is just a few scraps of material?"

"Well you are one to talk. You're still fully dressed in what we went out in," she said, folding her arms over her chest while she looked me up and down.

"That is easily remedied, Chloe."

I removed my T-shirt and unbuckled the belt on my new

jeans. Chloe's eyes grew wide when she realised I was about to strip naked.

"Gregor, what if some of your staff come in? Surely you don't let them see you naked?"

I shrugged my shoulders before pulling down my jeans and boxers simultaneously. I'd already removed my footwear and socks, so I stood completely naked before her.

"I'm keeping the bikini on," Chloe declared as she opened the belt on the bathrobe and shrugged it off her shoulders.

Anna had done well when selecting this swimsuit. The bikini was a halter-neck style, with ties at the back of the neck and each side of the panties.

Before my emerging erection became noticeable, I turned and dove in, doing a quick lap of the pool before coming back up for air. As I wiped my eyes, I saw Chloe descending the steps into the water. When she reached waist level, she pushed in and swam breaststroke towards me.

Before she could reach me, I swam away from her to the other side of the pool. I could see the confusion in her eyes, and I smiled a little before completing my lap.

Once again, Chloe swam towards me. When she nearly reached my end of the pool, I pushed away from the side— as if to swim back to the other end. Only, I didn't. This time I turned, grabbed her from behind, unhooked her bikini top and had it over her head in seconds, throwing it out of the pool before she could stop me. She gasped and spun around, but I swam away laughing.

"Oh, so it's like that, is it?" she questioned, treading water with her hands over her breasts.

"It is," I replied, still laughing.

When Chloe turned her back to hold on to the side of the pool, I swam towards her and pulled the ties on both sides of her bikini bottoms. They didn't come undone. This time it was Chloe's turn to laugh as she yelled, "Ha, double knotted."

Grinning, I released my claws, slicing through the material with ease. When I pulled them away from her and threw them onto a poolside chair, she slapped at my chest and shouted, "I can't believe you just did that. They were brand new, Gregor. I've only worn them for about twenty minutes."

"I will buy you more, *moya malen'kaya tsvetochnitsa*, if you wish. But for now, just swim. Feel the water flow over your entire body as you move through it. Feel how liberating it is, just for a while."

I swam away from her and watched her facial expression change when she realised I'd not stripped her of her swimsuit for a sexual purpose.

After a minute or so, Chloe swam steadily towards me, and just before she reached me, she smiled.

Yes, my love, I thought to myself. Letting go of that prudish behaviour would do my flower girl more good than she realised.

After completing the lap to my side of the pool, Chloe turned onto her back, her whole body rising to the water's surface as she opened her legs and kicked off into a perfect backstroke.

This time, it was her turn to laugh while I groaned at the captivating sight. I was determined to be a gentleman— until she requested otherwise—but seeing my Chloe bared before me was testing my control. I swam after her, circling my prey before she could reach the other end of the pool.

"What are you doing, Gregor?"

"I know what I would like to be doing," I said, backing her into a corner.

"And what would that be?" she asked breathlessly.

"Dancing with you, my love, what else?" I told her, pulling her into my arms and spinning us around in the water.

Chloe laughed out loud as we made our way around the pool, turning and swaying, chest to chest until I lifted her high above me and kissed her lower belly.

"Gregor," she whispered while gazing down at me.

I lowered her back into the water, our bodies temptingly close. She instinctively wrapped her legs around my back. Good. This was progress, but I needed more.

Chloe stared at my mouth. I knew she expected me to kiss her, but I denied myself the pleasure. I just held her body against mine, letting the water's ebb and flow rock us gently. My cock was hard and throbbing fiercely against the very place that would give it sweet relief. It would have taken only a slight movement to get where it so desperately needed to be. But again, I did nothing. I left it all to her.

I could sense her confusion over why I wasn't giving in to the lust I so obviously felt, and my cock seemed to have that same confusion as it flexed against her.

Feeling how deliciously tempting it was to have Chloe's naked body against mine, I thought it best to leave the pool. So I swam us to the steps and held her hand as we made our way to the loungers where I'd left our towels. After wrapping one around my waist, I crossed to a waiting, bemused Chloe, who was drying herself thoroughly.

"I have drinks and food for us," I said while picking up my bathrobe and then helping her put it on.

"Come, my darling, let us sit and eat. All that dancing has given me quite an appetite—for something," I told her with a wink. She blushed at my words but took my hand and let me lead her to the table.

Something I have always loved about Chloe is how easy it is just to be with her. Even though there was still such strong sexual tension in the air, we could relax in each other's company. She talked about the sights she'd seen today, so I asked her which one was her favourite. She told me it was St Basil's Cathedral because of its exterior architecture.

Chloe said it reminded her of a mixed floral display, with different flowers of various sizes and colours. Ones that you wouldn't think would go together, yet they'd look great all the same. She was so animated when she spoke and told me she was going to design a display with similar colours to remind her of her visit.

I didn't mention that because she was mine, she'd be able to visit the real thing anytime she wanted. I thought that little fact was better left unsaid for now. What my Chloe didn't yet realise was that the world was now her oyster, as they say. She had unlimited financial reserves and access to several jets that could take her wherever she wanted to go. My little flower girl will want for nothing.

"Someone had been in my room and hung up all my new clothes. I would have done it when we got back, Gregor. We were in too much of a rush to do it earlier, but now I feel so guilty that someone thought they had to do it for me," she said.

"Nonsense, Chloe. My staff are here to take care of this house and its residents. I pay them four times what they would be paid elsewhere and always treat them with a great deal of respect. It ensures loyalty and longevity in their employment with me. This is all very necessary with the secrets that many of my human employees have to keep. But I would be a generous employer anyway, even if I didn't have to safeguard my immortality."

"I know that, Gregor. But I'm just not used to it. I've lived by myself for some time now, and you get used to not having to rely on anyone else."

"Do you fear change, Chloe?" I asked.

"What? No, I don't think so."

"I think you do. But when you become mine, you will also become the mistress of this house, Rothley Manor, my palace in St Petersburg, and every other property I own. You will have to get used to having staff."

"You seem so sure that we have a future together, Gregor. But—"

"Shh, no buts, Chloe. You will be mine, and I will be yours. It's as simple as that. Whatever comes our way, we will face it together, and what haunts us from our past can stay there or be brought out into the open. I promise you, my darling, I'll take whatever steps are necessary to enable us to move forward and bind us together as one. Now, let us go and get ready. I have an evening planned at the Bolshoi Theatre. We will watch the ballet, then dine at my favourite restaurant. The current ballet is Don Quixote, and I'm told it has excellent reviews."

Chloe gasped—a look of pure panic crossing her pretty face. "Gregor, what do I wear? I've never been to a ballet before; I'm not sure it's quite me."

"You will love it, Chloe. There's a selection of dresses and gowns suitable for this evening in your wardrobe. Due to your height, Anna had the longer-length gowns altered, and they were delivered while we were out. Choose something floor-length and wear the jewellery we picked up today. Tonight, you will dazzle the whole of Moscow, *moya malen'kaya tsvetochnitsa*."

Chapter Twenty-Five

Chloe

The third act of Don Quixote had just begun, and I couldn't stop yawning. I was exhausted, and the ballet wasn't something that was holding my attention. Though the dancers, scenery and costumes were impressive, I prefer to see a story on a page or screen, with words, not dance.

The theatre, however, more than impressed me. It was huge. We had a fancy box all to ourselves, and from here, I could see the hundreds of people below us who seemed awestruck by the ballet. So what did that make me? I sat back in my plush red velvet seat and once again scanned my surroundings.

All around us, every bit of wall, ceiling, and other decorative mouldings was beautifully carved and heavily gilded. As were most of the women in the building. I wondered how some of them could even move, being so overloaded with jewellery. Most of them wore their jewellery and fur as status symbols, according to Gregor. But I thought it looked gaudy, and real fur offended, not impressed me.

Gregor tugged on my hand, which he'd held since I came down the stairs at his home. I was dressed in uncomfortably high heels and a beautiful, deep green Vivienne Westwood gown that I truly adored. I heard him make a low growling noise deep in his throat when he saw me, but I nearly fell the last five steps when I finally saw him.

Looking at Gregor in a tuxedo was like foreplay. He was made for suits like this. The confident way he wore it showed me that this sort of formality was a common event in his life. I knew from our walk through the theatre that the ladies we encountered lusted after my blue-eyed vampire, and I couldn't blame them. With the most kissable lips I had ever seen, abs that made me want to trace them with my tongue, and that huge...

I felt another tug on my hand and was pulled to my feet in front of a standing Gregor.

"I can scent your arousal, Chloe, and I know it's not the ballet that's doing it for you. You haven't even looked at the stage in the last ten minutes. So tell me, does tiered seating turn you on? Or has someone in the audience caught your eye?"

"Yeah, right, as if any other man in this building could compete with you, Gregor."

He stared at my lips as though they were the most fascinating thing on earth, and I expected him to lean forward and kiss me. Disappointingly, he didn't. He just smirked and tugged me towards the doorway of our private box.

Two of his guards, Alexei and Marat, were waiting for us out in the hallway; I'd been grateful for their presence when I finally found out why Gregor needed them. As we'd climbed the theatre steps, a gang of whom I assumed to be press began calling Gregor's name and taking photographs.

Alexei shielded Gregor and me while Marat pushed the photographers back. We also had a driver who was waiting in a limo at a side exit. Gregor told me how important it was that there were very few public photographs of him in circulation because of his immortality.

He explained the lengths he had to go to in order to reinvent his identity every thirty years or so, but he couldn't keep passing for the younger generation of Antonov forever. I asked him whether he'd ever retire. Gregor said he'd never fully retire, as that would make it a long life of doing nothing.

———

I popped to the bathroom while Gregor and his guards discussed our exit plan. Even the toilet stalls were beautifully decorated, and I felt like I'd stepped into another world. I knew Gregor wanted to take me to one of his favourite restaurants, but all I wanted to do was get back to his home and take off my shoes.

Gregor took my arm when I emerged from the bathroom, and we made our way towards a door with a sign that I assumed said Exit. Just before we got there, a stocky, grey-haired gentleman with his arm around a younger woman stepped out in front of us.

"Good evening, Gregor. There is yet another act to go, but you seem to be leaving. Is your young female not enjoying the ballet?"

"Semyon, you are speaking to me in English, which I assume is for the benefit of the woman on my arm. Tell me, how did you know she was English? Do you have your spies following us?" Gregor appeared calm, but the abrupt way he spoke said otherwise.

Semyon tutted loudly. "Gregor, you wound me. I just happened to hear her beautiful voice when you entered the theatre. Tell me, is she the reason you have been keeping away from your club? I haven't seen you there in months. I must say, you have left many subs disappointed in your absence."

Gregor tensed beside me; his anger clear for all to see.

"What is it to you, Semyon? Have you missed me? Is that it?"

Semyon laughed. "I just wanted to let you know my offer is still on the table. As long as you guarantee the full member list, I will purchase your club, and I will not haggle on the price. You know I am good for any amount you ask."

"Why?" asked Gregor. "You are a member and have been for many years. You are familiar with everyone who attends. Why do you need to own it?"

"There is nothing untoward in my need for this property, I assure you. However, as you say, I've been a regular attendee for many years. Centuries, even. Therefore, I feel I should have first refusal when it comes to the sale."

"I've not made any decision regarding my club. But I will notify every member in due course if I decide to sell. Now, please excuse us, Semyon." Gregor nodded towards the woman. "Ophelia."

He placed his hand on my back, ushering me hastily out of the exit door and down a long staircase. We reached another door that revealed our waiting car.

As we pulled out of the side street, I turned to look at Gregor. His face was like stone.

"Can we just go back to your house tonight?" I asked. "I'm exhausted, and my feet are killing me."

"You must be hungry, Chloe. The restaurant isn't far, and you'll see all the sights around Red Square lit up against the night sky."

"I'd prefer to head home and grab a slice of toast or something. It's way too late to eat out anyway," I told him as I slid my shoes off and sighed.

"Very well," Gregor replied grumpily. He tapped the glass partition on the limousine and uttered a few words in Russian when it opened. Then he unbuckled my seat belt before bending down and grabbing both my feet. I spun slightly so that my feet were resting on his lap, and I was facing him instead of just sitting beside him. Gregor's gaze never left mine as he began massaging my feet; his fingers finding the points that ached the most with relative ease.

"You're good at this," I told him. "Is it something you do for women at your club?"

He stopped massaging for a moment, then began again.

"I do this for Freya whenever we attend a function together. She always takes off her shoes as soon as we leave, often while we are there, too. She much prefers flat shoes, as do many women. But formal situations dictate you wear heels. And no, I never massage a woman's feet in my club... Unless they have been bound by them."

There was an awkward silence for a moment until Gregor asked, "Do you have any more questions about my club?"

"Not right now," I told him.

I did have a question, but I wanted to wait until tomorrow. Tonight, I wanted to talk to Gregor about my past. I wanted to see what his reaction would be, and how he would look at me afterwards. If it was with pity—or as a victim needing protection because he thought I couldn't handle certain situations—then I knew we wouldn't have a future together. Because I couldn't live like that, despite the love and obvious sexual attraction we had.

———

We were both quiet the rest of the way back, and it carried on into the house. Maybe it was an awkward quiet at first, but after I made a joke in his kitchen about me standing there buttering toast while wearing a Vivienne Westwood gown, the quiet was replaced by laughter and idle chatter.

When I yawned once again, Gregor took my hand and led me upstairs. He paused outside my room, and I felt quite disappointed when all he did was peck me on the cheek and wish me a good night's sleep.

I let myself into the bedroom and stayed beside the door long after it had closed, half expecting to hear his footsteps as he made his way back down the hallway so he could grab me and take me to his bed. But those footsteps never came.

I took off my dress, underwear and make-up before having a quick shower and donning one of my new satin nightdresses, courtesy of the wonderful Anna.

Sitting on the edge of the king-size bed, I contemplated my next move. Should I go to bed and have my talk with Gregor in the morning? Or should I get it over and done with tonight?

Even though I was tired, I found myself walking down the hallway and knocking on his door. Whether I would live to regret my decision remained to be seen.

Chapter Twenty-Six

Gregor

I heard her close her bedroom door and come to stand in front of mine. I opened it on her first knock and swallowed hard at the sight of my Chloe. She wore a black satin nightdress that skimmed her curves beautifully.

"Can I sleep with you tonight?" she asked hesitantly. "I don't want to have sex; I just want you to hold me while I talk."

"Of course you can. If it were up to me, you would spend every night wrapped in my arms. But, Chloe, seeing you dressed like that, feeling the satin material against your skin as I hold you... I'm going to have a hard time just holding you."

"I see. Should I take it off, then?" Chloe asked with a coquettish smile.

"If you want me inside you tonight, then by all means, take it off," I replied, praying that she would.

We stared at each other for a moment until she looked

195

down and sighed, then walked towards my bed. Leaving my boxers on, I got in beside her and turned out the light.

I lay on my back and held her against my chest as I ran my fingers through her hair.

"It's why I keep it short, you know," Chloe said. "Because of what happened. Because of him."

"How come?" I asked, trying to keep my voice calm as she sighed once more.

"The second and third time he attacked me, he grabbed my hair and pulled me back. I nearly got out of the door that last time, but he just managed to grab a handful of hair when I tried to run. He pulled me back with it and slammed the door shut. As I said, that's why I keep it short now, so no one can stop me from getting away."

"Oh, my love. I am so sorry you still feel that way about your hair. But if it's any consolation, the short style really suits you. You are too pretty to hide your beauty behind long hair, anyway."

"Thank you, Gregor. I may grow it again one day, but I do find the style more practical in my line of work."

"I can see how that would be," I told her, then waited with bated breath to see if she spoke again.

"I bet you wondered why I stayed and thought me a fool for doing so. You wouldn't be the first to think like that, nor the last, I'm sure. But there were circumstances—ones that are hard to believe I'd ever put up with. But everything happened so gradually that I didn't notice it for a time.

"Peter was sweet to begin with. Good-looking, great body, and so caring and thoughtful. Well, he was at first, anyway. He was a builder, and he had these big dreams of building us a house. He'd even drawn up plans for it. We got engaged after three months of seeing each other—he kind of sprung it on me, actually.

"We were out with my friends at a works party; he got down on one knee and proposed to me in front of all of them. He had the ring and everything. Of course, I said yes. What else could I say after everyone was oohing and aahing at his speech? I moved in with him two months later at his insistence so we could save the rent I would have been paying on my flat for our new home. My mum and dad got on really well with him, but my auntie Joyce warned me I was moving too fast and I didn't know him well enough. I knew that was true, but I went ahead with it regardless.

"The manipulation was one of the first things he started with. I see that now. At the time, I wasn't detached enough from the situation to notice. I used to go out to the pub with my friends from college on Tuesdays after our classes had ended. It was a tradition that we'd kept up, even though we all now worked in different areas of Nottingham. Tuesday night was quiz night, and afterwards, they played classic rock. I used to enjoy it. We all did.

"Pete would book us a table at a restaurant on Tuesday nights and say he'd forgotten about the quiz. Or he'd turn up to the quiz and sit there looking miserable all night, saying my friends made no effort to talk to him, even though they were welcoming and friendly. So gradually, my Tuesday nights out with the college gang began to trail off.

"He started to choose my clothes for me, saying he didn't like it when I flaunted my cleavage or showed my legs to get other men's attention. I told him he was being silly. I've never been body confident, even as a teen, so I would never purposely show off any part of my body like that. Being faithful in a relationship is something I strongly believed in, and I was loyal to the core. Pete turned it all around, saying I made him feel self-conscious and not attractive because I felt the need to dress flirty. He said it made him feel as though he wasn't good enough for me.

"That upset me because, as someone who had low self-esteem most of her life, I hated to think my actions would cause the same feelings in anyone else. So out went the skirts and anything that showed even the slightest hint of my cleavage, which was pretty hard going as I haven't got a small bust to begin with.

"Then came the accusations—like I had taken too long getting home from work, therefore I was stopping off somewhere to meet someone else. He'd look through my phone, checking my text messages, then he'd accuse me of deleting them when he couldn't find anything.

"In the end, it all became too much. I booked a flight to Spain and spent a week with my mum and dad to clear my head. I never told them about what had sent me there, just that I missed them and had some holidays at work.

"Pete turned up one day, apologising for his behaviour. He said he loved me so much and was scared he was going to lose me. He said he knew he needed to work on trusting me more, but because his ex-girlfriend had walked out on him for someone else, he was worried the same thing was going to happen with me, and it was eating him up inside.

"Once again, I felt sorry for him. I'd been cheated on in college, and I knew how painful it could be. I forgave him, but I realised I knew so little about his past, and if we were going to move forward in our relationship, that would have to change.

"When I left for home, he stayed behind and helped my dad with some building work on the B&B they were open-ing. My dad was raving about how great he was when I called them a few days later.

"When he came home, things were good for a few

months. We often went out together and socialised with friends more, too. After coming home from a party one night, he accused me of flirting with my friend Gary. I'd known Gary for years and would never think of him in that way, but Pete kept going on about it.

"We'd both had a lot to drink and began arguing. I can't quite remember the full build-up to it, but suddenly he was in my face, yelling at me. I pushed him away, and he stumbled back into the door. He righted himself quickly, slapped my face, and almost threw me onto the floor. I felt my wrist go straight away and screamed in agony. The neighbours started banging on the wall, and then Pete kicked the table over and left the house.

"I had to get a taxi to the hospital and sat in A and E for three hours before getting X-rays, but I knew it was broken. I ended up with a cast on my wrist for eight weeks. Being a medical secretary meant that doing my job was almost impossible. I had to be assigned different duties for some time, mostly phone work."

My anger was an almost palpable thing by this point, and I hoped Viktor had done what he'd promised and rid the world of this ogre.

"What did he say when he saw the cast?" I asked, trying hard not to show too much emotion.

"He was mortified. He said that when he was growing up, he'd witnessed his mother attacking his father frequently, so when I pushed him, he'd thought that would happen to him, and that's why he lashed out first—to protect himself.

"I didn't get on with his mother. She was a nasty, sarcastic bitch, so I was willing to believe him when he told me that. And I believed that, because I'd pushed him first, it was my fault that things had got physical.

"He cried on and off for most of the day. We both did.

In the end, we decided to make a fresh start. Yes, I know you think I was crazy for doing so... I think so, too. But that's what happened.

"For another couple of months, things were good again, and I ended up having a pregnancy scare. I was on the pill but had missed one by accident, and we hadn't used condoms. We were saving money to put towards a self-build property and had been living in his rented house together for a year, so money was tight. We couldn't afford a baby, but when I got my period, we were both disappointed. I think that feeling is natural, whatever the outcome you wanted. He began talking about us starting a family after that, and we tightened our belts even more.

"One of the doctors at work was turning fifty, and all the secretaries put twenty pounds in a collection to send her on a luxury spa weekend for her birthday. We were also having a big party for her at the pub next to the hospital. Pete wasn't happy about the amount of money I'd put into the collection and reminded me of it daily.

"My parents were having more building problems at their place in Spain. They'd paid a local contractor a hefty deposit, but he'd run off with their money without doing the work. Pete took time off from work and agreed to go over to finish the build with my dad as his labourer, so we had his flights to pay for and the loss of his overtime to contend with while he was out there.

"The night he was due to fly out to help Mum and Dad was also the night of the birthday party. Pete said I shouldn't go because I'd spent enough already on the doctor's gift, but I dug my heels in and got ready to leave. It was like someone had just flipped a switch. One minute he was saying I'd disappointed him, as calm as you like; the next minute, he started punching me in the face and stomach.

"I didn't even have time to defend myself. He must have only punched me five or six times, but they were enough to make my eyes black, bust my nose and bruise my ribs. I actually thought my nose was broken and made my way to the hospital when he left, but luckily it wasn't.

"Before leaving, Pete threatened me that if I told anyone what *'I'd caused him to do,'* or if I tried to leave him, he wouldn't go to Spain to finish the build, which would have left my parents in deep financial shit. I knew they were relying on his help, and I knew how much money they'd invested in the place. So I didn't report it or tell anyone as I should have.

"When he left, he took my bank cards, passport, and car keys, which left me with just the forty pounds I had in my purse and whatever I could find in my coat pockets and bags. I had to use the bus to get to work all the next week. I rang my colleagues and told them I'd fallen down the stairs as I was leaving for the party, so I couldn't attend because I was in a mess. My friend Gemma came and took me to the hospital. I think she was suspicious of my injuries, but she knew that Pete had left for Spain and I was alone in the house.

"I came home from work every night, both aching from my injuries and exhausted from all the thoughts that were constantly buzzing around my head. I knew I had to leave, but I also knew my parents were relying on his help. He was over there holding normal, light-hearted conversations with my parents while their daughter was battered and bruised from his hands. What kind of monster does that?" she asked.

"A psychopath, Chloe. He was a psychopath. I'm so

sorry for all that you suffered. You don't have to tell me any more of it," I said, praying that she wouldn't.

"No, I do need to tell you. If we have any chance at a future together, I need you to know," she insisted.

I stayed quiet and listened carefully as her breathing steadied once more. I could almost feel the cold detachment come over her when she began to speak.

"When he arrived back from Spain, he came into the room and kissed me as if nothing had happened. I still had some bruising under my eyes, but he never mentioned it. He said he had a few more things to finish off with the build before it was completed, but at least my parents could accommodate paying guests and could finally make some money from their chosen retirement project. Pete said he'd talked to my dad about us getting married and starting a family, and my dad gave him his blessing. That made me feel sick. I left the room and locked myself in the bathroom for an hour.

"I had to make a plan and get away from him somehow. I thought about going to my auntie Joyce, but she'd warned me about him, and I hadn't listened, so I didn't feel like running to her and hearing '*I told you so,*' even though I knew she would help me. After going over everything in my head, I decided to let him think things were okay between us. I needed him to feel a false sense of security, so he wouldn't suspect that I would leave him.

"The worst thing was faking affection—and the sex. He emptied my pill packet down the toilet and wouldn't use a condom. I suppose he thought that if I were pregnant with his baby, he would have a hold over me. But I made an appointment with the family planning clinic in the next town over and got the Depo injection without him knowing.

"That's what set him off that January. Unbeknown to

me, the wife of a friend of his had seen me going into the family planning clinic. His friend must have said something to Pete about it when he'd mentioned us starting a family. So when I got home that evening after work, he was waiting for me.

"You already know what my injuries were, and you've seen how bad it looked from the photographic evidence. If it wasn't for a neighbour calling round, I think he might have killed me that day.

"What hurt me even more than all the injuries put together were the looks on my parents' faces when I told them how long it had been happening—and my reasons for not reporting it sooner. They were distraught, seeing me lying all battered and broken in the hospital bed. But anger was the main emotion flying around that room.

"My dad was livid, as was my mum. But not just with Pete, with me, too. They were heartbroken that I hadn't confided in them about what was happening. Neither of them could believe their daughter had been weak and stupid enough to put up with someone like Pete when they'd taught me to be so strong.

"My mum actually asked, *'Where did we go wrong?'* Like it was all somehow their fault that their daughter was open to such manipulation."

"I'm sure you are wrong, Chloe," I said, holding her a little tighter while her body shook with held-back emotion.

"No, Gregor, I'm not. And it hurts to know my father was so stressed about it he had a heart attack on the day the case was due in court. My dad was a sergeant in the army, for God's sake. He was a strong guy, but all that trouble with Pete was too much for him. He ended up with a triple heart bypass."

"From experience, Chloe—and believe me, I've had

many human friends over the years—your father must have had serious problems with his heart if he needed a triple bypass. It can't have been just because he was stressed. It saddens me to think that you've carried so much guilt about that."

I felt her warm tears fall onto my chest, and my heart broke to know that she still suffered from her past.

"What happened to this Peter Finch, Chloe? The document I received said he was hit by a car. Do you know if someone tried to kill him?"

"They questioned my dad, but he was still recovering from his surgery, so it couldn't have been him. But who knows how many enemies he had?"

I wiped the tears from her cheeks before pulling her body higher up the bed and kissing her softly.

"Do you feel better for telling me all this, Chloe?" I asked.

"I don't know yet. I'll be able to tell you in the morning when you look at me in daylight. Then I can judge the expression on your face when you see me—after you've had the chance to think about it and process all I've told you."

"If it does change, perhaps it will be because I realise you are much stronger than I thought you were, having survived such a past to grow into the woman you are today. That's who I fell in love with, Chloe. The woman you are. Don't forget that when you look for ways to push me away.

"You're not the only one who has a painful past. I, too, have suffered. Maybe you will judge me and find me lacking for my actions or lack of them. Do not forget, my love, I've had many years on this earth, and not all of those were filled with things I'm proud of or want to relive."

"Why don't you share some of them with me, Gregor?" Chloe whispered, stroking my face.

Could I? When we went to St Petersburg, Chloe would realise how uncomfortable I feel when I'm there. If I told her, then maybe she would forgo the visit to avoid my distress.

After a moment of contemplation, I began to tell her about my past.

"My family had been part of the Russian aristocracy for many centuries before I was born. My father, who was also named Gregor, had married my mother after he'd taken human blood and became immortal. He was forty-eight when he did so, just over a year older than I was when I became immortal."

"Why did you wait so long, Gregor? I mean, wouldn't it make more sense that you'd want to stay young and virile— say, thirty, maybe?"

"Are you saying I'm not virile, my love?" I asked as I took her hand and ran it down my chest to my cock.

"No, I didn't mean in that way. I meant in the looks department. You don't look any older than forty, come to think of it."

"That's because we don't age as quickly as normal humans. Neither do we get ill. And we live much longer than a human would, even if we don't decide to take the blood and have full immortality.

"Back then, maturity held more respect in society, and the more mature you looked, the more knowledge you were thought to have. Many waited until they were around the age of fifty to become immortal; I waited because I wasn't sure I wanted immortality.

"My mother came from a well-respected Russian family, and although she was always very proper, she was also very hands-on when it came to my upbringing. I adored her. You could say I was a mummy's boy. I would pick up on her unhappiness easily, and although I knew my mother loved my father dearly, she often became sad when he returned from his business in the city.

"I was sixteen when my brother was born; my sister came along eight years later. My father had me working alongside him when I was seventeen—after I had finished my studies. It was on my third day of working in the city that I found out why my mother used to get so distressed.

"I thought we were on our journey home, but we made a stop outside some houses in a part of the city I'd never visited before. We made our way inside, and our hats and coats were taken by a gentleman my father obviously knew well, as he addressed him by his first name.

"My father turned to me and said, *'We'll be here for some time, Gregor, so relax with a drink or partake of the delights on offer if you must. But do not come looking for me. I will find you later when I am ready to leave.'* I was confused by his words, but also curious, so I decided to look around.

"There were many rooms throughout the house, and all had beds. Some of them contained women in their undergarments, and I apologised profusely for disturbing them. But they only laughed and beckoned me inside. I could hear strange noises coming from one room, and as the door was half open, I chanced a look inside.

"A woman was bent over the bed, naked, and a man was behind her, also naked. I watched, fascinated, as he fucked her hard. I was still a virgin, but I'd seen enough from the ancient Greek texts to know about sex. As young men, we'd passed about drawings from books showing various sex acts and positions, yet seeing it in the flesh was something else, and I felt myself grow hard in my breeches. The man spotted me and gestured for me to come inside and watch, but I walked away, embarrassed.

"I went back to where we had entered and asked the gentleman who greeted us for a drink. I was served a strong vodka, which was like medicine in its taste. It helped me relax, and after another glass, I took another look around.

"Upstairs was almost the same as downstairs, but more of the rooms were occupied. Many of those rooms were locked, but in one of them, there were several men sitting on chairs—as if waiting for a performance of some sort.

"I sat on one of the empty seats and waited, trying my best to appear nonchalant instead of a sweaty-palmed virgin. A few minutes later, a woman entered the room from behind a curtain. She was naked apart from a tasselled silver chain around her midriff.

"A man from the front row got up and walked towards her. I watched, riveted, as he bound her hands behind her back with a silver-coloured cord, then he knelt on the floor and bound her at the ankles, all the while kissing her bottom and the back of her thighs.

"I was uncomfortably hard again, more so than before, but I was momentarily relieved when the man got up and stepped away from her. My relief was only short-lived. The man told her to drop to her knees, then he unbuttoned his breeches and let his hardening cock hang free as he commanded her to take him in her mouth. The woman did as he asked, but he insisted she take him deeper. He took hold of her hair and forced her head forward. Instead of the sounds of distress I expected, the woman moaned on his cock in pleasure.

"After a while, he tapped her cheek, and she released him. The man then removed all his clothes and helped the woman to stand. He unbound her hands and ankles and told her to lie on the bed. She did so with eagerness. Then the man pulled down more cord from around the bed rail above. After fastening each of her wrists to the cord, the man got between her legs and fucked her. I came hard in my breeches at the sight, but I don't think I was the only one that did so from the grunts and sighs of the men around me. After he'd finished with the woman, he unbound her wrists and embraced her. Everyone got up and left the room, and I followed like the lamb that I was."

"Do you think that's why you like that sort of thing, Gregor? The kinky stuff, I mean. Is it because that was your first sexual experience, and it somehow made you that way for good?"

"It is wrong to think we have to be flawed to enjoy BDSM, Chloe. We don't have to have a terrible childhood experience or be sexually abused to want to seek out pleasure in such a way.

"I had an exceptionally happy childhood, full of love and laughter. Yet I knew seeing the woman bound and at that man's mercy did more for me than the straight fucking I had seen earlier. It's always been that way... Until I met you.

"I had some thoughts for a time after something that Maxim—my old bodyguard—had said. He thought I did what I did because I didn't like women. And I must admit, I compared myself to your abuser. But I would never lash out at a woman in anger, and it was ridiculous of me to contemplate the idea that we had any similarities."

"You are nothing like him, Gregor," she said vehemently. "Now, answer my next question honestly. Which did you prefer? Making love to me, or what we did in your cellar?"

"Both, but for very different reasons. I want it all with you because that's what I think we both need. But the furniture scared you, and that's why it had to go. Seeing you like that and knowing I had a hand in causing your fear wasn't something I could live with."

"But I really enjoyed what we did in there, Gregor, and I would have done it again, willingly. You never even considered asking me about it. You just assumed from my first reaction to the room—and on seeing the police report and photographs—that destroying the room was for my benefit. But all it did was cause you to get injured and will probably cost you a fortune to replace."

"You would have me replace it?" I questioned, not sure I'd heard her correctly.

"If we end up being a couple, then yes. It's obviously something you need, and as long as it's on the lines of what we did in there, I would like to do it again too. Does that shock you?" she asked.

"It both shocks and pleases me, *moya malen'kaya tsvetochnitsa*. And it makes me very happy because I know what Keeley has been trying to tell me was correct. All these years, I believed that the women who enjoyed my kink were not appropriate marriage material, even though I knew there were married couples who attended my club. You see, after that day when we went to—what was for all intents and purposes—a brothel, I knew why my mother was often so sad on my father's return. I questioned his love for her on our way home that day, and it is the only time my father ever raised his voice to me in genuine anger.

"He said that he loved my mother with everything he had, but she was a lady who was good and pure. He said the things he often needed from the women at that place were not acts that a woman such as my mother should have to perform. So he sated his need there and gave his love to my mother in the only way a woman of her standing deserved.

"I was still angry at him because his actions made my

mother unhappy. My father's best friend was Vasily Petrov, Sergei's grandfather, and he never went with us to the brothel. He would leave the city after work and go home to his wife and young son.

"Vasily's wife was from French royalty, and her name was Adelisa. She was beautiful, smart and funny, and when I looked at her and Vasily's marriage and compared it with that of my parents, I didn't like what I saw. I knew if I was to get married, I wanted the same type of relationship as the Petrovs. One based on mutual love and respect. And though I enjoyed attending the brothel weekly so I could indulge my desires, I knew I would give it up if I were to take a wife. But I never found anyone I wanted to spend my life with until now.

"Our palace is just outside the city, and it would take us at least an hour by carriage to get home. We didn't know it at the time, but vampire hunters had arrived in Russia and had been searching the land, trying to find out anything they could about the immortals who resided here.

"The vampire hunters were recruited by a secret holy order and have been known by many names over the centuries. Every hundred years or so, they would band together and build an army. They'd attack and take the head of anyone they thought was immortal and would kill the humans who protected them. One fateful day they attacked our palace and that of Vasily Petrov.

"Instead of going straight home as Vasily had done, my father had insisted we go to the brothel. By the time we arrived home, my mother, sister, and brother were already dead, as were ten members of our staff."

Chloe held me tighter than ever, warming the coldness that swept through me.

"My father fell to his knees weeping beside my mother

and sister, and his valet, Ruslan, also wept. I left them while I followed a chambermaid to where my brother's body lay, then I picked him up and carried him back to my mother and sister's side.

"As I approached, I saw a sight that haunts me to this day. Ruslan was taking aim at my father's chest with a sword. I cried out for Ruslan to stop, but my father said he'd compelled him to take his life because he could not live without my mother. I begged him not to let Ruslan finish his task, but all he said was, *'I'm sorry, my son.'*

"I was just a few steps away when the sword pierced my father's heart, and as soon as that happened, Ruslan fell to his knees, compelled no longer. To end a vampire fully, you also need to remove their head and burn them. Ruslan wept openly for my father and for what he'd made him do. But when he asked if we should remove the sword from his heart, I said no. It was my father's wish to be in the afterlife with my mother, and I would see it done.

"Ruslan told me to go. He didn't want me to see my father beheaded, and I agreed to do so. I took my sister's and brother's bodies to the palace chapel—where my mother used to sit for hours and pray. She was probably more devout than any of the hunters. They were the monsters that day, not the vampires and their families.

"My father's body was burned later that evening, and when he was nothing but ash, we collected it all and placed it in a box next to my mother's body.

"Vasily and his family came later that night. He'd lost a few servants and a cousin but had been in time to save his wife and son. If we hadn't called to the brothel, I might still have my family."

"I'm so sorry, Gregor. You must have been completely

devastated. To lose all your family in such a way is unimaginable."

"Two days after we had their funerals, I finally drank human blood. Ruslan was the donor. Three days after I awoke as an immortal, I turned Ruslan into a Made vampire at his request. So you can say we share our blood in a way.

"Some hunters died on our land when our staff tried to defend my family, and I believe my brother killed several of them. Many had been slaughtered at Vasily's palace, but we knew a lot who had escaped. So Vasily and I gathered as many Born Immortal vampires as we could and set off to find the rest of the hunters' army.

"We caught up with them near Rostov and slaughtered every single one. My family were not the only ones killed in St Petersburg, and we made sure the hunters suffered before their eventual deaths."

I felt Chloe shudder at my words, and I wondered what she thought of them. But she didn't offer up her thoughts, and I never asked. We lay there not saying anything at all, a real change from the last few hours, and eventually, just as daylight appeared through a gap in the curtains, we both fell asleep.

Chapter Twenty-Seven

Chloe

For the second time this week, the sexiest man on earth kissed me awake. How lucky was I?

"Good morning, beautiful," Gregor whispered in my ear before kissing around my jawline and back to my mouth.

"I could get used to waking up like this," I told him before kissing him right back.

"How about like this, my love?" He knelt between my legs and pushed my nightdress up my body, exposing my breasts.

"Oh, definitely like this," I replied breathlessly. He tugged hard on each nipple, almost to the point of pain. Then he soothed the ache away with gentle licks and sucks before kissing his way down my tummy. Parting my thighs further, he sank low between them and began an oral assault on my whole sex—with licking, sucking and gentle biting around my labia before turning all of that attention towards my clit. I came quickly but loudly, all the skill from my lover and the pent-up sexual tension from yesterday intensifying my pleasure.

I wasn't even aware that Gregor had moved until I felt myself being lifted in his arms and carried into the bathroom. He set me on the vanity unit between the two sinks, removed my nightgown, and then turned on the shower. He adjusted all the different shower heads before opening a drawer below where I was sitting and taking out a towelling bathrobe. Pulling the belt from the loops, he discarded the robe, then he placed my wrists and palms together in a praying position. He bound them together tightly, allowing no room for movement. Gregor stepped between my legs and tilted my chin so he could look me directly in the eyes.

"You were right about me looking at you differently today, my love. I will not apologise for doing so, or I will end up having to do that every day for eternity. Every time I open my eyes to a brand-new day, I will love you more. With each hour, I see something else about you that makes me want you in ways that you can only imagine. So tell me, Chloe. Will you be mine? Will you Bond with me and share my immortal life?"

In his eyes I saw many things. Love, lust, hope, determination. Combining all that with the honesty in his words made me nod my head and smile.

"Say the words, Chloe," he commanded, his deep masculine voice rising slightly with happiness.

"Yes, I will Bond with you, Gregor. I love you, and though logic and common sense should make me wait a bit longer, I feel something deep inside telling me this thing between us is right. But we're not going to do it here in the shower, are we?" I asked hesitantly.

Gregor shook his head, then smiled. "No. This is where

I show you I won't treat you any differently. Now come with me, my love."

He lifted me off the sink and placed me feet-first on the floor. After removing his boxers, he tugged on the belt that was binding my hands and led me into the shower. Gregor kissed me again and ran his hands all over my body. I wished for a moment that my own hands weren't bound so I could hold him.

When I ground my sex against his thigh, he spun me around and pressed my body against the wall. My breasts flattened slightly on the cold marble, and I shivered, despite the warmth of the flowing water.

I felt a tug on my wrists as my arms rose and looked up to see Gregor tying the other end of the belt to the shower head above. He traced his fingers through my sex and paused for a moment before pushing two inside me. I moaned out loud, pushing back on his hand as much as I could when he removed them. Before I could protest, Gregor slid a wet finger between the cheeks of my bottom.

"Gregor, what are you doing?" I asked nervously.

"Hush, my love. I don't intend to take you here," he murmured as he breached the tight ring of muscle. "Not today, anyway. Tell me, Chloe. Has anyone ever taken you here?"

"No, and I don't think I would like it either," I panted.

"Relax, my darling. I would prepare you to take me. There are many ways I can make it easier for you to accommodate my size."

"You mean a butt plug? Oh, no! I'm not having anything plastic or rubber pushed in my arse," I stated, raising my voice a little so he knew I meant it.

"I wouldn't dream of it, my love," he declared with mock outrage and a chuckle. "As my wife, any toys you have will be gold or platinum and decorated with diamonds and pearls."

"Gregor, if that was a proposal, it needs some serious work before I accept," I huffed.

With his other hand, he cupped my mound before flicking rapidly at my clit.

"Whatever that was, Chloe, I bet I can get you to say yes many times over before we leave this shower."

And he did. Bringing me to orgasm with his fingers, then by bracing my forearms on the wall as he fucked me hard from behind.

Chapter Twenty-Eight

Chloe

I was both exhausted and ravenously hungry by the time we got ourselves clean, and I devoured the tasty breakfast that the wonderful Andrei created.

Gregor was happy, and it showed. So was I, but I also had questions. He'd mentioned marriage in the shower—was that just a joke? Or did you have to get married when you Bonded? I wished I could talk to Julia about it, but I didn't want to disturb the new mum. And I didn't feel like I had the type of friendship with Gina or Keeley to ask them questions of that nature. So I knew I'd have to bite the bullet and talk to Gregor about Bonding etiquette.

After we'd finished our breakfast, Gregor received a call from Sergei.

"Sergei, you have a lot to answer for, and I haven't decided how I will deal with you yet," Gregor grumbled into the phone. After Sergei said something, he asked, "Why do you want to speak with her?"

Gregor put his mobile on speakerphone and placed it on the table in front of me.

"What can I do for you, Sergei?" I asked, still a little annoyed with him.

"Hello, lovely Chloe. Are you enjoying Moscow?"

"It's a beautiful city, Sergei, although the ballet wasn't for me, I'm afraid."

"I do not blame you. It is not becoming of a man to wear tight clothing such as they do. It is sometimes obscene, depending on the size of their...*endowment.* I often wonder why Gregor likes it so much..."

I laughed out loud, even as Gregor glared at me.

"Fuck off, Sergei," snapped Gregor. "Now, what did you want? We have a very busy day ahead of us."

"I called because I wanted to ask who had a key for Chloe's flat, other than Pamela and me. Pamela doesn't know of anyone else who has access, yet on my return after my half-shift at Night Movers, I picked up the scent of a male that had not been present before I left."

"There are no other key holders, Sergei, only me and Pam. Have I been burgled?" I felt sick to my stomach at the thought. Gregor took my hand, a concerned look on his face.

"I do not think there was anything missing, and as far as I could tell, nothing was out of place from before. Your cat was unhappy about it, too. The clever feline was pacing around where I could scent the intruder the most, which was in your hallway and bedroom. He is missing you, Chloe. He won't leave me alone, so I had to let him sleep in your bed with me. I could not find any food for him in your flat, so I bought some cat food from Mr Singh's shop. I will buy him some chicken and fish tomorrow as a treat."

"Sergei, I don't have a cat. I'm not sure whose cat you have there, but he's definitely not mine," I informed him.

"Oh," said Sergei, sounding a little confused. "Well, I will ask around tomorrow to see if anyone knows who his owners are. He can stay with me until I find them. In the meantime, I am going to set up cameras in your home. Whoever had been in here only ventured through the upper floor; he did not go to your shop on street level. Because it had rained heavily, I could not pick up any scent on the metal steps to your flat. It is all very strange indeed."

"Keep us informed of your progress, Sergei. Are you going to have the locks changed?" Gregor asked.

"Viktor and Josh suggested the cameras. They said that the man would know I was on to him if I changed the locks, and he could try something else."

"Yes, I see what they mean. But I also have an unwelcome thought about this, Sergei. Chloe has suffered regular household emergencies, including a small kitchen fire. Maybe this intruder had something to do with that," Gregor said as he looked at me.

For a moment, I thought my breakfast would make a sudden reappearance on the table, but before I knew what was happening, Gregor had picked me up and carried me to the door. After half a dozen gulps of fresh air, my stomach began to settle, and my nausea passed.

"Gregor, I think we should go back to Barrowfield. I need to speak to the police and—"

"Do not worry about this, Chloe; Sergei will handle it. Besides, how would you tell the police that you'd had an intruder? They would not accept that Sergei had scented him," Gregor reasoned.

"I know, I just... It's not safe for Pam or the others to be there, either."

"Do not worry about that, my love. Sergei won't let anything happen to those women. On that, you can count."

"Gregor, have you forgotten how we ended up here? That was all Sergei's doing. He used mind control on me, for God's sake. He could be making the whole thing up."

"No. That is not something he would do. Sergei is a joker, and sometimes his way of doing things is a little out of the ordinary. Yet he is a loyal friend and someone you can always rely on to do the right thing. I admit what he did the night we ended up here was wrong, but he wanted to give us a chance to be together. And as it stands right now, although I hate to admit it, we *are* together because of him. Yuri and Viktor, too.

"I would have given you time back in England before I pursued you again. But I would have pursued you; make no mistake about that. And because you were here, you were not alone in your flat when this mystery man gained entry."

"I can't understand anyone's motive, though, Gregor. I mean, why get into someone's home and do nothing? It doesn't make sense. I'm dreading going back there now. I don't think I'll ever get a good night's sleep in that place again."

"Of course you won't. You'll be living at Rothley Manor with me. And after I have finished with you every night, you won't be able to do anything but sleep," he said with a smirk.

"What are we going to do today?" I asked while closing the front door and leaning back against it.

"What would you like to do, my love?" Gregor questioned, pulling me into his arms and swaying gently.

"I want you to help me forget my troubles and make me feel better," I told him.

"I'd better take you back to bed, then, or maybe the pool," he said, raising his eyebrows suggestively.

Trust him to think of sex as the answer.

But maybe it was. Maybe a certain place in Moscow that Gregor owned would be enough to take my mind off anything else but sex. I looked into his piercing blue eyes and tried to find the courage to ask him.

"Gregor, I want you to take me to your club."

I watched many expressions travel across his face—disbelief, anger, confusion. Then he turned and walked away from me.

Staring at the fire, he asked, "Why?"

"I want to see what it's like. I'm curious, and I want to experience something that you've enjoyed for centuries," I told him firmly.

"BDSM is not a place; it's a way of doing things. An action, a state of mind, a way of life. I tied you up and fucked you this morning, Chloe. That's something I'll enjoy doing for centuries to come. You don't have to go there to experience that with me."

"But I want to go there, Gregor. I want to know what you're going to need from me in the future. I want to be mentally prepared. Please, I won't ever ask you again. We don't have to have sex there if you don't want to. I just need to see it," I admitted.

"Okay, Chloe. If you're sure, we'll go this afternoon. I want as few people to see me there with you as possible," Gregor said harshly.

"Because I'm not pretty and sexy enough? Is that what you mean?" I yelled, both hurt and thoroughly pissed off by his attitude.

"Do not fucking yell at me, Chloe. And do not make any assumptions as to why I wouldn't want you there, either. Do you know how many women I've fucked in that place? Do you know how many subs I've had kneeling on the floor with my cock in their mouths? Or how about how many women have begged me to wield the tail of a whip against their soft flesh so they can say their marks came from Master Gregor? I did not want to taint you with any of that."

"But I'm already tainted by it, Gregor. I'm imagining all those women in my head. How beautiful, obedient and willing they were for you. You have all those memories stored away from your time there, so let me give you a new memory of it to savour. One I hope will replace all the others."

Gregor closed the distance between us and grabbed my shoulders. For a moment, he looked like he was going to yell at me, but he didn't. He stared at my lips and said in a quiet voice, "Go and get yourself ready, Chloe. We'll leave in an hour." He turned on his heel and walked towards the pool area, his head down and shoulders slumped.

What had I done? Should I go after him and tell him we didn't have to go?

I debated what the best thing was to do, but I had made my choice, and although Gregor wasn't on board with it, I needed to put this to rest so I could move forward with our relationship.

I wanted to know how I'd feel if he kept the club. When Semyon had asked him what his plans were, he didn't say. What if it was something he couldn't give up? I'd never accept infidelity; I knew that for certain. But keeping the club would always be a temptation for him, one he might not be able to resist.

Up in my room, I went through the underwear Anna had purchased. I chose the raciest yet classiest ensemble I could find: a navy-blue lace bra and knickers set, with a red bow in the centre of each.

I thought about the underwear I'd have packed if I'd come here on holiday, and I couldn't have been more grateful for Anna's shopping spree. I had a few pretty underwear sets at home, but when it came to big knickers, my underwear drawer could rival that of Bridget Jones.

Though I'd had a shower an hour ago with Gregor, I ran the bath and filled it with some of the scented bath oil —yet another of Anna's purchases—along with a set of three ladies' razors. After I'd shaved my legs and under-arms, I tried making my lady garden look a bit neater. Unless I was working with real flowers, my work could be a bit hit and miss, and unfortunately, the attempt at creating a narrow landing strip with my bush was most certainly a miss. I ended up shaving the whole thing off, and I prayed the shaving rash wouldn't appear until we left his club.

By the time I'd finished getting ready, an hour and ten minutes had passed. Gregor hadn't come looking for me, so I walked down the stairs with my blue Dior high heels in hand, dressed in a pretty blue and white daisy-patterned shift dress.

Glancing around the great room, I found Gregor sitting on a sofa staring at the fire again, a glass of whisky in his hand. Yuri was glaring at me for some reason, so I shrugged my shoulders and mouthed the word *"What?"* at him.

Gregor stood and placed his drink on a side table before turning around slowly. I smiled at him tentatively, but he didn't smile back.

He came to stand in front of me and hesitated before saying, "Chloe, I must apologise for swearing at you. I can promise you it won't happen again, and I hope you can find it in your heart to forgive me."

He looked so despondent, and I felt awful about the giggle I couldn't suppress.

"Gregor," I admonished while hugging him tightly, "if we're going to be together for eternity, then rest assured, that won't be the last time we shout and swear at each other. We're allowed to get angry and shout. It's natural in an equal partnership of people who are used to being in charge. As long as the words aren't too hurtful and there's nothing physical involved, then it's a normal and healthy part of a relationship. Besides, you've said that word to me more than once, so I'm used to it by now," I said while raising my brow suggestively.

"It's different when it's used for those purposes, my love. It doesn't carry any offence that way." He bent slightly and kissed me on my cheek before whispering, "I will be saying it many times this afternoon, Chloe, and each time it will have the same meaning, so I hope you're prepared."

Gregor told Yuri and Dmitry to ready the car for us. I was nervous, but also excited to see the place. It was somewhere I'd have never considered visiting in England—in my normal life. How many ordinary people would? I was also happy that no one knew me here, so I wasn't concerned that anyone would be whispering about my secret world of kink while I sat in the hair salon in Rothley.

Chapter Twenty-Nine

Chloe

Gregor's club was a row of three normal-looking townhouses—from the outside. Inside the front door of the second house was where everything changed.

The houses had been knocked together but had a few columns separating them from where each entrance hall would have been. When we entered, a tall, sombre-looking man wearing a black suit greeted us. Gregor spoke to him warmly in Russian before handing him our coats.

Gregor asked if I wanted a drink—guiding me to a bar in a room to the left of the property. The man behind the bar was dressed formally in black trousers and a waistcoat with a crisp white shirt. Despite my dress and shoes probably costing more than I earned in a month, I still felt underdressed.

Gregor had a short conversation with the bartender, and the man smiled at me. I smiled back and decided to ask

Gregor to teach me a little Russian, so I wouldn't feel as ignorant as I did right now.

The club looked classy, maybe more so than any normal club would. For a minute or so, we were the only ones in the bar, but as the bartender handed me my glass of wine, I saw a man approaching Gregor.

The man had a loud voice and spoke to Gregor like he would a long-lost friend. In between all the Russian, I heard Gregor say my name, so I turned to the man and smiled. He smiled back at me as Gregor introduced us.

"Chloe, this is Fedor Kuzmich. He is interested in buying my club, and I have made the decision to sell it to him. He owns similar clubs in St Petersburg and Kazan, so I know it will be in good hands."

I told Mr Kuzmich I was pleased to meet him and held out my hand for him to shake. Instead, he kissed the back of it before bowing in front of me.

What should I do now? I thought. *Do I bow back? Curtsey?* I looked to Gregor for guidance, but he just smiled and carried on talking to him.

Two more men walked into the bar, followed by a woman dressed in a short, black, sleeveless cocktail dress. She wore high heels like me, though she towered above my height. She wasn't as super-slim as I'd pictured all the women who came here to be. Her arms were quite muscular, although not enough to lose her femininity.

I watched her as she approached the bar and saw how she lowered her gaze when she neared Gregor. After ordering a drink, she caught me looking at her through the mirrored wall behind the bar. She flicked her shoulder-length white-blonde hair away from her face, which I noted was quite ordinary in appearance.

I'd pictured all the women who came here to be model-beautiful, with slender yet curvy figures. But this woman was a revelation to me, and I instantly felt a little more confident.

When Gregor's conversation with Mr Kuzmich was over, he suggested we take a short tour. He took hold of my hand, and I placed my empty glass on the bar, casting one last glance at the woman who was speaking to the bartender. He nodded towards us, and the woman stared at me wide-eyed. I smiled at her and let Gregor lead me out of the bar.

"Did you know the woman in the bar?" I asked.

Gregor sighed. "Maybe," he replied.

"That's not an answer, Gregor," I muttered as we walked along a low-lit hallway.

"What do you want me to say, Chloe? If I tell you I fucked her, you might be upset. If I tell you I've never even spoken to the woman, you probably wouldn't believe me." He let go of my hand and ran it through his hair.

"How about telling me the truth, then?" I offered with a shrug.

Gregor folded his arms across his chest and stared down at me. "Okay, here's the truth. I can't recall if I did a scene with her or not. If that makes me sound bad, then so be it. I make no apologies for who I am and what I did before I met you." Then he shook his head and said, "Fuck the tour," before taking back my hand and pulling me along the hallway.

Gregor opened a door, revealing a room that resembled a shop. There was a counter, display shelves, and cupboards, although there wasn't anyone to serve you.

He rifled through cupboards and drawers, selecting a few things from each. When I asked what they were, he grunted something in Russian, ignoring me completely. I stood there waiting as I watched him cast aside different sex toys before selecting…*oh shit!*

"Gregor, that's a fucking horse whip. You can put that back. I didn't ask for that."

"No, my love. You wanted to be here, now you have to play by my rules. In this club, I am the Master. Whatever I say goes—and I say we use the riding crop, or *'fucking horse whip,'* as you so eloquently put it."

I looked towards the door, wondering if I should make a run for it. Of course, the shoes would have to come off so I could run faster, but…

"Don't even think about it, Chloe. As a vampire, I can run faster and much farther than a human."

Gregor stalked towards me and only stopped when we were chest to chest. He took a deep inhale, staring down at me angrily.

"You fear me, Chloe. Even after all I've said and done, you fear me. *You* demanded I bring you here. I didn't want to, but I gave in to your wish just to please you. Yet now you are here, you're feeling scared; your bravery and courage have fled. Tell me, Chloe, do I take you home so we can cuddle up on my sofa while you cry away your fear? Hiding like the victim you do not wish for people to see you as? Or do you face your fear head-on and trust in the fact that deep down inside, you know I wouldn't hurt you?"

Well, that surprised me. I hadn't expected him to say any of that. It was a challenge, really. A mental and most certainly a physical one.

He waited patiently while I decided what to do. I wanted to look down at the rest of the stuff he'd selected that he'd tucked under his arm, but I didn't. I looked into his eyes and watched the stern look soften.

Then I knew.

I knew it was safe to put my trust in this man.

He wasn't giving me any bullshit lies—just a few home truths, no matter how I felt about it. He was doing exactly what I wanted because he wasn't treating me like a victim. So I tilted my chin up, took a deep breath in and said, "Bring it on, Gregor."

He raised one eyebrow and smirked. Then he dipped his head and kissed me, softly at first, then with more passion than I'd ever experienced.

I heard the crinkle of packaging from under his arm, and the crop dug into my hip, but I didn't care. Kissing my big, sexy vampire was becoming so addictive, and I was determined to get my fix before the naughty stuff started.

When he had me moaning into his mouth, Gregor pulled away and caressed my cheek with his free hand.

"I love you, Chloe," he whispered, and my heart skipped a beat.

Before I could say it back, he set off walking towards the hallway and commanded me to follow him.

After descending a flight of stairs, we stopped in front of a metal door. Gregor took a swipe card out of his pocket and passed it through a card reader on the wall. The door clicked open, and we stepped inside.

The room was pleasantly warm and well-lit, high-lighting the exact same furniture that had been in Gregor's cellar back in Rothley.

The familiarity of what I saw seemed to ease my nerves a little, but when the metal door clicked behind me as it locked, I felt those nerves rise right back up.

The lights dimmed much lower than they had been previously, revealing small spotlights around each piece of furniture.

Gregor placed the items he'd brought on top of a set of

drawers before opening them. I made my way over to a large leather sofa and was just about to sit when I heard him say, "Strip."

I thought about questioning him, but in the end, I just got on with it, thankful that my underwear and the low lighting hid quite a few of my flaws. Gregor turned around with two leather-strapped who-knows-what in his hands and said, "I meant all your clothing, *moya malen'kaya tsvetochnitsa*."

I dutifully removed the bra, then the lacy knickers, which certainly wasn't easy over the spiky stiletto heels. Well, not for me, anyway. I stood there with my hands on my hips, trying to pull off an *"I'm so confident standing here naked"* look.

"You've shaved, Chloe. Was that for my benefit?" Gregor asked while running his fingers over my smooth mound. I was so glad the soon-to-come shaving rash hadn't appeared yet.

I shook my head. But he knew it was a lie.

"Now remove your shoes," Gregor commanded, suppressing what I could tell was one of his famous smirks.

"You've just watched me struggle to get my knickers off over these bloody heels, Gregor. You could have said something earlier."

"And spoil the show… Where would the fun have been in that, my love? Now, I am going to help you put these on, and while I do, I will explain the rules to you. In this room, you will refer to me as Master and obey me as such. You will give me your trust, your body and your thoughts, and you will not question my commands or actions. Do you understand, Chloe?" he asked.

Gregor knelt behind me and removed each shoe before helping me step into what were essentially crotchless knickers made from leather straps. I was so interested in the matching cup-less bra he was dressing me in I forgot to answer him.

"I asked you if you understood what I was saying, Chloe, and you failed to answer me. Do I need to repeat myself, or are you wilfully disobeying me because you want me to punish you?"

"What? No, Gregor, I mean, Master," I said with a giggle. I doubted I'd be able to keep calling him that and keep a straight face.

"So this is all a joke to you, *moya malen'kaya tsvetochnitsa?* A silly little game," he said while tightening the strap on the cup-less bra that made my ample boobs stand high and proud. This bra was definitely coming home with me. My boobs hadn't looked this young and perky for years, and I was desperate for a mirror so I could get a side view.

When I was fully strapped up in my barely there leather undies, Gregor led me over to the St Andrew's Cross. The wood was cool where it touched my body, and it brought me back to the here and now.

Gregor wasted no time at all, strapping me to the cross by the wrists and ankles. He reached behind the wood of the cross before bringing around a metal rod. It spanned the length of the leg piece and had a four-inch-long rod on the end that he positioned under the arch of my foot. He did the same to the other leg, and though I wasn't sure what was happening, I didn't question it. Obviously, I'd never been strapped to a St Andrew's Cross before, so maybe this was normal.

He worked silently and methodically, and I stayed as still as I could as he did so. But when he walked around the back of the cross and I heard the loud clanking of metal against metal, I wanted to know what was going on.

"Gregor, what are you doing back there? That's a lot of noise from something that's made of wood."

"How did I tell you to address me, Chloe?" he asked crossly. "Did I tell you not to question my actions?"

As he stopped speaking, I heard a thud and a clinking sound before feeling a soft padded surface against my back and head.

"I'm sorry, Master," I said, duly chastised.

"Are you, Chloe? Are you really sorry?"

"Yes, Master," I answered as I looked him in the eyes. Gregor nodded his head and came to stand in front of me. I tensed when I saw the riding crop in his hand.

"Tell me you trust your Master, Chloe. Tell me you trust him to know exactly what you need."

"I do. Erm... I mean, I trust you, Master. But don't I need a safe word?" I asked, thinking back to all those kinky books I'd read over the last few years. They never seemed to get into a situation like this without choosing a safe word first.

"Why would you need a safe word, Chloe? You just told me that you trust your Master will know exactly what you need. If that is so, you should not need a safe word. Or were you lying to your Master?"

"No, I wasn't lying... Master. I do trust you. I just don't trust myself not to have a stupid meltdown," I admitted sadly.

What if I wasn't strong enough for this? What if I panicked because I couldn't cope?

Gregor stepped towards me and placed his hand on my cheek.

"I'm your future husband, Chloe. You need only say stop, and I will release you. I'm not testing your limits here. Not today."

I nodded, and Gregor stepped away from me once again.

"Your Master is pleased that you shared your thoughts and feelings with him, so your indiscretions from earlier will be forgotten. However, any further insubordination will not be tolerated."

"Yes, Master," I found myself saying, and I could see this pleased him.

He traced the end of the crop up and down the inside of my legs, from my ankles to just below my labia. He did this for a few minutes, and I enjoyed the tingling feeling it created on the inside of my thighs. I closed my eyes and said a silent prayer that he'd go higher and touch my sex on the next trip up my thighs.

I heard the crack of the crop as a harsh sting hit the inside of my thigh.

"Oww, shit, Gregor, that stings!" I yelled, trying to close my legs, but I couldn't because they were strapped to the cross.

"Oww!" Another whack from the crop hit the inside of my other thigh this time.

"What the fuck was that for?" I shouted.

"First, you closed your eyes on me, Chloe. How can I tell if you like what I am doing if you close your eyes on me? The second was for addressing me as something other than Master. I told you the rules, Chloe. What am I to do if you keep disobeying them?"

"Oww," I yelled again, as this time the crop smacked against my stomach.

"And that one, my love, was for swearing at me. That will not be tolerated in here, Chloe."

"I don't like the crop, Master. It stings," I said with a

pout. I almost stuck my tongue out at him when his lips twitched in a semi-smile.

"But the crop can be such a pleasurable toy, my love. And today can be all about your pleasure if you just obey the rules. For instance," he said as he lifted the crop, the soft leather end tracing my cheeks and lips. "This part of the crop is called a keeper, but many call it a tongue."

He flicked the end of the crop all around my chin and jawline while he spoke.

"I'm sure you can feel why they call it that as it laps against your jaw, my love."

Gregor continued, working the crop with short, rapid flicks as he made his way along my collarbone from one side to the other, then down my chest towards my breasts. As soon as the keeper made contact with my hard nipple, I let out a gasp of pleasure and almost closed my eyes again, but I remembered just in time.

He flicked the keeper across to my other nipple, and this time I moaned. To my embarrassment, I felt wetness seep out and coat the entrance to my sex. The embarrassment increased tenfold when I saw Gregor's nostrils flare as he scented how aroused I was.

I don't know precisely why that embarrassed and bothered me so much. Maybe it was because I was in such a vulnerable position and couldn't close my legs to hide the evidence of what he did to my body?

"I'm going to remove my clothes now, Chloe, and while I do, I want you to tell me what's causing you to blush."

He put down the crop and removed his shirt. As always, my mouth watered, seeing his beautifully sculpted chest and abs revealed to me, button by button. He tossed the shirt to one side and unfastened his belt buckle before unbuttoning his jeans.

"I see you still cannot obey the rules, Chloe," he said before removing the rest of his clothes.

"I'm sorry, Gre…I mean, Master, but I get so distracted when I see you undress," I admitted.

Gregor, now naked and hard, picked up the crop and whacked the outside of my thighs.

"Ow, ow, I'm sorry, Master. I'm embarrassed because I know you can scent how wet I am."

"Why would that embarrass you, Chloe? It is good to know your body is ready to take me. It means I am doing something you enjoy. And I love the scent of you here," Gregor said as he traced the leather keeper down my tummy until he reached my hidden clitoris.

He ran the keeper sideways through my slit and back up to my clit. It felt strange and completely different from the rapid flicking he did earlier. I liked the slightly rougher feeling and tried to push my clit against it every time it reached the needy bud.

Gregor stepped away from me for a moment before studying my lower half. A few seconds later, he bent down and reached into his jeans pocket, taking out a remote control like the one at the manor.

The first thing I felt was a slight jerk as the cross sprang to life. I heard a low whirring noise, and then the metal bars under my feet rose up the wood simultaneously, taking my feet and legs with them until my knees were fully bent and my heels rested against the back of my thighs.

"Gregor," I cried out, shocked at this new position and how I got into it. He didn't chastise me for not using "Master" this time.

"Hush, my love. I know you can do this. Try to relax and accept this new position. I've placed you in it for a reason, *moya malen'kaya tsvetochnitsa*. In this position, you are fully exposed to me. I know how much you like the feel of my tongue all over here," he said, once more running the crop over the whole of my sex. "So I wonder if you'll like this tongue just as much?"

Gregor didn't fool around and tease this time, targeting the rapid flicks of the keeper directly against my clit, and less than a minute later, with no build-up whatsoever, my body was propelled into a powerful orgasm that had my core clenching almost painfully.

A few moments after Gregor took the crop away, the cross tilted backwards. The relief I felt was instantaneous, as some of the heaviness from my lower half abated.

"Over the centuries, I have seen many flowers, my love. Some are so rare and incredibly pretty that you have to stop and breathe in their scent. Yet I have never seen anything as beautiful as your flower, Chloe," Gregor said while kneeling between my legs. After running his nose up the inside of my thighs, he added, "Although the scent is enough to attract me, it is nothing compared to the sweet nectar it secretes when it blooms."

I cried out when he licked from the entrance to my sex, up to my clit and back down again. But he didn't stop there. His tongue ventured further back along the seam of my bottom to the hole he'd breached earlier before coming back to lap against my sex.

"I want to devour this most beautiful orchid, Chloe. I want to feast on the outer and inner petals before finally taking this bud at the top. Do you want me to devour your pretty flower?"

Every syllable seemed to vibrate through my core, and before I knew it, I was crying out for my Master to do what he wanted, to devour me and take away the ache that was growing inside me.

Gregor had shown me many times over the past week that he had excellent oral skills, but today's demonstration was something else entirely.

His tongue speared inside me firmly before lapping all around the inside and outside of my labia. He sucked and flicked at every bit of my sex before doing as he promised, settling on that throbbing bud. I screamed out my release before spiralling into another immediately after.

Before I could come down from the orgasm-induced high, Gregor stood and tilted the cross back a little further before ramming his hard cock deep inside me.

I didn't want to come again; I honestly didn't think I could, but as soon as Gregor sank his fangs into my neck, I orgasmed almost immediately—before falling into a pleasure-filled haze.

This must be heaven, I thought in my dreamlike state. I felt myself being lifted and carried, then wrapped in something warm and fluffy. Someone was speaking to me, but it sounded like they were in the distance, and I wanted them nearby.

Something cold and wet touched my mouth, then dribbled down my chin.

Water.

Warm lips pressed soft kisses all over my face, and I smiled.

He was here. My lover was here in heaven with me. But wait a minute. Gregor was a vampire. Would God allow him in heaven?

"Chloe, my darling, can you hear me?" Gregor asked.

"Shh," I whispered. "I don't think you're allowed in heaven. We don't want to let God know you're here."

"*Moya malen'kaya tsvetochnitsa*, not even God could keep

me away from you," he said. I opened my eyes to see him smiling down at me.

We sat on a large leather sofa opposite the St Andrew's Cross, which was still tilted backwards. Gregor cradled my naked body against his. A large fleecy blanket covered me from shoulder to toe. I was grateful for its comforting warmth, yet I was still shivering.

"Gregor, what's happening to me?"

"You'll be fine, Chloe. You went into subspace for a while, and now you're coming out of it. It's like coming down from being high. Not everyone experiences it, and it's not always the same for everyone who does. The glass of wine so early in the day probably didn't help, but you'll benefit from rehydrating yourself and eating something sweet, like fruit or chocolate."

I nodded in understanding, too weak to do anything else. But I so desperately wanted to get dressed and leave.

I'd had the experience with Gregor that I needed. I just hoped I'd given him a memory he'd want to keep.

"Did I disappoint you, Gregor? I kept forgetting to call you Master, and then I kind of floated away at the end. I wanted your last memory of this place to be with me, and I'm not sure whether it was something you enjoyed enough to want to think about again."

"Chloe, my love, you have given me the most pleasure I have ever felt in this or any club like it. You are wilful and stubborn, yet you surrendered to me and allowed me to control this encounter. In doing so, you experienced enough pleasure to go into subspace. My darling, the trust you needed to give me to achieve that after all that you've been through was immense, and I am humbled by your strength and courage.

"You are beautiful, my love, but today, gazing at you all

spread out before me in submission, your beauty seemed almost ethereal. So it is fitting that you thought you had entered heaven."

"Thank you, Gregor, for bringing me here. I never thought I'd enjoy this sort of thing. But you can replace the furniture in the cellar at Rothley Manor as soon as we get back. Not the stocks, though," I said with a grimace. I'd never willingly be fastened into them.

"No, not the stocks," he agreed.

Chapter Thirty

Chloe

I can highly recommend travelling by private jet. In fact, I'm annoyed that I didn't get to experience my journey to Russia due to Sergei's mind control more than I'm mad at him for doing it.

We arrived in St Petersburg on a Bombardier Challenger, and I spent the entire flight remarking how comfortable the leather reclining seats were; how beautiful the walnut panelling was, and how it fitted seamlessly down the sides of the plane—converging into separate side tables that slid away when required. It was pure luxury. I loved it!

Gregor had joked I could have the plane as part of his wedding present to me. At least, I think it was a joke. He kept mentioning a wedding, but as yet, I'd had no proposal.

Ruslan had sent a car to meet us at the airport, and I was tempted to ask for the car, too, as I felt like a film star in it. Who'd have thought that Chloe Davies, a florist from Yorkshire, would be chauffeur driven around St Petersburg with two bodyguards and one of the world's sexiest men by her side? How I wish my old school friends could see me now.

As we were closer to the city than the Antonov Palace, Gregor took me sightseeing for the day. I was pleased that we were seeing some of the beautiful places he'd promised to show me, but I also thought that this could be a stalling tactic because he didn't want to go home.

———————

Our first stop in St Petersburg was the Church of Christ our Saviour on the Spilled Blood. It was similar in decoration to St Basil's in Red Square, with exquisitely designed domes of swirling colours highlighted with gold. It was adorned with mosaics of religious scenes that rivalled others I had seen in Greece and Cyprus. But there was still something about St Basil's that drew me more than this church did. Maybe it was because it had Red Square as its backdrop? Or maybe it was because the tenseness emanating from Gregor was starting to rub off on all of us, preventing me from seeing the beauty in this historical landmark.

St Petersburg was built around a canal system and appeared to be in blocks of little islands, so driving around the city was a slow process.

Palace Square was thoroughly breathtaking and had so much going on around it. In the middle was the Alexander Column, which was topped by an angel holding a cross. But that wasn't what drew me in the most.

The walls and buildings surrounding the square were decorated in delicate pastels: lemon and white, cream and white, and all so pretty and feminine. The Winter Palace was painted mint green and was adorned with heavily gilded decorations on the exterior. It dominated the majority of the square. I was informed it was the legacy of Catherine the Great, but it had also been the home of several empresses and tsars over the years.

The inside of the palace was truly spectacular. Part of it was opened as a museum, and it once suffered extensive fire damage that luckily hadn't spread to the palace art collection. My favourite room by far was the Armorial Hall, with its creamy white walls and gilded columns, watched over by military statues and lit with golden chandeliers. I wasn't usually into such heavily gilded fretwork and architrave, and there was so much of it here that it could have looked gaudy. But it didn't.

I was so impressed by the Winter Palace, and I asked if we could come back again to see things I was sure we'd missed. Gregor, of course, agreed.

When he suggested we go for lunch in a restaurant overlooking the river, my tummy rumbled as if on command. I'd spent most of the morning and early afternoon looking up at buildings and artwork, so my neck ached, and my eyes were starting to feel heavy.

I was surprised I felt so tired after all the sleep I'd had yesterday. After we came back from Gregor's club, I went straight upstairs and climbed into his bed. I slept until just before midnight. Then, after eating what Gregor informed me was his chef's version of Russian lasagne, we watched a film he'd streamed through his laptop before falling into a contented sleep. Well, mine had been contented. I hadn't asked Gregor about his when he kissed me awake before making love to me this morning. Looking at him across the table at this very fine restaurant, I felt a little selfish that I hadn't enquired.

"I thought we could visit the Peterhof Palace after

lunch. I'm told the cascading fountains are a wonderful sight to see," Gregor said with about the same level of enthusiasm he'd had all day.

"I'm tired, Gregor. My neck hurts, and I want to put my feet up. Can we go to your home and chill out for a while?"

"You do realise that Ruslan will want to take you on a tour of the palace, don't you? He's been looking forward to meeting you since Viktor so kindly informed him we'd be coming to stay."

"And I look forward to meeting him, too. I can't believe he's Anna's grandfather. I wish she could have come with us."

"She visits often. Ruslan has a full wing of the palace for himself and his family. He took so much pride in restoring it after the hunters came. The front of the palace was altered again years later, so it was more in keeping with the fashion during the time of Catherine the Great. As immortals, it is essential that we fit in with the rest of the human population. It can be a problem if you or your property are so different that people start to take notice. It's better to blend in, even if part of your history is lost."

"That's a sad way to live," I told him. But I'd have to live that way once I Bonded with Gregor. When I looked up into those beautiful blue eyes, I knew it would all be worth it. We would find our way together from now on and accept the years of change as two parts of a whole.

A lot of traditional Russian food comprised dishes I found unpalatable—I wasn't keen on fish or cabbage, certain spices or pickled food. So I opted for the nearest thing to a traditional British Sunday lunch I could find, although I will admit to having two traditional Russian desserts to finish off with.

One thing I noticed was that wherever we ate, Gregor

made sure that Yuri and Dmitry, or whoever his body-guards were on that day, ate either with us or at a nearby table. He was a fair employer, and I got the impression that Yuri was more to Gregor than just an employee. I knew that Yuri was a Born Immortal vampire, like Gregor, but Dmitry had yet to *"take the blood,"* as Gregor liked to put it.

After our meal, we went back to the car and proceeded over the many bridges out of the city, making our way to the Antonov Palace.

The driveway up to the property had pristinely mani-cured lawns on either side, and there were urns filled with an array of summer plants and trailing ivy. The palace itself was huge and reminiscent of the buildings in Palace Square, with cream walls and white windows, door architrave and frames. I was seriously impressed and remained speechless for a time.

"Come, my love, let us say hello to Ruslan and his wife, Kristina."

As we exited the car, I noticed the ornate double doors of the palace open. A tall, blond-haired man stepped over the threshold, a petite brunette beside him.

"Gregor, it is so good to see you, and I am thrilled you have brought your Chloe with you."

"Ruslan, my friend," Gregor replied. The two men hugged and held each other for a moment before pulling away with tears in their eyes.

Ruslan pulled me into a big bear hug while his wife grabbed Gregor's hand.

"It seems like forever, Gregor. You must not stay away for so long next time. I have to get updates on your welfare from Anna and Viktor instead of seeing you in the flesh."

"Well, I'm here now, Kristina, and I have brought you a

gift," he said, reaching into his pocket and pulling out a familiar velvet box. I recognised it as one of Mr Yanev's.

"Chloe, I see that Gregor is distracting my wife with jewellery so that she doesn't stay angry with him for not visiting. While he does so, I will take you inside and introduce you to everyone. Of course, you know who I am, even though Gregor has failed to introduce you formally to my wife and me." Ruslan tutted and shook his head while guiding me up the stone steps, but he glanced back at Gregor with a fond smile.

Inside the doorway, there were a dozen people lined up to greet me, and I had a moment's hesitation regarding my place in Gregor's world. But everyone was smiling as they waited for Ruslan to introduce us. Most spoke English, or at least they tried, and it bolstered my resolve to learn a little more Russian than I would need to just say hello or order food.

When Gregor entered the hallway, he was greeted so warmly by all the staff and was hugged by many of them. One lady—the cook, I believe—kissed his cheek twice, then admonished him for staying away, just as Kristina had done outside. Once again, I was saddened by Gregor's reluctance to come here.

After managing to pull Gregor away from everyone, Ruslan led us through a large arched doorway, and my jaw dropped. In front of us was a double staircase that met on a mezzanine level at the top. The balustrades were the same dark oak as the stairs themselves and were so different to the opulent marble of the Winter Palace. For a home that you lived in, I preferred it. Although, with the beautiful vine carvings, it still looked very grand.

At the bottom of the stairs was a portrait of a young Gregor, holding the reins of a white horse. He was so handsome as a young man and was obviously someone who got even better looking over time.

"This is you!" I exclaimed. "How old were you in this painting?"

"Twenty-two, I think," he answered, a faraway look in his eyes. Ruslan nodded.

"I think that horse's name was Zvezda, wasn't it, Gregor?"

"Yes. It was my mother's horse. My own horse would not stand still long enough for the painter to do his thing, but Zvezda was such a patient and gentle animal. Zvezda means star, in case you are wondering. She had the shape of a star in grey under her belly. It was strange because she was pure white everywhere else. We bred her with one of my grandfather's horses, and my brother had the foal. Such a good horse. Very obedient. There is a painting further up of my brother on his horse. Demyon was exceptionally good with them. A horse whisperer, you could say. Come, I will show you."

We passed more paintings before encountering his brother's portrait about ten steps up. Demyon was similar in looks to Gregor, but he had blond hair instead of brown— although they both shared those piercing blue eyes.

Next to Demyon was a portrait of Elizaveta, Gregor's sister. She was extremely pretty with the same blue eyes as her brothers, although her hair, which was up in a kind of chignon, was brown like Gregor's.

"She was very beautiful," I remarked as Gregor walked further up the stairs.

"That was painted six months before her death. It still hurts so much to look at it—even after all these years. I wanted to take them all down."

I ran up the steps and threw my arms around him.

Tears filled my eyes, and I had a lump in my throat. I didn't know what to say, so I said nothing at all and let my embrace do the comforting.

Ruslan touched my shoulder and pointed at the next two portraits. I knew immediately that they were Gregor's parents. Gregor was his father's double—uncannily so. They had the same hair colour, although his father's hair was long and tied back in the portrait. But those eyes...that same piercing blue that could look deep into your soul. There was no mistaking who Gregor belonged to.

His mother had blonde hair, though it was lighter than Demyon's. Her eyes were a much deeper blue, yet no less beguiling. She was beautiful; her pale skin had a radiant glow.

"They made a very attractive couple," I remarked, gesturing at the paintings. "So this is where you got your good looks from?"

Gregor turned to look at the paintings. He seemed deep in thought for a moment, then shrugged it off. I couldn't bear the distant look in his eyes. I tried desperately to think of something to say that would lift his spirits and couldn't think of anything at first. But as I glanced up and saw another painting—an older woman with a baby on her lap—an idea popped into my head.

"I want these portraits to stay, Gregor. When we visit with our children, I want them to see their grandparents, aunt and uncle every time they go up and down these stairs. I want them to know they have family in heaven who love them dearly and watch out for them every day. Like my grandparents and Auntie Joyce will, too. Just because they're gone, it doesn't mean that they, and the good times you had with them, should be forgotten."

Gregor looked at me for a moment, then glanced back

at the paintings. I smiled at him before turning towards Ruslan, saying, "I want you to tell me all about Gregor and his brother and sister when they were growing up. I bet they got up to all sorts of mischief in a home as big as this."

"Oh yes, my dear Chloe," said Ruslan, grinning. "I remember Gregor and the gardener's son, Dima, having races right here. They each would stand at the top of one of these staircases and slide down them on feather pillows, mostly on their bellies. Then Gregor discovered you could slide quicker on your back on the rugs his grandfather brought back from Persia. Olga, Gregor's mother, was just coming out of the drawing room when Gregor slid straight into her. He knocked her right off her feet. It was lucky his father had quick vampire reflexes and was able to catch her, or she would have had quite a landing."

"Did you get into trouble?" I asked Gregor, wanting to involve him in the conversation.

"I had to go to bed without supper, and I wasn't allowed to ride my horse again for a week. It was my standard punishment."

Ruslan chuckled. "I remember later that night, his mother, father, her chambermaid and I had a great time trying to race each other down on different rugs. Of course, his mother won most of the races. She was so very competitive. Although his father said it was only because Olga had the better rug."

I laughed at that, picturing these people in the portraits doing something so childlike and fun.

"I didn't know that," Gregor remarked, looking from the portraits to the stairs.

"Of course you didn't. You had gone to bed without supper. We couldn't let you see us doing something we said was dangerous."

Again, Gregor looked back at the portraits, puzzled but smiling.

"Demyon was terribly mischievous," said Ruslan as he glanced back down at his portrait.

"Every day as a young child, he would roam the gardens, finding caterpillars, worms, and beetles. He would bring them in to show his mother, even though he knew she hated them. And he was always trailing muddy footprints through the kitchens. It used to drive Olga and Mrs Garina, the housekeeper, crazy. Every day you would hear them yell *'Demyon,'* and then chase him through the kitchens to get him to take off his shoes, which would, of course, leave even more muddy footprints."

"What was Elizaveta like?" I asked.

"She used to put on shows all the time," Gregor said before Ruslan had the chance to speak. Ruslan gestured for Gregor to carry on.

"Father and I built her a puppet theatre. Mother had kept the puppets from when she was a child. My brother and I hated them. I thought they had strange faces, and Demyon agreed. They were dressed in huge pantaloons, and my sister wanted them to have different outfits. So she and my mother made new ones from Elizaveta's old dresses and lace from a tablecloth. Nearly every night for weeks, we had to watch different plays and dances. It would take hours to unravel the strings afterwards, and the first time I didn't do it, she said I wasn't her brother and she was never speaking to me again. She was such a little woman at times," he said with a huff. Then he laughed.

Finally, some progress, I thought.

"Can you remember when she went through her wedding phase?" asked Ruslan.

Gregor groaned. "I think she was about eight years old.

Mother had shown her our grandmother's wedding dress; Elizaveta preferred it over what our mother had worn. Our grandparents had moved to their palace in Germany. They said the air by the Rhine was better than in St Petersburg, and we had relatives there. Our grandmother gave Elizaveta some of her rings and pendants, as well as the tiara she'd worn at her wedding. Elizaveta was obsessed with it.

"She had everything planned—from the food that would be served, the wedding cake, what fabric her dress would be made from. She wanted to be married in the palace chapel in early spring so that she could have spring flowers all around her and in her bouquet."

"Elizaveta said her future husband would be the next tsar of Russia and would rule the world." Ruslan laughed loudly and pointed at Gregor.

"What's so funny?" I asked.

"Elizaveta said Gregor looked like a tsar, so she made him dress up and wear a crown she'd created from gold-coloured ribbon and a bread tin from the kitchen. He had to pretend to ask her to marry him. He went along with it and got down on one knee. Elizaveta said his crown didn't fit right, so while he was kneeling, she hit the tin, forcing it further down his head."

Ruslan laughed again, louder this time. "The tin was stuck on his head and wouldn't come off. Elizaveta stormed off in disgust, saying Gregor would never be a tsar of anywhere because he was silly."

"Several hours later, and with my head heavily greased in goose fat, the tin finally came off. It took six washes to remove the goose fat, and my father kept telling me he could smell it for days," Gregor recalled while rubbing his head.

"We have all your grandmother's jewellery and the tiara

in the new safe we installed last year. Your mother's jewellery is in the old one," Ruslan informed him. "I know you favour a jeweller in Moscow, but if Chloe wanted to wear any of the family heirlooms on her wedding day, I think it would be a fitting tribute."

"I'd love that," I said, taking Gregor's hand. "I could wear your grandmother's tiara like Elizaveta planned to, and we'll have the day she never got to experience. We could do it here, in springtime, and have spring flowers surrounding us, just as she wanted. It sounds magical, and something I would have chosen to do myself."

Gregor frowned. "I thought you'd want to be married in the church in Rothley, with your parents and work colleagues around you."

"Can we bring them here?" I asked.

"Yes, of course, if that's what you want. But you don't have to do this. I know you're trying to make me feel better about being here, but you don't have to go along with my sister's childhood plans," he insisted.

"But I'd like to, Gregor. I was an only child, and so was my mother. My dad had a sister, my auntie Joyce, but she couldn't have children. So I had no cousins or any other family members to grow up with. I made some friends during the time we travelled with my dad when he was in the army, but no one I could say was like family to me. I want to do this.

"I want to hear all about the fun times you had as a family growing up here. You've told me about the bad times; now tell me all the good. All the times that you laughed, played pranks, sang and danced. Show me where you played and where you slept when you went to bed without supper. Tell me how many people tried to pull the bread tin off your head, and how long it took for your sister to forgive you for not making a good tsar. And tonight, let's race down the stairs on a Persian rug—though I insist on having the same one your mother used."

I was breathing heavily by the time I'd finished my little rant, but that's nothing compared to how I was breathing after Gregor grabbed me and kissed all coherent thoughts away.

He lifted me so I could wrap my legs around his waist, and then he carried me up the rest of the stairs—still kissing me, although more softly now. When we reached the top, he turned and said, "Ruslan, we will retire to the east wing for the night and do not wish to be disturbed."

I didn't hear Ruslan's reply because Gregor pressed my back against the wall and gave me more of those addictive kisses. I was aware we weren't behind closed doors, yet I couldn't help grinding my core against him.

Gregor growled in response to my movements, and the sound thrilled me. He walked me down one hallway after another, every now and again stopping to kiss me against a wall—soft sighs and deep moans our only accompaniment.

We reached his apartment on the east wing, and I was grateful when the door locked behind us. I thought Gregor would take me to his bedroom, but he sank to the wooden floor and declared, "Here, now!"

Gregor tore my cropped trousers from my lower half, along with my white satin knickers. I heard the clink of his belt buckle hitting the wooden floor and the pop of buttons before he lowered his jeans and boxers.

There was no foreplay or teasing, it wasn't needed. Instead, he rubbed the head of his cock through my very wet sex, then thrust hard inside me. I came within thirty seconds, clawing at his shirt as I did so. Gregor rode out my orgasm with deep, rhythmic thrusts, then whispered in my ear, "You know what I want, Chloe."

I nodded my head in response, and he pushed up on both arms so he could look down at me.

"Bed?" he questioned.

I shook my head and replied, "Here, now."

Gregor smiled, but his expression changed when I took hold of his shirt and ripped it open. I heard pinging as buttons hit whatever furniture was beside us. He held his position with one forearm while lazily tearing through my T-shirt and bra with an extended claw. Strangely enough, I found the tearing sound a turn-on; the influence of a kinky vampire rubbing off on me, I supposed.

With the same extended claw, Gregor made a cut in the side of his neck, then lifted my head so I could lap at it. As soon as my mouth made contact with his skin, he groaned out the sexiest sound I'd ever heard, and it thrilled me to think I'd given him pleasure by doing this.

When I felt his fangs slide into my neck, I sucked harder at the puncture wound he'd created for me. I tried so desperately to concentrate as he drew my blood into his mouth, but as always, my clit throbbed with every suck. I orgasmed again, even though Gregor was hardly moving inside me, just rocking into me gently. After pulling away so I could take a deep breath, I lapped at the blood that ran from his neck. Another orgasm began to build, but this one felt stronger somehow. Deeper. More intense.

Gregor's movements became rougher as he thrust more forcefully inside me. I heard him say, *"I love you, Chloe,"* but it wasn't words he used. He was in my thoughts: a kind of telepathy.

When the orgasm finally hit, I swear I saw stars, and when he gave me one last thrust—burying his cock as deep as it would go—I felt the pleasure of his orgasm right along with him.

It took a few moments to gather my thoughts, and I wondered if Gregor felt the same way as I did. Happy, content, sated.

"Yes, I do, my love," Gregor said against my throat when he finally let go of my neck.

"My darling Chloe, I feel all those things and more. I finally have someone to share my immortal life with—a reason to exist. I can relinquish the painful events that have haunted my past because I have you to guide me to a better place," he said.

"I feel the same, Gregor. It's not been easy. I tried pushing you away because I was scared of letting anyone else in, of giving them my trust. But I know it was inevitable, really, us being together. It was always going to happen, one way or another."

"I'm sorry I didn't make our Bonding more comfortable for you. I should have waited until we were in bed, but I had to have you immediately. You were lucky I didn't take you in the hallway."

I'm not that brave, I thought, and Gregor laughed before telling me telepathically, *"My love, you are one of the bravest humans I know. And now you are mine, for always."*

"For always," I replied before kissing him again.

Chapter Thirty-One

Gregor

It was late afternoon, twenty-four hours after I'd Bonded with my flower girl. Ruslan had seen to it that my kitchen in the palace apartment was well stocked, for which I was grateful. It meant that Chloe and I didn't have to leave our bed for long.

I made love to her most of last night and three times today, and I felt the fourth time wouldn't be too far away. Our Bond was strong. We had no issues conversing telepathically, and the emotions I could sense in her pleased me greatly.

Chloe was happy with our Bond, with our love, with me. And I felt the same, if not more so. But there was one thing missing. I wanted Chloe to be my wife. I had a ring ready for her to wear, but I hadn't proposed to her.

We'd made plans throughout the night about our wedding day. But I felt I should organise something grand where I spoke pretty words, something befitting my great love for her. I wanted Chloe to know I would worship her every day, forever.

"I don't need anything grand, Gregor. You already know I'll marry you. And the thoughts I've just heard carried pretty enough words for me. I've had proposals before. They were done for show, for selfish reasons. Right here, right now, there's just you and me. And when everything is said and done, that's all a marriage needs."

I got out of bed to collect my luggage that Yuri had left outside the door last night. My apartment occupied the upper floor of most of the palace's east wing, so we were completely alone here.

I unzipped a small suitcase and retrieved the ring old Yanev had brought while Chloe slept the night before we arrived here.

We hadn't sized her ring finger, but the old jeweller had estimated the size from our visit the other day.

The ring contained two diamonds on either side of the apatite stone that matched my Chloe's eyes. Old Yanev had worked for nearly twenty hours to get the stones set into the gold band perfectly, and he was paid extremely well for his time.

I took a deep, calming breath, preparing to return to Chloe to make my proposal, but I realised I was still naked. Neither of us had been dressed since we Bonded last night, but it seemed crass to propose when my cock was on show. I dug into my luggage and retrieved some boxers before putting them on and heading back to where my flower girl sat expectantly on the bed.

I opened the box and showed her the ring. "Chloe, my love, will you do me the honour of becoming my wife? Will you swim naked with me after a stressful day? Do you promise to visit supply cupboards in community halls with me whenever there's a meeting? Will you—"

"Yes," she said, laughing. "Yes, I'll marry you, Gregor. But only if you promise to replace the cross in your cellar, and the horse thing. And get me a riding crop with a longer, softer tongue on the end."

"Done!"

I picked up the ring and placed it on her finger. It was slightly too big, but Chloe insisted we keep it that way because her fingers often swelled when she was working. I resolved to get Yanev to make a replica in a smaller size, just in case.

Chapter Thirty-Two

Chloe

Gregor had just proposed, and we were about to *get busy* again when his phone rang. He would have ignored the call, but it was Sergei, and I wanted to know if he'd had any progress regarding the intruder.

Gregor put the call on speakerphone before saying, "Hello, Sergei."

At first, there was no answer, just rustling in the background. Then we heard, "No, Boris. Come down from there."

"Sergei!" Gregor yelled, and this time Sergei answered.

"Hello, Gregor. Do you have the handset on speakerphone? Is Chloe with you?" Sergei asked.

"Yes, she is here," Gregor replied, then added, "Sergei… Chloe and I have recently Bonded, and she has just agreed to become my wife, so we need to make this phone call a quick one."

"Ah, congratulations, both of you. I have the perfect

Bonding gift for you, Chloe. I had a very interesting evening yesterday. There is much to tell you. Boris, stop that!"

"Sergei," Gregor yelled, "who is this Boris you keep shouting at?"

"Boris is my cat. I have claimed him as mine. Boris is normally very well-behaved, but he does not appear to like flies. Chloe, I need to know whether you were fond of the curtains in your sitting room?" Sergei asked hesitantly.

"Yes, I am. Why?"

"Well, Boris was chasing a fly, trying to defend your home against the winged invader, and clawing his way up your curtains was the best way to do that. He is such a clever cat, but he has very sharp claws."

"Sergei, don't let him wreck my stuff. If he keeps running up the curtains, he's going to have to go. He sounds feral," I said, already picturing the damage.

"Boris isn't feral, Chloe; he is just very young. And he has an aversion to flies and bees. Spiders, too."

"Spiders?" I said with a shudder. Even the word made my skin crawl.

"Yes, he hates spiders. A big one ran out from under your sofa last night, and Boris caught it immediately. He flicked it around the floor for a while after he'd killed it, which was uncalled for. So I had to be stern with him and explain that playing with your prey was in bad taste. The one he killed in your bathroom this morning, he left straight away. So my Boris is learning to be a good cat."

Sergei sounded so proud of this stray animal; I was just grateful he'd killed the spiders that had been waiting on my return.

"Well, then, if he's a spider catcher, he can definitely stay."

"Sergei, did you call just to talk about your cat, or was there another reason?" Gregor asked.

"It does concern my Boris in a way. I went into the butcher's yesterday to buy him some chicken, so I could cook it for him today. But as I stood in the queue, I recognised the same scent I'd picked up off the intruder.

"There were two men in front of me, and it wasn't either of them. But when the butcher came out of the back with a large cut of pork loin in his hands, I recognised it was him straight away.

"I knew the butcher had upset Keeley at one of the meetings a few weeks ago, and I thought it was another way to get back on her good side. So I called her and told her what I knew I had scented. Keeley and I waited in the back of Chloe's shop until we saw the butcher lock up and start walking to his car.

"I used mind control to get him to come into Chloe's flat and explain why he'd been trespassing, and how he had done so. The butcher said he'd been loosening bolts on her pipework to cause a leak. He also caused damage to some of Chloe's electrical wiring and started a fire in her kitchen, amongst other things."

"How did he get into her flat, Sergei? Did he have a key?" asked Gregor.

"No, he did not need one," replied Sergei. "As the flats are upstairs in a row of old terraced properties, their attic spaces are all connected. There is only a single row of wood panelling separating each roof space, so all the butcher had to do was take the panels away to gain entry into Chloe's flat."

"But why?" I asked, dumbfounded. "Why would anyone want to do something like that?"

"Using mind control, Keeley got him to tell her why he

wanted to damage Chloe's property. He said it was because he wanted to extend the pies and pastry side of his business and make Chloe's shop into a café. There wasn't one in the village since Milly's Tea Room had closed down, and he thought it would be profitable. He wanted you to get so fed up with all the costly repairs on your property that you would sell it to him cheap."

"I can't believe it," I said, shaking my head. Gregor looked livid.

"Sergei, tell me you made the man suffer for this," he demanded angrily.

"I compelled him to sell me his shops for less than a third of the market value, so as not to arouse suspicion. With my...*help*, he made an appointment to see his solicitor to get the sale underway. I will gift them to Chloe in celebration of your Bonding."

"Thank you, Sergei," I gasped.

I was shocked, angry, and also quite upset that Dave Higgins, someone who I thought was a friend, could target me this way.

"You are most welcome, my dear Chloe."

"Sergei, I feel that the butcher has got off lightly," Gregor snapped.

"On the contrary, my friend. As I said, Keeley was with me when we apprehended this man. She made sure he would not only have to sell his businesses, but that he would also have to sell his home on the lane just past the Night Movers depot—because he will be too embarrassed to stay here."

"What did she do?" I asked, curious as to what a sweet woman such as Keeley could do to a despicable man like him.

"Using mind control again, Keeley told the butcher that

his balls were itching because he had crabs, so he needed to keep scratching them. She told him to go into each of the local pharmacies and ask for the lotion to get rid of them, and to offer to show the staff where they were.

"She also told him that if anyone asked why he'd sold the shops, he was to tell them he needed the money to get the penis extension he'd always dreamed of because his was no bigger than a discarded cigarette butt. I added that he should make an announcement at the next council meeting that this was his plan, and that he should also do it in the Red Lion. It will make for good entertainment, I feel."

"I will have to be satisfied with that I suppose. But I would still like to make him physically suffer," Gregor said. "The fire and electrical problems he caused in Chloe's flat could have killed her."

"Oh, he is suffering physically," said Sergei. "He was with us at least an hour before we let him go, and he scratched his balls constantly during that time. When I saw him this morning, he was wincing when he scratched them. The man will need them bathing in ice if Keeley doesn't reverse her compulsion in the next hour or so."

"Good!" Gregor huffed, a little more appeased than he was before.

"Goodbye, my friends, and don't get married without me being there. You know I deserve all the credit for getting you to Bond so soon, although I will admit I had Viktor and Yuri's help. Perhaps you'll consider calling your firstborn son Sergei in thanks for my help?"

Gregor shook his head and was about to say something when we heard, "Boris, no! Leave it alone." Then the call ended.

"I can't believe Dave did all that, Gregor. I was so fed up with having to foot the bill for a lot of the repairs. And I *had* considered if it was all worth it. If I hadn't come here, what would he have done next?"

Thinking about him being in my flat without my knowledge, poking through my things, made me feel sick. Had he ever done it when I was there?

"Shh, please, Chloe. My anger is hard to contain as it is, and at this moment, I want to go and tear the man apart," Gregor said, taking me in his arms and holding me close.

I thought back to the rest of Sergei's conversation and realised at the end, he'd mentioned our firstborn. I hadn't thought about it before, but since Gregor and I Bonded, we hadn't used any contraception. What if I got pregnant? Would Gregor want that so soon in our relationship? Would I?

"Gregor, now that we've Bonded, you could get me pregnant. I do want children, but I'd like to spend some time as a couple first. We didn't discuss it beforehand, but what if I end up pregnant?"

"I had forgotten," he said as he placed his hand on my lower belly. "You could be with child right now. My child. Would that disappoint you, Chloe?"

"No," I answered truthfully. "I wouldn't be disappointed, but it would mean I'd be waddling down the aisle ready to give birth at our spring wedding. And I don't think you're supposed to fly after your sixth month."

"So buy a bigger dress and stay here in St Petersburg."

"What? No, Gregor. I want our day to be special."

"It *will* be special, Chloe. We will celebrate our love with everyone *we* love. You are already mine, but marriage will cement our Bond in a human way. You'll become an Antonov, and in human law, that is important. You own half of everything I have already because we are Bonded. But a human marriage will confirm to all your family and friends that you love and value me enough to make a commitment to me. And I to you. If you happen to bring along another Antonov to the event, so be it."

"Another Demyon or Elizaveta?" I queried.

"You would do that? Name our child after my siblings?"

I nodded and smiled before adding, "Or Damian and Eliza. Whichever you prefer. But not Sergei."

"No, definitely not Sergei," Gregor agreed. Then he smiled and added, "There could only ever be one of him."

vinci-books.com/sergeisangel

A mysterious vampire. A tragic past. Can two broken souls find solace in each other's arms?

Devastated by loss and struggling to care for her little brother, Holly Fraser reluctantly accepts a job from the enigmatic Sergei Petrov. Sergei, a Born Immortal known for his mischievous nature, finds solace in Holly after recent chaotic events. But as secrets threaten to unravel their budding connection, they must confront the truth and discover if their love can withstand the challenges that lie ahead.

Turn the page for a free preview…

Sergei's Angel: Chapter One

Sergei

Snow fell silently from thick grey clouds while we waited for the undertakers to carry the coffin into the old village church. A young woman stepped out of a black funeral car, and an odd sensation struck me. I studied her closely, watching snowflakes settle on her halo of golden hair blowing in the cold winter breeze.

As befitting a funeral, she wore black. Her azure-blue eyes glistened with tears, and the surrounding skin was red and puffy. She gripped the hand of a small boy who appeared dazed and maybe a little scared as he studied all the people making their way into the church. Once again, an odd feeling came over me when I watched them take their seats. It was a feeling I couldn't decipher but felt fiercely nonetheless.

I was at this funeral at Maggie Saunders' insistence. She'd said that because the recently deceased Beryl Fraser had worked for Night Movers for so long—before her retirement three weeks ago—at least one of the owners should attend.

It appeared I'd drawn the short straw because I was standing here on this cold winter's day at the funeral of a woman I had only met twice.

Beryl Fraser had sought me out after she'd made up a mixture of oils and cleaning products that removed blue dye from my hands. Yuri and I had a bit of a mishap with Daisy during a day out, and we all ended up with blue dye staining our skin. Keeley had asked the woman if she knew how to remove it.

Beryl had been a cleaner at Night Movers for twenty years, so she knew plenty about removing dirt and stains.

Keeley told her not to tell me she had a way to remove it, but Beryl found me and gave me a bottle of something she'd made up herself. It removed the stain after leaving it on my hands for ten minutes, although I do not know what it was.

I thanked her with an enormous bouquet of seasonal blooms I made up myself. I was filling in for Chloe at her flower shop at the time, and the only other occasion I'd conversed with Beryl was when she came to thank me.

I sent Chloe to Russia with a drunken Gregor to get them together after they'd had a falling out. Less than a week later, they were Bonded, and three weeks after that, Chloe found out she was pregnant. So my interference proved positive in more ways than one.

I am happy for my friend, and I look forward to having another child around for me to love and be an uncle to. But since they found out, Gregor has become extremely over-protective, which is getting the typically independent Chloe down.

I'm staying at her flat until the cottage I'm having built

on Night Movers' land is ready to move into. It's situated next door to Nik and Gina, although I'm not sure if that's a good idea now. The build is being held up temporarily by the wintery weather.

Since my move to Chloe's flat, I've spent little time with Nik and Gina—other than when we are at work. Instead, I visit with Josh, Keeley and Daisy, and, surprisingly, Alex and Julia.

Their baby, Rory, is so pleasant. I pop by whenever possible, and it's great to see him as often as I do. It enables me to witness every new development he makes, no matter how small.

Rory is just over four months old and can push himself up on his hands and roll over from his belly to his back. Alex and I have videos of this on our phones and will often argue over which is the best. But half an hour with the baby every couple of days is not enough to fill up my week, so I spend more and more time with the humans in this small Yorkshire village.

I'd taken on a partnership in Night Movers during the summer and have worked some of Joshua York's evening shifts for him on a four-on, three-off night shift pattern.

He's recently Bonded with his love, Keeley, and wanted to spend more time with her and her daughter, Daisy—whom he's adopting—but the night shifts he worked didn't allow for much of that. I was happy to take on a partnership because I considered everyone to be a great friend and, in Nik and Gina's case, family.

But months have passed since I made that decision, and as time has moved on, I've been much less comfortable with the situation than I was previously.

Most of my immortal friends are busy being a couple

and have little time to spare—wedding planning and babies taking precedence over their social life.

I used to rely on Nik and Gina to keep me company on my days and nights off, but after some revelations I made when Keeley was attacked, Nik—someone who I always thought of as a brother—had become distant and seemed to resent my close friendship with Gina.

I have always loved Gina. Many years ago, I thought she might have been it for me. But Nik had met her first, and I would never come between them.

Over the years, I realised while my love for Gina was strong, it was not, and had never been, as powerful as the love between true soulmates destined to Bond. I think Nik understands this, but his vampire side probably still sees me as a threat.

Yuri is over from Russia with Dmitry, one of Gregor's human guards. We've been out drinking together, but I feel that something is not right between the two friends, although they hide it well whenever Gregor's around.

I've seen how Yuri looks at Mel, the bar manager of the Red Lion—the pub he owns in the village. But the last time I was with them, I noticed Dmitry share the same look with her. From experience, I don't think that will go down so well.

Because of all this, I have been integrating more with the humans of this village, and I thoroughly enjoy their company. I've made good friends here, and if it were not for that and my position within Night Movers, I would have gone back to Russia.

I have trusted staff to manage my business dealings in my home country, but I feel I should do more to oversee the business that my grandfather created.

Sergei's Angel: Chapter Two

Sergei

After the funeral service, the mourners walked along a flagstone path from the church to the graveside. The young woman crouched in front of the tearful boy, offering words of comfort before taking him in her arms while he cried.

The child was scared and grief-stricken, and my heart ached to see his tears. I turned to Maggie, who was sobbing at the sight of the little boy's distress.

Taking her in my arms, I stepped aside with her to let the other mourners pass.

I asked why there were no other family members to support the young woman and child, whom I assumed to be Beryl's grandchildren.

Maggie told me that Beryl's husband had passed away just after their grandson, Matthew, was born. She said that Beryl had raised Matthew and his sister, Holly, after their mother committed suicide when Matthew was a baby.

Beryl's friend Moira took a weeping Holly and Matthew

into her embrace when they lowered the coffin into the ground.

It took everything I had not to walk over and carry them away from here. It felt wrong that there were no other living relatives around to help.

Their father, maybe? Maggie informed me that their mother "*had been a bit flighty in her youth*" and had taken off to some protestor camp. She came back heavily pregnant with Holly two years later.

Maggie said Matthew's father was rumoured to be a married man from Lincolnshire, and as far as she was aware, he'd had little to do with the child.

Their plight disturbed me. I felt I could relate to them somewhat.

Nik and I were orphaned when we were babies. Our parents had been killed by the vampire hunters—a religious group who sought out and killed immortals and their families. Our mothers, who were cousins, had left us with a relative named Petre—a priest who ran an orphanage some miles from where they lived in Romania.

Our fathers had joined the immortal army and had met our mothers over 294 years ago. But the vampires had been betrayed by one of their own, and the hunters' numbers were much more than anyone had expected, backed at the time by Rome itself.

We stayed in the orphanage with Petre until our grandfathers came to take us away years later when the hunters had finally been defeated.

The orphanage had been a way to hide us in plain sight, and I never forgot my roots—despite my reasons for being there. But as good a man as Father Petre was, I missed having a family to care for me.

Nik and I were as close as brothers and always had each other's back. Until now, it seems.

Maggie and I were told a funeral buffet was being held in the local community hall. We went along so we could speak to Holly and offer our condolences.

She moved around the room, thanking everyone who'd attended. Moira sat with the little boy, who now seemed more settled. Maggie said that Holly must only be eighteen or nineteen; no age at all to take on the sole responsibility of bringing up her seven-year-old brother.

Before Holly got to speak with people on our side of the room, she filled up a plate of food and took it to her brother, ensuring he had everything he needed. Unable to take my eyes off the beautiful angel in black, I watched as she went back to the table and wrapped more food in a napkin, which she placed in her handbag. She glanced around, ensuring no one was watching, before doing the same again.

This was her grandmother's funeral, most likely paid for by her or from funds put away by her grandmother for this very occasion. So she wasn't stealing food, as I often had to do in the orphanage when hungry.

When that memory hit me, my gut clenched. Holly was hungry and was taking food for her and her brother for later. My suspicions were confirmed when she came over to thank Maggie and me for attending.

Maggie embraced Holly and then turned to me.

"Holly, this is Sergei Petrov. He's one of the new partners at Night Movers. He's also the one who sent your grandmother that huge bouquet of flowers that she was so thrilled about."

Holly turned to me and smiled. It was genuine and was the first I had seen on her pretty face all day.

"Thank you, Mr Petrov. My gran loved them. They filled two of her favourite vases and lasted for weeks. It was very sweet of you."

"Not at all, my dear Holly. I was grateful to her for helping remove the blue from my hands," I told her, and she looked at me, confused.

"Don't ask," voiced Maggie. "You would never believe how his hands came to be blue even if he told you."

"Oh, okay," Holly replied, a little puzzled but still smiling.

"Maggie, I wanted to ask you something," she added before taking a deep breath. "Do you have any vacancies at Night Movers? I did my business administration course at college, so I'd be happy to take on an office role or perhaps even my gran's old cleaning job. I need something in the daytime when Matthew's at school."

"I'm sorry, Holly, we don't have anything in the office in the daytime, and we filled your gran's old job the day after she retired. Doesn't the hotel you were working at have any places nearby that you could transfer to?"

"No, it wasn't part of a group or chain, which meant I had to hand in my notice so I could look after Matthew. I've been without work since she passed away."

"What about your boyfriend? Paul, wasn't it? Is he still at the hotel? I thought he would have been here with you."

"Paul and I split up before Gran died," Holly said, looking down at her feet. She took a deep breath, then looked back up at us.

"If any daytime jobs come up at Night Movers, or if you hear of anyone else hiring locally, will you let me know?" she asked.

Maggie nodded and told her she would before hugging her once again.

"It was nice to meet you, Mr Petrov. Maybe next time it will be under better circumstances," Holly said as she held out her hand to shake mine.

As soon as I placed my hand in hers, I felt a deep yet familiar connection. My heart skipped a beat, and my mouth went dry. If Holly's gasp was anything to go by, she, too, felt the same as I.

I knew I had to see her again. In fact, I didn't want to let her out of my sight. I quickly thought of a way for this to happen, one that would benefit her, too.

"Holly, did you say you were familiar with business administration?" I asked.

"Yes. I did a two-year college course on the subject when I left school, and I've been working in a hotel up in the Lake District for the last five months—on reception and in the back office. Why?"

"Because I need a PA with experience in business administration to help manage some aspects of my business dealings in Russia. It's paperwork mostly."

"I'm sorry, Mr Petrov, but I don't speak Russian," she said with a sigh. I heard her words as soon as she uttered them, but I found myself staring at her full, pink lips as she spoke, so I didn't immediately reply.

"Sergei," prompted Maggie.

"What? Oh yes, Russian. Well, all my staff speak English and can also communicate any paperwork and emails in English. I need someone who's competent and reliable and can work during the day because I do the evening shifts at Night Movers. I will understand if you need to take some time to grieve, and I'll hold the job open for you until you feel you are ready—if you are interested?"

"Yes, of course I'm interested, and I can start immediately. It's Friday now, so I have Matthew off until school on Monday, but if you want me to work the weekend, I can ask if Aunt Moira will watch him tomorrow."

"No, Holly. You need to take this weekend for you and your brother—to come to terms with what has been a very distressing time for you both. It would be unfair to ask you to work," I told her.

"Actually, Mr Petrov, I need an income as soon as possible. So if I could start tomorrow, that would be great for me," she replied with hope in her eyes.

"Okay, but only if you are sure," I reiterated. "I'm currently living in the flat above Chloe's Flowers and Gifts in Barrowfield Village. I will expect you around eleven o'clock, and you can bring your brother. We'll find something to entertain him while I go through what I need you to do."

"Thank you, Mr Petrov," Holly said as she went on her tiptoes and threw her arms around my neck.

I closed my eyes while breathing in her scent, savouring the exquisite fragrance while hugging her back.

"You are more than welcome, Holly," I told her in a deep, throaty voice, much lower than my usual tone.

I felt her shudder before she loosened her arms and tried to step away from me. I held her a little longer before letting her go, and after brushing her golden hair out of her stunning blue eyes, I said, "Until tomorrow, Holly."

Then I left the hall without looking back.

Grab your copy...
vinci-books.com/sergeisangel